More Than Us

by Dominique Wolf

More Than Us
Copyright 2021 Dominique Wolf
All rights reserved.

ISBN: 979-8-476713-59-3

Published by Dominique Wolf
Formatting by Bob Houston eBook Formatting
Editing by TC Media
Cover design by Dominique Wolf (Picture supplied through Canva ProLicense by Thais Compte from Getty Images)

TO THE READERS

THIS ONE'S FOR YOU.
MAY ISABELLA AND GIOVANNI'S LOVE STORY LIVE IN YOUR
HEART THE WAY IT'S GOING TO FOREVER LIVE IN MINE.

CHAPTER 1:

Isabella

"**A**re you ready for another surprise?" Giovanni leaned closer to my ear.

Another one? Giovanni proposing to me was the best surprise of my life, and I was still reeling from it. I couldn't stop smiling the whole time we watched the show. I was pretty sure my cheeks were going to hurt tomorrow.

I turned around to face him. "What do you mean by another surprise?"

He chuckled and leaned down, planting a small kiss on my lips. "Follow me, baby."

He slipped his hand in mine and a new refound electricity coursed through my veins. My heart was bursting, and I was overwhelmed by the emotion working its way over me. The sun had set a long time ago, and the nighttime air had settled around us. It was packed with people scattered all around, enjoying the ongoing gymnastics of the water. The music from the show was blaring around us causing the perfect Saturday-night-out atmosphere. Hand-in-hand, I followed Giovanni as we slipped through the crowds past the fountain. I thought we were headed back to the car but instead, we headed in the opposite direction.

"Are we walking?" I asked, unsure of where we were going and if I was going to regret wearing my high heel boots.

"Yes." He pulled me closer to him. "It's not too far."

I lifted my left hand up again, making sure that this was all real. I stared down at my beautiful engagement ring and shook my head.

"I can't believe we're engaged," I gaped.

Giovanni laughed. It was my favorite sound. I glanced up at my fiancé who was already smiling down at me. His deep brown eyes were shining with the love that I knew we both shared. How was it possible that I got to call this man mine?

"Well, believe it, *mi hermosa.*" He lifted my hand to his lips. "It's you and me forever, Isabella."

Tears swelled in my eyes again. I must have done something right to deserve someone like Giovanni. The kind of man who thrilled my body and set my soul on fire. Between his witty charm and dirty jokes, I fell in love and I haven't stopped falling since.

"This is the only time I am happy to see you cry," he joked.

I giggled and wiped my tears. "I can't stop. I'm so happy."

"That's all I want, baby."

We moved with such ease together as we made our way up the cobblestone street. I watched the double takes as we passed a few groups of women. Some of them were less subtle than others when gawking at Giovanni and honestly, I couldn't blame them. He carried himself with a confidence you couldn't help but be drawn to. Hell, every day I was amazed by him and the way in which he commanded attention so effortlessly.

And I got to call this man my fiancé.

Fuck, I seriously hit the jackpot here. We started to approach a building that already had people lined up outside of it. I had never been here before, but Giovanni led us straight to the bouncers that were standing in front of the entrance. I could already hear the music coming from upstairs. Giovanni stopped and exchanged a few words in Spanish with the large men before the one nodded and stepped back, allowing us to enter.

"Did you just jump the line?"

"It's not jumping the line if you have a booking."

Of course. He was so prepared. As we entered, he led us straight to the staircase in front of us. Our hands were still intertwined and I followed closely behind him as we reached the top, entering a rooftop bar that was already packed with people. Giovanni led us through the people that had gathered on the dance floor until we reached the outside area of the bar. The music surrounded us and as Giovanni stopped and stepped to the side, I was suddenly greeted by a chorus.

"SURPRISE!"

"Oh my God!" My hands flung up to my mouth as I was greeted by the excitement from the six people closest to us.

Reyna, Katrina, Sergio, Diego, Penelope and Alvaro all stood in front of me, cheering and smiling. Of course, I would want to celebrate our engagement and Giovanni knew that. He knew me. He always knew what I needed.

Reyna was the first person to throw her arms around me. "Congratulations!"

The tears didn't stop as I went around greeting everyone. Each of them congratulating us and wishing us well. My heart was so warm. The most important people in my life were all in one room to celebrate the best day of my life.

Well, one of my best days. I was pretty sure I had more to come with Giovanni.

"Let's see the ring!" Katrina exclaimed and reached for my hand before turning to Giovanni. "You did well, sir."

Giovanni chuckled and slipped his hand around my waist, pulling me closer to him. "I would take credit but Reyna helped me pick it out."

I turned to Reyna, gawking at her. "You knew this whole time?"

"Of course I did!" she jumped excitedly. "And don't even lecture me about not telling you 'cause you know I couldn't give away a surprise like this."

"And here you were telling me we should make plans for tomorrow," I said, remembering our conversation at *Aroma* yesterday.

"Yes, well I had to do whatever I could to throw you off." She smiled.

I chuckled. "You're right."

Penelope threw her arms around me next. "I am so happy for you! I didn't think I would ever have a sister-in-law."

I squeezed her back. "Everyone was convinced this one would be a terminal bachelor."

I nudged Giovanni playfully and he tugged at his bottom lip before letting out a small laugh. "Trust me, I had convinced myself of that, too."

He pulled me closer, leaning down to my ear, "You changed it all for me, *mi hermosa.*"

I was so in love with this man it hurt. Every fiber of my being was consumed by him and the love we shared. It came so naturally to me. Loving him was like breathing. I didn't have to think about it, it just happened.

I brought my lips to meet his before Alvaro called for our attention.

"Champagne all around!" Alvaro shouted and started handing out glasses from the tray the waiter was holding, *"Gracias."*

Giovanni reached over and grabbed two glasses, handing me one before securing his arm around my waist again.

"A toast," Alvaro announced, *"Felicidades, hermano*! I never thought I'd see the day where this guy got engaged."

A chorus of laughter surrounded us. Giovanni's previous reputation preceded him but he had come a long way from being the man who was afraid of commitment.

"But when I met Isabella and saw the way they were together, I knew he had found someone special."

Giovanni looked down at me before leaning over, kissing my forehead. I swear my heart was so close to bursting right through my chest. I had never felt happiness quite like this before.

"Isabella, Giovanni," he started to raise his glass, "Wishing you two a lifetime of happiness. No matter what life throws at you two, if you stick together, you can conquer it all. *Salud!"*

We all lifted our glasses in celebration before bringing them down again. I lifted the glass to my lips and sipped on the bitter taste. I looked up at Giovanni who was already looking at me with a big smile on his face, that dimple of his on full display.

"Look at you and your goofy smile," I teased and reached up, his rough beard against my hand as I cupped his cheek.

"I've never been happier." he leaned his forehead against mine, "Seriously, I can't believe I get to call you mine for the rest of my life."

"Giovanni, you're going to make me cry again."

"From this day onwards, you're only allowed to cry happy tears, okay?"

I giggled and stretched up to meet his lips again. He wrapped his arms tightly around my waist and I sunk into the kiss. My body was calling out for him. With the amount of love working its way through me, I was just about ready to devour him.

He pulled away but leaned closer to my ear to whisper, "Fuck, I'd take you right now if I could."

I was open for business. The heat spread across my cheeks and I flicked my eyes up to meet his. They were swimming with love and desire. When he looked at me, everyone else disappeared. He was all I saw.

And right now, my body was calling out for him and as much as I wanted to drag him out of here so I could have my way with him, we had a celebration ahead of us so that was going to have to wait.

"Patience, Mr. Velázquez," I murmured, "Delayed gratification."

He cocked an eyebrow, "Wait till I get you alone, future Mrs. Velázquez."

I was so ready.

CHAPTER 2:

Giovanni

"You ready to get out of here?" I leaned down and murmured in her ear so she could hear me over the music.

She pulled away; a naughty look immediately settled over her face. Her arms were wrapped around my neck and I had her body pulled up close to mine. I could feel the heat between us as the tension presented itself. I already knew where her mind had headed and given the heat working its way to my groin, she could feel what I was thinking.

I had shared her enough for tonight.

"Oh, yes." She tugged at her lip before smiling. "Looks like you're already ready for me."

She leaned against my erection. It didn't take much for her to turn me on. Just having her body close to mine was enough to get the blood flowing. Being in love with her caused the same reaction. An emotional boner, if you will. I leaned down and gave her a quick kiss before subtly shifting to hide what was already obvious to her.

It didn't take long for us to say our goodbyes as we worked through our crowd. We had been here for hours, partying and celebrating till it was the early hours of the morning now. The place was still packed with people and with the music still blaring through the speakers, there was no sense that it was slowing down anytime soon but I was ready for Isabella and me to have a party of our own. I was too high on the anticipation of taking my fiancé home so I could have my way with her.

Fiancé.

Who would have thought? If you had told me years ago that I would be engaged to the most beautiful woman, I wouldn't have believed it. I didn't believe this was something that was meant for me but then Isabella waltzed into my life and changed it all. She captured my heart and I knew there was no one else for me.

She was my person.

"This way, baby." I guided her as we reached the bottom of the stairs and Isabella turned in the opposite direction.

She giggled and pulled herself closer to me. "Whoops."

She had a few drinks throughout the evening and I could tell she was on a level. I allowed her to do the drinking since I was driving and I loved watching how playfully clumsy she became whenever she was intoxicated. She also found everything amusing and I got to listen to that laugh of hers for most of the evening. God, I loved that sound. It was genuine and I loved hearing how happy she was. That's all I want.

She stumbled over her own feet and gripped onto my arm tighter as she burst into laughter again at her own clumsiness. I tightened my grip around her waist as she leaned against me.

"Am I going to have to carry you?" I nudged her playfully.

She smiled and shook her head. "I promise I'm not that drunk, I just missed my step."

"Suuuuure," I teased. "So, those dance moves you had going on back there had nothing to do with drunk Isabella?"

"Actually, that was I'm-so-happy-cause-I'm-engaged-Isabella."

I chuckled and placed a kiss on her temple. "God, I love you."

She looked up at me. Her hazel eyes were shining and her bright smile on full display. Her cheeks pulled upwards, creasing the corner of her eyes the way it always did when she was happy. She was so beautiful. I could spend hours tracing every little thing about her. The small beauty spot she had on her right cheek. The curve of her lips and the way she tugged at her bottom one whenever she was deep in thought or holding back a dirty desire. The light freckles that were barely noticeable across her cheeks unless you were close enough to find them against her skin. I knew they were there. I paid attention to everything about her. She was shining with genuine happiness that was picture perfect - I would remember her like that forever.

I slipped my hand into hers, intertwining our fingers as we made our way through what was left of the crowd by the fountain. It was fast approaching two in the morning but there were still people scattered throughout. There was a slight chill in the air that surrounded us now and I was thankful we weren't too far from the car. We turned down the, now, deserted alley towards where I had parked. After my accident, my car was a total write-off and instead of replacing it with what I had before, I decided on something less flashy. A black Audi RS7 with a Sportback had just the right amount of sophistication and speed that I needed.

I fished my keys out of my back pocket and went over to open Isabella's door for her. She slipped inside, closing it behind her as I went around to the driver's seat. I turned the car on and the engine roared to life as I pulled the seatbelt across me. Isabella followed my lead and turned in her seat to face me.

"I just realized I'm going to have to tell my parents." She tugged at her lip nervously.

"Oh, you don't need to do that." I shrugged casually.

Her face pulled in confusion. "What do you mean?"

I leaned my arm over her headrest and looked back as I started to slowly reverse. "I didn't actually go to Valencia yesterday. I went to London."

I pulled the car out of the parking spot and brought my hand from behind her headrest to rest on her inner thigh instead as we made our way down the street. I glanced at her as she gaped at me.

"What?" I chuckled. "I knew that would be something you'd want them to know about and although I didn't need their blessing. I knew it was the right thing to do."

"No way!" Her hand went to cover her mouth, hiding a smile behind it. "There's no way you went to London."

"I promise I did." I laughed at her reaction. "I'd do anything for you, *mi hermosa,* and I wanted them to know that I was going to take care of you."

I looked over at her again as a few tears escaped her eyes. Her big hazel eyes looked up at me with disbelief. Almost like she couldn't believe I would do something like that but how couldn't I? It was the right thing to do and I would always do right by her.

"I made you cry again," I pointed out.

She laced her fingers with mine. "I can't believe you would do that. I don't know how I got so lucky to have you, Giovanni."

It was like hearing my name roll off her tongue for the first time. I love it. I love her. I was completely consumed by her in every way. She was addictive to me.

"I'm the lucky one." I brought the back of her hand to my lips, loving the sight of the ring around her finger.

She was mine.

Forever.

CHAPTER 3:

Isabella

As the elevator doors opened to our apartment, I threw myself at Giovanni.

The alcohol was still working its way through my system, igniting my desire like it was something I had never felt before. I was consumed by it. His strong arms came around me lifting me to wrap my legs around his waist as his hungry lips found mine. He wasted no time pinning me up against the nearest wall and I gasped as my back hit against it. I loved his intensity. I wanted his hands all over me. I wanted his lips to explore every part of me. I wanted to hand myself over to him. My love. My fiancé. My forever.

His lips quickly left my lips and grazed against my jaw before starting to work its way down my neck. The throbbing between my legs was very much alive as the pressure increased with each touch. My hands found his hair and I tugged at it as he brought his lips back to mine. I nipped at his lower lip and he let out a deep growl. Fuck, that was enough for me to come undone.

I started to push his jacket down his arms, dropping it to the floor. He pulled his shirt over his head before he lifted me and started to walk through our apartment, never once breaking the kiss until I caught his bottom lip between my teeth again, this time applying a bit more pressure.

"*Joder*," he groaned and placed me on the kitchen counter, the cold of the granite seeping through my jeans.

I wrapped my legs around his waist and pulled him closer to me, feeling how hard he was for me. I lifted my hips and rocked against him, causing a rush of desire through me. I was aching for him.

"Giovanni," I breathed as his lips sucked on my neck, sending an overwhelming amount of heat through my veins making my toes curl.

"Yes, baby?" He reached for the bottom of my shirt and pulled it over my head, tossing it on the floor before bringing his lips against my chest.

He was not gentle about it. He was devouring every part of me he could get his hands on and I couldn't get enough of his touch. His hand came around my back and unclasped my bra. I slipped it off me and his lips came down on me again. They found my one nipple and between the licking and biting, I was struggling to contain the moans escaping my lips. He always knew how to make my body feel good. He had mastered it but I wanted to do the same. The sudden urge to take control overcame me and I pushed him off me.

"What are y-?" he started to ask but I turned him around, pushing his back up against the counter before reaching for the button of his jeans.

He rolled his eyes back before looking at me with a lascivious smirk. He knew what was coming next. I pulled his pants and underwear down, freeing himself to me.

God, he was so ready for me.

The throbbing between my legs only intensified at the sight of his erection. I wanted him inside of me, filling me up in all the right ways.

But right now, I wanted nothing more than to please him.

I lowered myself and heard him suck in a small breath as I wrapped my hand around him. I was slow at first, moving up and down him as he leaned his head back, soaking in my touch. Without warning, I brought my mouth over him and was rewarded with a husky moan coming from deep within his throat. He jerked his head forward again, looking down at me as I worked my way over him. My tongue doing the work around him. His hand gripped my hair and I looked up at him.

"God, I love this sight," he moaned, tightening his grip on my hair which only made me increase the pace.

I was just about ready to explode as the aching between my legs continued to throb as I watched how he soaked in what I was doing to him. I quickened the pace, taking him deeper as I went.

A twirl of my tongue around his tip sent his head back again, the veins on his neck displaying themselves as his orgasm built up. "I'm close."

Another increase of pace and one last push against the back of my throat,

Giovanni released himself. I had just enough time for one last twirl around him before he grabbed me and pulled me up, his lips crashing down against mine. His greedy tongue pushed its way into my mouth as he caught my lip between his teeth, making me whimper as the throbbing continued. I needed him.

"I need to be inside you, Isabella," he groaned and reached for the button on my pants.

I quickly pushed them down my legs, my underwear following. I stepped out of them and his hand cupped me, feeling how ready I was for him.

"Oh, baby," he murmured into my ear as he nipped at it. "How about you turn around?"

I rolled my eyes back, almost coming undone at just the thought of what he was going to do to me. I turned around and he pushed me gently against the counter, the cold granite against my body. Between the arousal working its way through me and the cold against my breasts, my nipples hardened. He ran his hand down my bare back before cupping me again, this time slipping a finger inside of me.

I couldn't stop the moans from forming on my lips as he teased me, sliding slowly in and out of me. I was pretty sure he could feel the throbbing against his finger. He slid up my opening to reach my clit and started to slowly rub his finger against it, sending my body into a frenzy.

"Do you like what I'm doing to you, baby?"

I tugged at my bottom lip and nodded.

"I need to hear you, Isabella." The seduction in his voice washed over me. "You have to tell me."

"I love what you're doing," I breathed.

He increased the pace and pressure against me causing the orgasm to build deep inside of me. I pushed up on my tiptoes as he continued to push me further and further.

"Do you want me inside of you?" he breathed into my ear as he pulled my hair back, forcing me up against his body.

"Mh-mm," I murmured.

"Say it."

"I want you inside of me, Giovanni," I groaned. "Now."

He snickered and let me go, pushing me down against the counter again.

I was wet in anticipation. He removed his hands from me but not before I felt him hard against my entrance. Skin against skin. I was burning for him. He positioned himself before pushing deep inside of me. I tightened around him as we both let out a satisfied sigh. This is exactly where he belonged. He started to move inside me - trying to be slow and gentle at first but I wasn't having it. I needed him. My desire craved it harder. I pushed myself up against him, forcing him deeper.

"Someone's eager," he chuckled.

"Don't be gentle," I commanded.

"Oh?"

The words were on the tip of my tongue. Giovanni had no problem expressing to me exactly what he wanted - dirty or otherwise and I had always wanted to allow that part of me out. The voice of my desire lingered in the background but he made me feel comfortable to share all the parts of me. Even the part of me that may have a filthy mouth.

I turned my head to look up at him. "I need you to fuck me, Giovanni."

It was like music to his ears. His face twitched in arousal and his eyes darkened with desire. There was no holding him back now. He grabbed my hips and started to push harder into me, the sound of our bodies colliding filled the room. His hand buried itself in my hair and he pulled it back, causing me to arch my back as he pushed deeper inside of me.

"Yes, yes, yes," I moaned, not wanting this to end.

And he delivered on what I asked. He didn't stop once and he definitely wasn't gentle about it. Between pulling my hair and sucking at my neck, I was moaning his name as my orgasm rolled through me.

But he didn't stop.

He reached around me and found my clit again. Circling it as he continued to move in and out of me, each movement harder than the one before. He was giving me exactly what I wanted and he didn't stop as the orgasms continued to roll through me. I couldn't hold back moaning his name. My legs were already shaking but he held onto my hips, pushing deeper inside of me before finally reaching his own climax again. For a few moments, we stayed like that. He was still buried deep inside of me and I was leaning against the counter, trying to catch my breath. He pulled out of me, leaving me feeling empty before turning me around and lifting me back onto the counter. The cold was no longer an issue - my body was far too hot now.

He positioned himself between my legs and wrapped his arms around my waist, trying to catch his own breath. His dark hair had fallen over his eyes and I lifted my hand, pushing it back. I ran my nails through his hair and my hand found the back of his neck. I slowly scratched against it. His eyes were closed as he soaked in my touch. He looked happy and satisfied. I couldn't help but smile.

He slowly opened his eyes. "You keep surprising me, *mi hermosa.*"

"How did I surprise you now?"

"By telling me to fuck you. God, just those words were enough to make me come."

I giggled as the heat spread across my cheeks.

He noticed and couldn't help but laugh. "Oh, are you embarrassed now?"

I shook my head, pretending I was still just as confident as I was a few minutes ago. "I've never been one for dirty talk. I'll let you do all that."

"Not anymore. You must tell me what you want." He leaned closer to me, his hand cupping my breast as he squeezed my nipple between his fingers. "I want to know all the dirty thoughts going on in your mind."

I lifted my head and tugged at my lip again. The embarrassment was momentary. Giovanni made me comfortable to explore all the parts of me. He made me want to explore my deepest desires.

I wrapped my arms around his neck. "Well, we have years to explore that."

"We have the rest of our lives, baby."

CHAPTER 4:

Isabella

I woke to the distant sound of a calm Spanish guitar melody filling the room. It was faint at first but then started to slowly seep its way around me as the volume increased. I stretched across the bed and found Giovanni's side empty. My eyes slowly fluttered open and adjusted to the day. The curtains were drawn closed and the only light slipped through the bottom of them. I lifted my hand to wipe my eye and stopped as I noticed the ring on my finger. A huge smile spread across my face.

I'm engaged.

And not just to anyone but to the man of my dreams. The connection Giovanni and I had was the most natural thing I had experienced. We fell into a rhythm with each other that worked and we knew that no matter what, he and I were meant to have found each other. I could be the best version of myself with him. He loved me in ways I had only dreamed of being loved and I count my blessings every day that this man is the one I get to spend the rest of my life with.

I sat up and set my feet down the side of the bed, the cold of the tiles against my bare feet. I grabbed the sheet and wrapped it around my naked body. We spent hours exploring each other and soaking in the euphoria of our engagement before sleep finally found us. I had never been happier and my body was still feeling the after-effects of the multiple orgasms. I was at ease in every way.

I slowly wandered out of the room and down the stairs as I followed the sweet melody. I turned in the direction of the music and in the corner of the lounge, Giovanni sat with the guitar in his hands. The sun was peeping through the curtains in the area, landing on him. He was looking down at the guitar, his hair falling forward as he played. He didn't notice me as I reached the bottom of the stairs and I didn't move. I soaked him in. He was wrapped up in the melody he was playing and didn't notice me. His fingers moved effortlessly across the strings. He was shirtless and the muscles on his arms slightly flexed as he continued to play.

He was perfect.

I could sit for hours staring at him. I could get lost trying to take in every marking over his skin. He was the only kind of art I was interested in. Slowly he approached the end of the song he was playing and his head lifted, his gaze landing on me.

"I'm sorry, did I wake you?" He set the guitar down next to him and gestured for me.

I smiled and walked over to him, dropping onto his lap. "I don't mind being woken up like that."

I draped my legs across his lap and wrapped my arms around his neck. He pulled me closer to him and I breathed in that familiar smell of his. I could never quite place exactly what that was but it smelled like home to me.

"It's nice to hear you play again." I slowly ran my nails over the back of his neck the way I knew he liked it. "That was beautiful."

He leaned his head back and brought his hand gently over to push a few stray strands of hair out of my eyes. "Thank you, baby. Just woke up and felt like playing again."

He was looking at me with such love that it made my heart burst. I felt like I was exactly where I was meant to be.

"Did you sleep alright?" he asked.

I nodded. "I thought yesterday was a dream until I saw this."

I lifted my hand to show my ring and he smiled, revealing that deep dimple of his.

"Me too. I thought there was no way I was actually engaged to the most beautiful woman in the world but look." He lifted my hand to his lips and kissed the ring.

"You don't think I'm the most beautiful woman in the whole world." I nudged him playfully.

"In my world, absolutely." He leaned into my neck and started leaving kisses against my throat.

A small blush presented itself across my cheeks as I smiled. He made me feel so warm inside and the lingering desire reminded me of its presence. I could never get enough of him. I was addicted.

I leaned down as he pulled away and planted a small kiss on his lips. "I love you so much."

"I love you, *mi hermosa.*"

"You know this means we have to plan a wedding now? All the flowers, the venue, the music, the photographer..."

My mouth was running away with me as I started listing all the things that started to pop into my head. I had to plan a freaking wedding. Where do I even begin?

"Whoa there baby," he chuckled. "We don't have to plan everything today but knowing you, you'll already have an action plan by the end of the day."

"No, I won't." I pursed my lips.

He lifted an eyebrow. "So you have no desire to sit down with your notebook and pen and write a list?"

I absolutely had the desire to do that. The organized control freak in me knew it was the first place to start.

I tugged at my bottom lip. "Nope."

"Oh? So no list about the engagement party or the fact we need to pick a date or all the people we need to call?"

I shook my head.

"You liar!" He exclaimed and chuckled as he leaned closer to my neck again, making me laugh. "I know you and you love making lists. In fact, you need to make lists."

I caved. "I'm a compulsive list-maker."

"We may need to send you to see someone about that."

I giggled and leaned down to meet his lips again. This time we soaked it in a little longer and my heart fluttered in my chest. I was perfectly content.

He slid his hand under the sheet I had wrapped around me, moving up my bare skin. "Someone's naked."

"Mm-hmm," I murmured.

His hand reached the top of my thigh and instead of heading where I wanted him to, he brought his hand back out.

"What are you doing?" I asked.

"It's Sunday. Your dad is going to call at exactly 09:30 which is in." He glanced past me to the clock hanging on the wall in the kitchen. "Exactly six minutes from now."

"You don't think we could do stuff in six minutes?" I challenged.

"I think your body deserves more time, baby."

He was right. Giovanni wasn't one to rush things like that. He enjoyed soaking in every part of me and the way my body handed itself over to him. I felt desired. I felt worshipped. I felt loved.

"You never told me what happened when you went to go see my parents," I said. "I still can't believe you did that."

"It was the right thing to do," he shrugged.

"I can't imagine my mother was very happy to see you."

"She was surprised. Your dad and sister too 'cause I didn't tell them I was coming but they're your family, they just want you to be happy."

I scoffed. "My dad and sister - yes. My mother, I'm not so sure about. I don't think our relationship will ever truly recover."

My relationship with Gloria Avery was complicated. She hated that I went against everything she wanted for me. It didn't matter that I was happy or successful in my own way, she still kept me at arm's length. After the brief conversation, we had the night after Giovanni's accident, I made sure to limit our interactions. I didn't have it in me to continue to be disappointed by her.

"I wouldn't be so sure," Giovanni commented. "While your mother was definitely less than impressed to see me, I kind of called her out on her bullshit."

My jaw dropped. "You didn't!"

"I did. I told her that she was wrong thinking I'm not the right man for you and that her treatment was pretty unjust considering I hadn't done anything wrong."

I was amazed. The one thing my mother needed was to be called out on her bullshit but when it came from me, she was too dismissive of it. She was stubborn and refused to understand where I was coming from. It infuriated me.

"And I think she actually respects me for calling her out," he continued.

"I didn't go there to ask for their blessing - so sorry if that's what you were hoping for - I just went there to let them know I was going to take care of you."

I smiled. "I don't care if we don't have their blessing. I'd marry you in a heartbeat."

He pulled me closer to him. "Then it's a good thing I got it anyway - from your dad and sister at least. Your mother said she respects me going there so that's basically code for welcome to the family."

I chuckled. "That's more than I've ever gotten from her so you're definitely winning."

Just like clockwork, my phone started ringing as soon as the clock hit half-past nine. We had stuck to weekly catch-ups over the last year. At first, it was just my dad and I but then Camila started to get involved when she could. My mother popped up briefly but we never engaged further than polite pleasantries.

"That's my cue," I announced and slipped off Giovanni.

My feet were cold against the floor as I shuffled over to the kitchen where I had left my phone to charge. I reached for it and swiped up, putting the call on loudspeaker.

"Hi, Dad."

"Hello my Bella, how is everything going?"

We went through our usual check-ins. I told him I was doing well and he updated me on the same. He was doing much better with his health and said his doctor was happy with his recent check-up. He asked about the coffee shop and I was excited to share how well it had been doing recently. I loved getting up in the morning to go to my space. It constantly reminded me that this was what was meant for me. A simple life where I was happy.

"And how's Giovanni?" My dad asked as Giovanni returned from upstairs, pulling a shirt over his head.

"He's actually just walked into the room," I said as Giovanni came around to the counter.

"*Hola,* Mr. Avery."

"How many times must I ask you to call me Oscar? I think we're past the Mister part, don't you?"

Giovanni chuckled as I walked over to the kettle, bringing it to boil. "Yes, sir but you know me, I always want to be respectful."

"He's too polite for his own good," I interjected and wrapped my arms around his waist from behind.

I turned my head in the direction of my phone. "We actually have some news."

"Oh?"

"Is mom with you?"

"She's in the kitchen - I can call her- wait, let me quickly." He pulled away from the phone and shouted for my mother.

A few seconds later I heard her voice in the background asking what's going on.

"Isabella?" My dad asked, appearing clearly on the other end of the line again. "Your mother and I are listening."

"Hi, mom," I said awkwardly.

"Isabella," she replied as curt as ever. "I believe Giovanni is there too."

"Hi, Mrs. Avery."

"I was telling dad that Giovanni and I have some news." I paused to see if either of them would say anything but they didn't so I continued. "I know you already knew this was going to happen but we got engaged last night."

"Congratulations!" My dad exclaimed. "Giovanni did come to see us but I had no idea it would be so soon, that's wonderful news."

I was so relieved by my father's reaction. I don't know why I feared it in the first place - he was always the one that wanted the best for me. Giovanni moved over to the kettle to make us some coffee and I leaned against the counter, over my phone.

"Yeah, he told me he went to see you guys."

"He did," my mother replied this time. "It was greatly appreciated."

I glanced up to meet Giovanni's smug face. He had his eyebrows lifted and he mouthed, "She loves me now." I had to hold back my giggle.

"We are very happy for you, Bella," my dad said.

"Thanks, Dad."

I heard my mother's voice away from the phone. "Love, could you give me a moment? I just want to speak with Isabella."

"Yes, of course," my father replied before bringing himself closer to the phone. "Your mother wants to speak to you, Bella, so I'm going to go. I need to speak to the new gardener we hired. I'll chat to you next week."

"Okay dad, I love you."

"Love you too," he said. "Goodbye, Giovanni."

"Bye sir." Giovanni handed me my cup of coffee and leaned closer to me. "Do you want me to leave?"

I shook my head and mouthed. "Stay."

He leaned down and kissed my hair before returning to lean against the counter on the other side of me.

"Isabella?" my mother said.

"I'm here."

"I know things have still been a bit rocky between us and I'm -," she paused and took a breath in, "I'm sorry for my part in that."

I was surprised. Stubborn-ol' Gloria Avery apologizing. That was unheard of. I glanced up at Giovanni who was just as surprised as I was.

"Giovanni came all this way to speak to us and he reminded me of how unfair I've been to the both of you."

"Mo-"

She cut me off. "You don't need to say anything right now. I just wanted you to know that and to know that I am happy for you - both of you."

Well, I'll be damned. I used to believe hell would freeze over before I heard the inclination of an apology from my mother but I was wrong.

How's that for character development?

"Thank you," I murmured. "I appreciate that."

"And I hope the both of you will consider joining us for the holidays this year. I know your father would love to see you, Isabella."

I glanced up at Giovanni and he nodded.

"Of course. We'll be there."

"Wonderful!"

I was still trying to process the entire conversation with her and I was at a loss for words.

"Well, I must go now. We'll talk soon, Isabella."

"Yes, definitely."

"Alright. Goodbye."

"Bye, mom."

Still no I love you as she disconnected the call but I had to count the small victories.

"Your mom loves me," Giovanni announced.

"Love? That's a bit of a stretch."

"I'm serious. She said she was happy for us - that might as well have been a declaration of the fact she loves her new son-in-law."

I threw my head back in laughter. "I would love to know what goes on in your mind. Seems like a fascinating place to be."

Giovanni walked over to me and leaned his hands on either side of me as my back leaned against the counter.

"I think the fact she said she's happy for us means she accepts our relationship now." I said.

"That was never going to stop me from being with you. Even if she had thrown me out of her office yesterday, it wouldn't have changed a thing."

"Not many people call her out on her shit so I commend you." I wrapped my arms around his waist.

"Well, if you think about it, I've actually done nothing to her, she just hated that she didn't choose me for you."

He wasn't wrong. She attempted to puppet master every aspect of my life and Giovanni is the furthest thing from the man she would have picked for me which is exactly why he was perfect for me. I knew what I needed in my life - not her.

I leaned up and my lips met his before I pulled away. "Breakfast?"

He nodded. "What do you have in mind?"

CHAPTER 5:

Isabella

Over the last few months since our engagement, things had started to already come together quite nicely. It turned out that my great organization skills and compulsive list-making proved to be helpful when it came to planning a wedding. Many people dream of their wedding day - I was not one of them. I had never really thought of what I wanted so I had to figure it out as we went along. Giovanni was far too blasé when it came to the details of our wedding - he was more focused on planning the honeymoon which he refused to tell me about. He had asked to take control of that and I had to trust him. We had already picked a date.

15 August.

Giovanni was adamant about not getting married in autumn or winter and I refused to have our date slap-bang in the middle of summer. I had experienced the Barcelona heat before and it wasn't my favorite. Excessive sweating was not what I wanted in attendance when I walked down the aisle. We eventually agreed on a date that we hoped would be past the peak of the heat but not too close to autumn either. We had already sent out the save the dates and the RSVPs were rolling in. Luckily our wedding wasn't going to be a big one. With our families and friends, we were well under sixty people and I was happy to keep it that small. Every time I thought about marrying Giovanni, my heart swelled with the overwhelming love I had for him. Just when I thought it wasn't possible to fall even more in love with him, he had a way of surprising me. I was never going to stop falling for him.

I had just brought the soup I was making off the hot plate on the stove when I heard the sound of the elevator doors opening.

"Oh, that smells amazing!" Giovanni shouted as he appeared from around the corner. "Hello, baby."

I smiled and walked over to greet him. He was all suited up as he had a number of meetings with his investors about the *Mala Mía* expansion. The success of the Barcelona and Valencia branches had cemented *Mala Mía* as a brand worth franchising. He was hard at work at the possibility of an opening in Sevilla.

He pulled me into his arms and his lips met mine. This was what home felt like.

"Hi." I smiled.

"What are you making?" he reached for the tie around his neck as I made my way back over to the stove.

"Reyna's famous tomato soup," I announced proudly. "I don't know if it will be as good as how she makes it but it's not a bad attempt if I do say so myself."

He placed the tie on the counter and shrugged his jacket off revealing the white button-up top underneath that sat perfectly around his toned arms. "I've never had Reyna's version so yours will be my only point of reference."

"Then this is going to be the best soup you've ever had."

He chuckled as he strolled over to the cupboard above the sink where we kept our glasses. He reached for a whiskey glass. "Can I pour you some wine?"

I nodded and leaned down, opening the oven to the smell of the freshly baked bread I had in there. "Yes, please. I had actually opened a bottle of red but I wasn't sure if you were going to have that or whiskey."

He turned around with the glasses in his hands and made his way back to the counter where I had left the open bottle of wine. He pulled himself onto the stool in front of me as I brought the bread onto the counter.

"Fresh bread too?" he gaped. "Looks like I made the right choice proposing to you."

I chuckled. "Yeah, it was definitely my cooking skills that drew you in right?"

"Yup, the first time you cooked for me I knew I had to marry you."

I rolled my eyes and smiled. That was one thing that changed when I moved in. Giovanni had relied heavily on pre-cooked meals for the longest time but I was more than happy to take on the role in the kitchen. I made sure that he learned as we went along and eventually he even got good at it. Coming home to him trying out some meals on his own was something I loved. He may not be the best but it was the fact he put in the effort at all that I appreciated.

I fanned the bread on the counter. I needed it to cool down before I could slice it into pieces. I stopped, and instead, I reached for the whiskey behind me and handed it to Giovanni as he handed me my now full glass of wine.

"How did your meetings go?" I asked and leaned against the counter as I brought my glass to my lips, allowing the bitter taste to spread across my tongue.

I was never a big wine drinker until my palate had matured enough to acquire the taste. Giovanni loved his wine so he introduced me to all his favorites. I started with rosé then moved onto white wine and now I had reached prime maturity with the red wine being my choice for the evening.

"Really good actually," he said as he poured his own drink. "They have a few locations in mind for the Sevilla branch so we're going to have to take a couple of days to go and visit them."

"Oh no, a trip to Sevilla - how will I survive?" I teased.

"We have such a tough life, Isabella."

I couldn't help but laugh. I had completely fallen in love with Valencia when I went with Giovanni. We had been back there a few times but he promised that Sevilla had a strong possibility of stealing my heart. I had been so excited to go there so I was looking forward to our weekend away.

"And how was your day?" He brought his glass up to his lips and tilted his head slightly as he took a sip.

"Not bad, thanks. It was pretty busy today but we're training our new hire - her name's Savannah and I think she's going to fit right in."

It had been months since *Aroma* first opened its doors to the public and I couldn't be happier with how well it was doing. The agreement with Reyna and I was never for her to take on a full-time role. She enjoyed popping in over the weekend and she helped when it came to some of the behind-the-scenes admin but I was the full-time presence. We opened just after ten and we were closed by four. I had started to become friendly with some of the recurring locals and we had already hired a couple of people to work full-time. Savannah was the latest hire and I had previously hired a student named Federico to work as a barista. The two of them were enough to help for now. If we continued to grow the way I was hoping we would then another pair of hands was going to be inevitable.

"And Federico? You never fired him?"

"Of course not."

"Not even after he spilled that coffee on that customer?" he eyed me playfully over the glass.

"Firing someone because they had clumsy tendencies would be wrong."

When Federico first started, his nerves had gotten the better of him. The mistakes he made behind the counter were still fine but it got a bit difficult to let them slide when he was spilling coffee all over the customers. I couldn't just let him go, so instead, he put in extra hours of training and he finally became comfortable enough. It took me a while to let him serve the tables again but he was much better now.

"You're just too nice."

I shrugged and took another sip of my wine before setting the glass down. I walked over to the other end of the counter where I had some papers scattered across it. All of them had something to do with the wedding.

"When are we supposed to decide on the menu?" he asked and walked over to join me in front of the countless lists in front of us.

He stood close to me, his arm brushing up against mine. I could smell what still lingered of his cologne as I turned to lean into him.

"By this weekend. I also need to confirm the flower arrangement and the guest list is starting to come together."

"Really?" He took another sip and walked over to the other side of me, glancing down at the papers, "That's a good thing."

"Should I be concerned that your father hasn't RSVP'd yet?"

"Nope."

"What do you mean 'nope'?"

"I mean 'nope' because I never gave him his save the date."

"Giovanni," I retorted. "What do you mean you never gave him his save the date? Do you not want to invite your father to our wedding?"

"I'm still debating it."

I sighed. Although things had been better for the Velázquez family since his parents got divorced. It had not been better for Giovanni and Cecilio. The damage his father had done to their relationship made it difficult for Giovanni to look past. Especially since his father refused to apologize for anything that transpired between the two of them. He was still angry that his father had treated his mother that way. Granted, Marcina ended up having an affair of her own but if Cecilio hadn't done it first, she probably wouldn't have had her own. The blurred lines of that situation could often lead to a debate about two wrongs not making it right but that was never a conversation that I had a place in. I stood by Giovanni as his parents went through a divorce and eventually ended up with other people. It became ironic when it was revealed that Cecilio's partner was also married and had decided against leaving her husband. He ended up alone and it proved that the grass was, in fact, not greener on the other side. The interactions between Giovanni and his father had been brief but I never thought he wouldn't want his father at the wedding.

I placed my wine glass down and went to stand behind him, wrapping my arms around his waist as I leaned my chin against his back. "I know things have always been rocky with your father but I think you'll regret not inviting him."

He sighed and brought his glass back up to his lips.

"Just think about it," I said and left a small kiss on his back. "In the end, it's your decision and I'll respect that but just give it some thought."

He remained silent the way he always did whenever he didn't feel like continuing to speak about his relationship with his father. There were rare moments where he spoke about how it made him feel and I knew he hated that their relationship was the way it was but I also knew that they were very similar. They shared a stubbornness that was equal in measure which meant that neither of them was likely to budge on the situation.

I strolled back to the bread that had started to cool down. Steam was still rising from it but I leaned my hand against it and found the heat had started to subside enough for me to start cutting. I pulled a bread knife from the draw and started to slice it into pieces.

"Alvaro has invited us to his place for Christmas day," Giovanni said as he turned to face me, still leaning against the counter. "Have you decided how long you want to stay in London?"

"I was thinking just for the day. Have Christmas Eve at my parents' and then leave early the next day to make it back for Christmas day with your family."

"We don't have to. If you'd prefer to stay with your family longer, I don't mind."

"Thanks but I think one day with my mother is enough for now. We may be in a ceasefire but she and I have always managed to bump heads so I know if we stay too long, then we'll find something to argue about and I'd like to keep the peace until the wedding."

When my mother had invited us for the holidays a few months back, we had accepted. It was a step in the right direction for our relationship but I wasn't delusional. I had grown up constantly in a battle with my mother so I was under no illusion that everything was going to be all sunshine and roses all of a sudden. We still had various traits that clashed and I wasn't about to poke the bear. I didn't want a hiccup at my wedding so I needed to keep this neutral ground going as long as possible. Maybe in the future, she and I would get to a place where our relationship was more than just polite pleasantries but only time would tell.

"Can we agree that we're not going to make the same mistakes our parents made with our own children?" Giovanni asked, stepping closer to me.

"You think about us having children?" I turned to face him, unable to stop the smile that had formed on my lips.

"What smile is that?" he chuckled and pulled me into his arms. "Of course, I think about that. Don't you?"

"Of course." I tugged at my bottom lip nervously. "We've just never really spoken about that."

"Now might be a good time considering we're getting married."

I giggled. "Yeah these are usually the things people cover before getting engaged."

"I want a family with you, baby. You can decide how many babies we have since you're the one that's going to have to do all the pushing."

I burst out laughing. "I'd be happier if I could just sneeze and they'd slide right out."

"That's quite a visual," Giovanni chuckled. "But seriously, I'll take as many babies as I can get. You know I have no problem with the baby-making process."

"That you do not." I smiled and leaned my head back to face him. "Honestly, I'm actually surprised we haven't had any pregnancy scares. Especially lately since we've been forgetting to use a condom. I don't know if I should be thankful we've been so lucky or concerned."

Giovanni laughed and leaned down to kiss me before pulling away, still keeping his arms around me, "We're just lucky. But seriously, I'd be more than happy if you had to fall pregnant, *mi hermosa*. I can't think of anything better than bringing a child into the world with you."

I swear my heart was just about ready to explode. I had always thought about what it would be like to start a family with him and it warmed my soul that he had thought the same. I had seen how Giovanni was with Mateo and it made my ovaries explode every time. He was going to be a great father and I was looking forward to that part of our future.

"Me too, but I'm in no rush." I pulled away from him. "I am in a rush to eat though because this smells great if I do say so myself."

He chuckled and reached over for the spoon I had been using. He leaned over the stove and placed the spoon inside, filling it with just enough to taste. He brought it up to his lips.

"Oh fuck, that is good." He placed the spoon in the pot again.

"If you grab us some bowls, you can have as much as you want." I gestured to the cupboard.

He turned to grab us two bowls from the cupboard. He stepped back next to me and handed me one as I started to dish up for him.

"And then after dinner, I think we should get started on that baby-making process."

I turned to him. "Sorry, can't. It's that time of the month."

He groaned and I couldn't help but laugh at his reaction. I nudged him playfully and handed him the now full bowl of soup.

"Why do you think I decided to make bread?" I reminded him. He was well-aware of my month-to-month cravings of devouring all the bread in the house.

"I forgot that your go-to craving is bread." He walked around on the counter and placed the bowl down before pulling himself onto the barstool. "You know, we could always try some other things that would definitely not get you pregnant."

I stopped and eyed him. "What the hell are you talking about?"

"You've never thought about the back door?"

"No!" I gaped at him. "Why? Would you want to try that?"

He burst out laughing and shook his head. "No thanks. Not my cup of tea but your reaction was priceless. You can put your eyes back in your head, Isabella."

"Let's stick to the hole we know, please."

He threw his head back in laughter again as I came around to sit next to him. He pulled my barstool closer to him and leaned closer to my neck, leaving a few kisses against it. "Fine, that's my favorite one anyway."

CHAPTER 6:

Giovanni

We landed in London, and yes, you guessed it - it was raining. I couldn't wrap my head around how Isabella had lived here growing up. I had only been here a number of times before and I was yet to see the sun make an appearance. The airport had been packed with people. The holiday season saw tons of passengers making their way through the gates either landing to visit their families or leaving for that same reason. Or just some people on their own mission I'm sure.

Isabella had been anxious the whole flight. She hadn't seen her family in months and I could sense her apprehension at having to be around them again - mostly her mother. For days she tried to talk us out of going but I reassured her that things would be different now. At least I hoped they would be. Gloria Avery was difficult but I had seen the thaw in the ice with her. She had come to accept Isabella and I together. Fuck knows why she had a problem with me in the first place but I maintained my respect and was almost certain that I had won her over. Isabella was less likely to believe that. Her relationship with her mother was a lot more far-gone than I had realized. I had booked a hotel room in the city at Isabella's request. She didn't want to stay at her parent's home and instead opted for our own space.

"I had felt like a stranger in that house growing up so I don't feel like staying there longer than I need to," she said.

It saddened me to hear how she spoke about her childhood. She grew up feeling like a complete outsider. While I had my own fair share of moments where I questioned my place in my own family, I still had a good childhood. It was when I was old enough to see the real shit going on that things started to change. That's why I was adamant to do things differently with my own children when that time came. I would not follow in my father's footsteps.

We were in the cab on the way to her parent's house when Isabella tightened her grip on my hand bringing me out of my own thoughts.

I squeezed her hand. "You okay?"

She nodded but tugged at her bottom lip nervously which was a dead giveaway of how she was really feeling. She tended to pull at it and keep her eyes down at her hands in her lap whenever she was nervous. She tapped her foot against the ground and I slipped my hand over her inner thigh.

"Baby, why are you so nervous? Your family is excited to see you," I reassured her.

"I know that. I just haven't been back here in well over a year and it's just weird to think about how much has changed."

"Well, I'm here with you and if at any point you want to leave, we'll leave." I squeezed her thigh again. "But I guarantee you're not going to want to do that. I know you've been wanting to see your father."

"Of course, and Camila."

"And your mother."

She scrunched her nose. "What if she starts her shit again?"

"There's no way. It's been how long since everything with Nate? Seriously, that's got to be water under the bridge."

She snorted. "I probably sound so stupid being nervous about this but I just never liked the way she made me feel about myself. Like I was never good enough. I was constantly seeking her approval."

"You don't need it. You're happy with your life aren't you?"

She glanced up and smiled. "Of course. The happiest I've ever been."

"Then nothing else matters. Your mother is going to be happy for you." I leaned down and kissed her temple.

I could still sense her weariness as we pulled up the bricked driveway up to a large white house. Your eyes were immediately drawn to the abundance of natural light that flowed through the generous floor-to-ceiling windows. I was taken aback by the luxuriousness of the house. Isabella never spoke much of how well-off her parents were and if their house was anything to go by, they were doing incredibly well for themselves. The driver stopped in the driveway just outside the large dark brown door. We thanked him and I paid our fare before slipping outside the cab. I walked around the back of the car with the umbrella open as he drove off and reached for Isabella as she stood staring up at the house.

"This is the right house, right?" I nudged her playfully, pulling her underneath the umbrella to shelter her from the annoying drizzle that the rain had become.

She turned to me and nodded. "Welcome to the Avery family home."

"You never told me you were rich."

"I'm not," she answered quickly. "My parents are."

She turned back to the house and I took a moment to soak her in. I loved to steal little moments like this where I could appreciate her beauty. Her dark brown hair was tucked underneath a beanie but the long curly locks hung over her shoulders. She pulled her coat closer to her and I watched as she clenched her jaw. I just wanted to make her feel at ease.

I turned to face her. "Hey, I'm here and everything is going to be fine."

"I know," she sighed. "Don't know what's wrong with me."

"Nothing is wrong with you, *mi hermosa*." I slid a finger underneath her chin and lifted it as my lips met hers. "Shall we?"

She gave me another quick kiss before leading the way to her front door. As soon as we were under the roof, I brought the umbrella back down and shook it off. Isabella took it from me and closed it up, dropping it in a long bronze pot that sat just outside the right side of the door. She reached for the handle, opening it up to welcome me into her family home.

"Dad, mom," she shouted. "We're here."

The inside was just as fancy as the outside. It was a beautiful open-plan interior with high ceilings. A staircase stood to my left and my eyes drifted to the second floor where Camila was leaning over the white banister

"Merry Christmas!" she exclaimed and quickly made her way to the bottom of the stairs, walking over to greet us. "It's so good to see you."

She pulled her sister in for a hug. The last time I had seen her in person was back at the London Herald offices. She hadn't changed much except for the haircut she must have gotten. Her light brown hair brushed just over her shoulders. There was no questioning whether she and Isabella were sisters. There was a similarity in their facial features that no doubt showed their similar genes. Especially their noses. They had the same delicate noses but

Isabella had a beauty that I was biased too.

"Hi, Giovanni." Camila stepped over to hug me next. "It's nice to see you again."

"*Hola,* Camila. Merry Christmas."

She turned back to Isabella and reached for her hand. "Giovanni showed me the ring when he came to the office but it looks even better on your hand. Congratulations you guys!"

"Thanks, Camila." Isabella looked over at me and smiled. "Where's Smith?"

"He's with Dad in the TV room. There's a game on and you know how Dad gets."

Camila led us through the house and I was impressed with the place. Everything was meticulously placed. Not a single thing seemed out of place. Must be Gloria's control-freak nature. She led us into the kitchen that had a large granite counter in the middle that was scattered with plates of food across it. An older woman was tending to something that was brewing on the stove before she noticed our presence.

"Ah, Isabella!" she exclaimed and waddled over to pull Isabella in for a hug. "It's so lovely to see you!"

She was a short, round lady who exuded a warm and welcoming energy as soon as she smiled at us. She was much older than Isabella's parents but she had kind eyes. She didn't have a British accent so I figured she wasn't from here but Isabella embraced her like her family.

"It's so good to see you, Maria." She pulled away and turned to me. "This is my fiancé, Giovanni."

"Ooo such a good looking man!" she gushed and reached for my hand. "You know, I've worked for the Avery's since this one was just learning to walk."

"Maria has been around since I can remember. Remember I told you I used to call her my second mom?"

I nodded and smiled. She had such love for Maria. I could see it in her eyes and the way she held onto her hand. They shared a mutual love for each other that I had never seen with her actual mother. When we shared stories from our childhood, Maria's name had popped up a few times. The few times that Isabella felt truly comfortable growing up, she had Maria to thank for that. When she wasn't in the kitchen with her father, she was in it with Maria. It was nice to be able to put a face to the name now.

"It's great to meet you, Maria. I'd love to hear some stories about when Isabella was younger, I'm sure you've got some great ones."

"Oh yes!" she exclaimed. "She was such an energetic little child. Made me run up and down chasing her."

Before we could continue our conversation, Oscar Avery walked into the kitchen with such excitement as he rushed over to his daughter. He pulled her in for a big hug and I swear I saw him tear up as they greeted each other. He pulled away and extended his hand to me. "Welcome to our home, Giovanni. It's a pleasure to have you here."

"*Gracias,* sir," I shook his hand. "It's great to see you again."

He nodded and smiled before turning back to Isabella. "I'm so happy you're here, Bella. I've missed having you around."

"I'm happy to be here too, Dad. You're looking good and healthy."

"I don't know for how much longer because that bloody team is driving my blood pressure through the roof." He flung his arms as he gestured towards the TV across the room.

Isabella chuckled. "Who are the Spurs playing? I've been so out of touch with the fixtures lately."

"Man City and they're already one goal down." He shook his head. "Kane needs to pull his head out his arse and get us a goal already."

I couldn't help but laugh. "I'm sure you've heard the talks about him leaving the club at the end of the season."

Oscar shook his head. "Don't talk to me about that son, I don't want to even think about what the team is going to be like without him."

Son? There was something endearing behind his use of that word to refer to me. One thing about Oscar Avery, he had always welcomed me with open arms and I was thankful for that. It was entertaining to watch the way he huffed around the room talking about the game. He was as passionate about football as they came. I knew my fair share about my teams but he was a walking Tottenham Hotspurs encyclopedia. Camila's husband, Smith joined us and as the conversation flowed freely between everyone, I watched Isabella start to relax. She was showing Maria her ring and I saw the light in her eyes as she spoke, smiling and laughing the entire conversation. That's what I wanted to see.

"Wine, beer or whiskey?" Smith asked.

"I'll take a whiskey, thanks."

He nodded and made his way into the kitchen as he tended to our drinks. I walked over to join Isabella as Gloria Avery walked into the kitchen. Her shoulders were pulled back the way they always were. She carried herself with so much tension in that upright position that I was pretty sure she would need a chiropractor. The grey had continued to present itself in her hair and she peered over her glasses.

"Isabella, Giovanni," she announced formally as she walked over to us. "It's lovely to have you here."

Isabella tried to contain the surprise on her face. "Thanks for having us."

"You have a lovely home, Mrs. Avery," I said politely as I slid my hand around Isabella's waist.

"Thank you, Giovanni. We had plenty of room here for the two of you."

Isabella shifted nervously. "I know but I was happy for us to stay where we're staying."

I half-expected an argument to ensue but instead, Gloria nodded and said nothing more. She turned to say something to her husband before making her way over to Maria who had stopped by the stove again.

I turned to Isabella. "You okay?"

She nodded and glanced up at me. "I mean I could definitely use a drink or three."

I chuckled and leaned down, placing a kiss on her forehead. "You should ask Smith to organize you one. There's nothing stronger than whiskey though so maybe you should consider making that your drink of choice."

She pulled a face. "I've just matured to wine, I don't think I'm ready for that just yet."

"I forget how immature your palette still is. Maybe by the time you're my age, you'll be ready for that."

Isabella snorted and eyed me. "You're speaking like an old man. You're not that much older than me."

"Four years, baby."

"Exactly. Four years, not forty."

I laughed as Smith handed me my drink. I thanked him just as Isabella placed her own order for a glass of red wine. Smith was polite and helpful and had no problem making his way back to where he came from to organize a drink for Isabella.

"So, do we get to fool around in your childhood bedroom later?" I asked low enough for just her to hear.

"We won't be doing any fooling around here." Her eyes widened.

I brought my drink to my lips and sipped on it. "Oh c'mon, it would be fun."

"Absolutely not. We are leaving that room perfectly un-christened."

I leaned closer to her ear. "Boring. I'm sure that room has never seen any action before."

"Of course not."

"Not even when you were in high school?" I gaped. "Or university?"

She shook her head.

"God, baby, your sex life must have been so boring," I lowered my voice, playfully teasing her with my words. "At least that's not the case now."

A smile played on her lips as she looked up at me, a naughty look crossing her eyes. She opened her mouth to say something but Smith interrupted, handing her a wine glass. She thanked him before turning back to me.

"Definitely not boring now," she murmured.

Her family started to make their way towards the TV area. I hung back and slapped her ass playfully earning myself a wide-eyed reaction that I couldn't help but laugh at. She was so easy to tease. I loved it.

I pulled her back to me and leaned closer to her ear. "Don't act like you didn't like that."

She couldn't hide it in her eyes that she loved that. A playful smile formed on her lips. "Let's get through this dinner and then we'll talk about incorporating that."

Oh, fuck yes.

CHAPTER 7:

Isabella

I stood outside on the patio overlooking my childhood garden and it was just as I remembered it. It was a large garden with beautiful rows of various flowers along the sides by the walls. My father loved gardening and his flowers were something he was always incredibly proud of. When I was little he tried to get me to join in on his hobby but after I stood up screaming when a worm ended up on my hand, he realized I was never going to be his gardening buddy. I hated the feeling of my hands being dirty so instead, I would sit on the stairs of the patio with a good book while he gardened. The rain had subsided but there was a winter chill in the air. I didn't mind it though. Breathing in the smell of the rain was oddly calming to me. It always has been. It was a smell I had associated with growing up. I would often find myself outside here when I needed a break from my mother or sister. Whenever we bumped heads or a fight broke out, I would escape to the patio with either my books or my music. Anything that would allow me the escape I needed in those moments.

We had been mingling around drinks and the game and all the interactions had gone off without a hitch. I was pleasantly surprised at how normal everything felt. Giovanni fit right in with my father and Smith once they started talking football. When he started spitting facts on the various teams, my father's face lit up. He was definitely impressed by Giovanni's knowledge of the league. He handled himself with such ease. He kept his hand on my knee the whole time as we sat in the TV room. He would squeeze it every now and then to remind me he was there. He would turn and smile at me in moments before returning to the conversation. I loved watching him. I couldn't wrap my head around how it was possible to be this in love with him but I was. He made my world better in every way.

My mother had engaged in polite chit-chat about what it's like living in Barcelona. She even went as far as to ask Giovanni about *Mala Mía*. He excitedly explained the expansion and how well it had worked out in Valencia. She nodded along as Smith engaged more in the business behind franchising. I appreciated my mother's attempt at being civil. Not once did I see a judgemental eyebrow or a rolling of her eyes in any way. She kept her face neutral and a small smile escaped every now and then. I was pretty sure I had riled myself up for nothing. Everything seemed to be going better than I could have expected.

"Aren't you getting cold out here?" My mothers voice brought me out of my own thoughts.

I shook my head as she came to stand next to me. "I don't mind it. We've definitely experienced colder than this."

"That we have."

I couldn't help the lingering apprehension that presented itself around her. There was still so much I wanted to clear the air with when it came to her but I also didn't want to ruin the ceasefire. It's the longest we've ever been this civil so I refused to be the one to mess that up.

"Thank you for inviting us to the wedding," she said.

"Of course. You're my family." I glanced over at her. "As long as you're not coming all that way just for the 'does anyone object' part."

She laughed. My mother actually laughed. *What the heck.* She pulled her coat closer to her and turned to me. "I would never do that. I think I was wrong about Giovanni."

"You think?" I lifted an eyebrow.

"I know," she corrected. "I know I was wrong about him. He's a very good man."

I didn't believe Giovanni when he said that he had won my mother over but it would appear that he was right. He had done the unthinkable and I couldn't help the smile that spread across my lips.

"He's the best and I'm glad to see that you can admit you were wrong."

"We've always had a difficult relationship, Isabella," she sighed.

That's an understatement.

"And I know a lot of it was due to my own stubbornness," she continued. "I had worked so hard to try and make sure that you and your sister would make a success out of your lives that I missed the part where I was meant to be your mother. I have become like your grandmother."

I couldn't help but feel a little bad now at her vulnerability. My mother hardly ever brought up her side of the family. There were a few moments growing up when my father would explain what had happened when she wasn't around. My grandmother was difficult and overbearing. It was mind-blowing to me that my mother couldn't see how similar they actually were. My father told Camila and I once what had happened between her and my grandmother after we asked why we never saw my mother's side of the family. When she was growing up her older sister, Antoinette, who was only a couple of years ahead of her, ended up falling pregnant at seventeen. My grandmother kicked her out of the house and all the pressure fell on my mother to be the perfect child they so desired. Over the years, I sympathized with the fact that my mother had a great amount of pressure on her shoulders but instead of being the opposite of my grandmother, she became her. She feared we would become like her sister. I understood her reasoning for everything but I didn't agree with it. The fact my grandmother kicked her daughter out was enough for me to not want anything to do with her anyway. I just couldn't imagine doing that to my own child.

"I wished things had been different growing up," I admitted, looking down at my feet to avoid her gaze. "I tried to be the daughter you wanted but I ended up being the woman I didn't want to be."

She remained silent so I continued, "And I know you just wanted what was best for me but look at me now. I'm happy and successful in my own way. It wasn't the way you wanted but it was exactly what was meant for me."

And I truly believed that. I was meant to have found my way to Barcelona. I was meant to meet Giovanni and go through everything we went through together. My life played out exactly the way it was supposed to because it brought me to this point and I had never been happier.

"I know," she sighed. "I'm not proud of the way I had behaved towards you and Giovanni so I'm hoping that we can put that behind us and move forward."

I looked over at her and I noticed a sense of nervousness in her eyes. I had to commend my mother for what she was doing. For as long as I could remember, she was never one to even apologize so this was a big step for her. It would take time but I needed to work through the resentment I had built up against her. She was making an effort so it was only right for me to try, too.

"I'd like that." I smiled at her.

She nodded and smiled before turning to face the garden again. For a few moments, we just stood there in comfortable silence before we heard a celebration from inside. I turned and watched as my father was jumping up and down excitedly.

Giovanni laughed as he peeped around the open glass door. "Your father's team is winning if you hadn't already picked up on that."

I chuckled and extended my hand out for him to join me outside. He smiled and walked over to me, slipping a hand around my waist as my mother headed back inside.

"Dinner will be ready soon," she said before slipping through the door.

"We'll be there now."

"You look much calmer than you did earlier," he commented.

"I feel calmer. I got an admission from my mother that she was wrong about you."

He lifted an eyebrow. "What did I tell you? Your mother loves me now. Smith better watch out, I'm coming for the favorite son-in-law spot."

I giggled and turned my body towards him, slipping my arms around his waist underneath his jacket. "What time is everyone going to your brother's place tomorrow?"

"They'll be there from the morning but I have to warn you now, the *Velázquez* family take forever to get the food out so we may have to grab a snack beforehand."

"Are we supposed to bring anything?"

He shook his head and tightened his arms around me. "Trust me, between my mother and Penelope, they have everything sorted. We do have to stop by our place though because I forgot Mateo's gift."

Giovanni went searching for a Real Madrid kit for his nephew. He was adamant that he would teach the little one about - what he calls - the best team in the world. That sparked countless debates between him and Alvaro, who was a die-hard Barcelona fan so I couldn't wait to see his face when his son came out wearing the kit of his fiercest rivals.

"Your brother's going to accuse you of brainwashing his child."

"Probably," Giovanni chuckled, "I can't wait to see his face."

For a moment we just stood there holding onto each other. I was at ease in his arms and any previous apprehension I had about anything had slipped away. I had enjoyed my first Christmas Eve in years with my family and I was looking forward to spending Christmas Day with Giovanni's family. This was what our future looked like and I was happy to welcome it.

"Okay, I tried to stay out here and pretend it wasn't cold 'cause I know how much you weirdly enjoy the cold, but please can we go inside?"

"Fine." I glanced down at my watch. "We can't stay too late tonight. Our flight is an early one, remember?"

Giovanni groaned. "You're torturing me with these early morning flights."

I rolled my eyes and pulled away from him. "You can nap on the plane."

CHAPTER 8:

Giovanni

"On a scale of one to ten, how much do you think Alvaro's going to want to kill me?" I asked Penelope as I called her to Mateo's room where Isabella and I had dressed him up in the Christmas gift I got him.

Penelope brought her hands to her mouth and couldn't hold back her laughter. "You did not buy your brother's son a Real Madrid kit."

I lifted Mateo up and perched him on my side, admiring how cute he looked in the kit. "Of course, I did and you can't even deny he looks fucking adorable in this."

"Language," Penelope warned.

"He doesn't understand what the word "fuck" means, Penelope," I whispered.

"Look at his little shoes," Isabella gushed as she walked over to playfully grab Mateo's foot. "I swear, Penelope, this is the most adorable child I have ever seen."

Mateo was pretty cute. The strong Velázquez genes dominated with his dark skin and dark hair. His eyes were a light brown that he shared with Penelope but other than that, he was all Alvaro. I had taken to my nephew from the first time I laid eyes on him and I could tell that I was becoming his favorite person. He cried when I left and never left my side when I was around. I used to think I'd be awful with children but I took to Mateo quite easily.

Mateo had his fingers in his mouth and I grabbed them and slowly pulled them away. "Now your hand is full of spit, Matelio, why would you do that?"

"Matelio?" Isabella said and burst out laughing.

"Where did you get that nickname?" Penelope asked.

I opened my mouth to answer, but Isabella jumped in. "Oh, we've been watching *Jane the Virgin*." She turned back to me. "I knew you were enjoying it!"

"It's a good show!" I retorted.

"That's what I told you." Isabella laughed.

I wiped Mateo's hands and straightened his shirt as I got ready to present him to Alvaro. He was downstairs with my mother as they organized dessert. After a successful Christmas Eve dinner at Isabella's family, we were on the first flight out this morning to spend the day with my family. Most of my family was back in Madrid so it was just my mother and Sebastian that joined for dinner this year. I had promised Isabella that next year we would host Christmas ourselves and we would have the entire family over. I had aunts, uncles and cousins all across Spain - it was getting everyone in the same room together that proved to be a trying task.

After my parent's divorce, my mother was reluctant to introduce us to the new man in her life. She wasn't proud about how their relationship came to be but who were we to judge her decisions? Sebastian was a quiet old soul but he treated my mother right and she had changed since being with him. She was lighter and brighter. She laughed more and for the first time, she seemed genuinely at ease. I just wanted her to be happy. I had seen her broken more times than I needed to and it was a relief to see her the way she was now. Even after everything that went down between her and my father, she still tried to get me to mend my relationship with him. I had thought about it. I tried to be the bigger person but there was still too much resentment to allow it to be water under the bridge.

Alvaro had invited him to join us today but he refused to be around Sebastian. When his new relationship fizzled out as quickly as it started, his pride refused to allow him to accept his ex-wife's new boyfriend. He distanced himself from his family because of it and I was not about to be the one to run after him. That was his problem.

"I'm going to see if your mother needs help." Isabella reached up and left a kiss on my cheek before disappearing downstairs.

"Isabella told me you haven't invited your father to your wedding."

Penelope eyed me as she tied Mateo's shoelace that had come undone.

"Technically, I said I was still debating it," I clarified.

"I know you probably don't want my opinion," she continued. "But I think your father is lost, Gio, and not being invited to your wedding is going to hurt him."

"I think he's inflicted enough hurt on this family, don't you think?" I asked, now annoyed.

"Yes, but look at where you guys are now. The divorce was good for your parent's but Alvaro says your dad has been struggling lately. He's too stubborn to admit it but it's true."

I remained silent. I didn't want to be so heartless towards him but he had done a lot to destroy the relationship we had. I'd say getting punched by your father one too many times tends to leave a bad taste in your mouth.

Penelope picked up that I had nothing more to share in the conversation and instead of pushing it like I expected her to, she turned to Mateo instead. "Shall we go show your daddy your new outfit?"

Mateo laughed as Penelope tickled him.

"Watch what he does now," Penelope said with a huge smile on her face before lifting her hand close to Mateo, *"¡Dáme cinco!"*

Mateo stared at her at first, not moving but when she repeated it, he lifted his little hand up and gave her a high five.

"Look at you little guy." I squeezed him as Isabella called for us from downstairs to join them for dessert.

"You ready to watch your husband throw a tantrum?" I asked Penelope excitedly.

She rolled her eyes and laughed before turning to make her way downstairs. I followed closely behind her with Mateo still in my arms. The sound of the chatter from the kitchen surrounded us as we walked into the kitchen. Alvaro had his back towards us but turned as soon as my mother started to gush over how adorable Mateo looked.

Alvaro turned around and his face dropped. "You didn't."

I burst out laughing at the dumbfounded look on my brother's face. "I did."

"You're trying to turn my own child against me."

"No, I'm just trying to make sure that he's correctly educated when it comes to supporting the right team." I brought Mateo down to the floor, allowing him to stand as he wrapped each of his hands around my index finger on each hand.

"Isabella helped me pick it out," I announced.

"Don't bring me into this," Isabella laughed and brought her wine glass to her lips. "This was all you."

"You're going to have to take that shirt with you when you leave," Alvaro instructed. "We will not allow that in this house."

Everyone burst out laughing at how dramatic Alvaro was about this. He had always been passionate about football growing up. We often ended up in fistfights with each other for nothing over the passion we shared for our teams. We were older and much more mature now but he still had a strong distaste for my team.

"*¿Alguien quiere café?*" My mother asked, changing the subject.

Penelope took Mateo from me as we all started to make our way onto the patio again where the various desserts had been laid out. My mother shuffled around inside with Sebastian organizing the coffee. Isabella was leaning against the door frame looking out onto the patio, her wine glass still in her hand. She looked tired but still just as beautiful.

"You look like you're just about ready for bed," I commented.

She glanced up at me with a smile on her face. "I really am. I've eaten more over the past two days than I have in my entire life. It's going to take a few days to digest all that."

"You're going to have to stay up if you want your gift."

"My gift?" she eyed me curiously, "You didn't have to get me anything."

I scoffed. "Of course, I did. It's Christmas and you're my fiancé."

"Can you believe that in a few month's time we're going to be married?" Her eyes lit up whenever she spoke about our wedding and I loved to see it. There was pure happiness in her eyes.

"I can't wait." I reached for her and pulled her into my arms, leaning down to leave kisses against her hair.

And I genuinely meant that. I couldn't wait to be her husband. I had never thought that would be something I would look forward to but with her, I wanted it all. Every day I got to wake up next to her was a blessing and I would never understand what I did to deserve someone like her.

"Giovanni, *tu café*," my mother said, handing me my cup.

I pulled away from Isabella and reached for it, careful to hold onto the handle to keep it from burning my hand. Penelope called Isabella to go see something she was showing Alvaro on her phone and I stood with my mom as we watched our family.

"It makes me happy to see you happy, *hijo,*" she said.

"I could say the same thing to you, *Mamá.*" I placed my arm around her shoulders. "I can see you're happy with Sebastian."

"He's a good man." Her eyes lit up as she looked over at him.

He sat with Mateo on his lap, playing a redundant game of peek-a-boo that brought on a wave of laughter from Mateo. Kids were so easily entertained sometimes.

"Your father is a good man too," she commented. "He has made his fair share of mistakes, there's no denying that but he's not a bad man."

"Did you guys all have a meeting about dad and me?" I quipped. "You're now the third person to bring him up."

"We were just talking about the wedding earlier and Isabella mentioned him," she explained. "And don't be mad at Isabella for that. She just doesn't want you to have any regrets about him."

I knew that. She was doing to me what I did to her with her mother. She wanted me to give him a chance and I couldn't be mad at her for that.

I sighed. "*Mamá,* you of all people know that dad and I have our issues. I want my wedding to be a happy occasion. He's still never apologized to us for what he did."

Was it delusional of me to hold out for something as simple as an apology from him? Not just for what he did to our family or to my mother directly but for the way he treated me because of his own wrongdoings. I was pretty sure I had every right to have my reservations about him but with everyone bringing it up, I had a feeling I was going to have to be the bigger person in this scenario.

"I just want you to know that I don't want you to not have a relationship with him because of me. Everything that happened between your father and me is over now. I'm not angry anymore. I've made my peace with everything so if you want to, you can too."

I squeezed her and leaned down to kiss her forehead. "I'll think about it, *Ma.*"

CHAPTER 9:

Isabella

With our wedding less than a month away, I couldn't contain the building excitement inside of me. Things had started to come together nicely and I couldn't wait for our special day. I was shuffling around at the back of *Aroma* as I finalized an order for a new type of coffee we were going to try out. I heard the indistinct chatter inside the shop continue to grow. It was a hot summer's day today but that didn't stop people from coming in. We had recently introduced a couple of iced coffee drinks on our menu and they had proved to be quite popular.

My phone buzzed in the pocket of my dress. I pulled it out to reveal a text from Reyna.

Reyna: So, when you said no stripper at your bachelorette party this weekend, you didn't really mean that, did you?

I rolled my eyes and chuckled as I typed my reply.

Me: You've already organized one, haven't you?

A couple seconds later, her reply came through.

Reyna: This weekend is going to be GREAT!

Classic Reyna. I guess that's what I get for making her my maid of honor but honestly, there was no one else more fitting. She was my best friend and I knew she was going to make sure my bachelorette party was nothing short of an excessive celebration. Giovanni and I had decided that we would both do separate parties but we would all stay in the same hotel. We had rooms booked at one of the hot new hotels on the beach. Reyna was in charge of my bachelorette party and Alvaro was in charge of Giovanni's - with the help of Sergio. I was actually looking forward to letting loose and celebrating the fact

I was getting married. With Reyna spearheading the planning, I knew we were all in for a treat. Even Camila was coming up for it. I had never seen my sister party in her life so being around Reyna was going to be a shock to her system. They couldn't be more different.

I slipped my phone into my pocket and made my way back to the counter where Savannah was serving a young couple. A short line had formed and I noticed an older couple seated at one of the tables on the floor.

Mr. and Mrs. Morales had become regulars at *Aroma* since it first opened. Every second day they would come in and order two regular sized coffees. They would sit at the table closest to the bookshelves and chit-chat for hours. I watched the way they were together and it warmed my heart. They had clearly been together for the longest time but there was no mistaking that there was still so much love between them.

I walked over to greet them. *"Hola, Señor y señora Morales,"*

"Hola, hermosa," Mrs Morales said and reached for my hand. *"¿Cómo estás?"*

"Estoy bien, gracias." My Spanish was still pretty non-existent but I was trying. I glanced down and noticed their table was still empty. "Have you been helped yet?"

"Sí, sí. The young man took our order." Mrs Morales gestured towards Federico who was grabbing mugs from the one cupboard. "How is your- your fiancé?"

I had spoken to her so often when she came in that she was well aware of my upcoming nuptials.

"He's good, thank you. We're just under a month away from our date."

"¡Qué emocionante!" she exclaimed. "Fernando and I will be married for - for how long this year?" She turned to her husband to answer.

"Forty-five 'ears." His Spanish accent cutting off the 'y' in the word.

"That's so exciting!" I exclaimed. "You got any advice for me?"

Mr. Morales thought for a moment. "Don't go to bed angry with each other. Talk, talk, talk!"

"And keep the bedroom things exciting." She lifted her eyebrows playfully and I couldn't help but laugh.

"I'll keep that in mind, *gracias.*"

Federico brought their order and I said my goodbyes before I disappeared behind the counter. I kept thinking about them and how they had been together for as long as they have been. It was beautiful to see that kind of love. I smiled and my hand immediately went up to the necklace that now had a permanent place around my neck. I thought back to that night after Christmas dinner when we arrived home.

"I was walking back to my car after a meeting and it just caught my eye in the window," Giovanni explained as he walked back over to me, a small black box in his hand.

He dropped down next to me on the couch as I waited in anticipation. He had a slight nervousness to him. I wasn't sure why he was so nervous but it was adorable to see.

He took a deep breath in. "I remembered how much you loved that one emerald-colored jersey I used to have. You said how much you loved that colour on me and when I saw the same colour diamond, I don't know - I just thought you might like it."

He opened the box to reveal the most beautiful necklace I had ever seen. My jaw dropped. It was a single silver chain and hanging on it was a silver-plated infinity sign with a solitaire-styled emerald diamond on the inside of it. Just next to it, against the infinity sign were two separate diamonds. It was so elegant. And so so beautiful.

"Giovanni," I gaped.

He placed the box in my hand. "I just wanted you to have something that always makes you think of me. It's my way of always being with you."

Tears swelled in my eyes. It wasn't the gift that made me emotional - it was him. Everything about him and his heart were so good. Too good for this world. Too good for me. He was everything to me and I was overwhelmed by the love I had for him.

"You know I could never not think of you right?" I reached out and cupped his face. "You didn't have to do this."

"I know I didn't have to but I wanted to. I want to spoil you, baby. I want you to have everything your heart desires."

"I just need you. As long as I have you, I'll be happy."

He leaned down and his lips met mine. "Well, now you have me and this necklace."

I couldn't help but giggle as I caressed his cheek gently with my thumb.

"You do like it, right?" he asked.

"Of course - I love it!" I exclaimed. "It's beautiful."

His face relaxed and he looked pleased with himself. I don't know why he was worried in the first place - apart from my engagement ring, this was the most beautiful piece of jewelry I had ever owned.

"Can I help you put it on?" he offered.

I handed the box back over to him, "Yes please."

And I hadn't taken it off since that day. I had no plans on taking it off at all. It rested perfectly against my chest and I often found myself reaching for it throughout the day. A happiness spread throughout whenever I held it. I definitely didn't need any reminders of Giovanni to think about him - he consumed my every thought but this was special to me and I would treasure it forever.

Savannah shuffled past me from the back to bring out the freshly baked muffins that Federico had been working on. After his clumsiness debacle, he bounced back and even introduced us to his baking skills. We had decided to start selling some of his goods and the customers loved it.

"Oh, those smell amazing," I gushed as she placed them on the counter.

"Right? He did a great job with them."

My attention turned towards the entrance as the bell above it jingled as someone entered. My eyes landed on Giovanni as he casually made his way towards me all suited up.

"You look very handsome." I smiled.

He was wearing his well-fitted navy suit that knew exactly how to sit on his body. He had recently neatened up his beard but it was still thick enough for me to run my fingers over it.

"Thank you, my baby." He leaned over the counter to give me a quick kiss.

I breathed in that cologne of his that I couldn't get enough of. Every time I smelled it, it reminded me of what it felt like to smell it on him the first time we met. It was just as intoxicating as it was that night. I loved it when he popped in unexpectedly. He often stopped by to say hi whenever he got a free moment.

"Are you headed to a meeting?" I asked.

He nodded. "With my father actually."

I was surprised. The last time he spoke to his father was when he had finally decided to invite him to our wedding. He mentioned it briefly back at Christmas when his mother and Penelope tried to get him to invite him. I could see it wasn't something he wanted to deal with at the time so I left the subject and didn't bring it up again. I tried to help but in the end, it was up to him to decide. If he wanted him there, I would support him and if it didn't, I would support him just the same. A couple of months back after a conversation with Alvaro, he had a change of heart and finally decided to invite him.

"Your dad wants to meet with you?"

"*Sí.*" He leaned against the counter. "He called Alvaro and I and asked to meet at his office."

"What do you think he wants?" I ducked under the counter as Giovanni came around to the side, allowing the small line of people that had now formed behind him to get their orders in.

"No idea but I can say hi to Nate for you while I'm there."

I scoffed and rolled my eyes. "You think you're funny, don't you?"

He smirked and reached for me, wrapping his arms around my waist. "I'm hilarious and you can't even deny that."

I had almost forgotten about Nate. There wasn't much of a reason to give him any thought.

"When does his project finish with your dad?" I asked.

"I'm not too sure. I can find out but there's a chance of him staying on a permanent basis."

I gawked at him. *Seriously?* I hadn't seen Nate since the Christmas party and I wasn't thrilled about him working for my future father-in-law. What kind of telenovela shit was that?

"Nothing like having your fiancé's ex-boyfriend working for your dad," he joked. "You know if we really want to put the -" He stopped for a moment to think. "What's that American show where everyone goes on to fight?"

"Jerry Springer."

"Yes! If we really want to put the Jerry in Jerry Springer then we should hire Lorenzo."

Another person I hadn't thought about in months. I had enjoyed Lorenzo's friendship. He was a good man but he was right to end our friendship when he did. His intentions with me went far beyond friendship and I would never be able to give him what he wanted.

"Or Casey," I pipped up.

Giovanni rolled his eyes at just the mention of her name. "Don't remind me of that one."

"That was an experience."

It wasn't long after Giovanni's accident before Casey made an announcement correcting the news outlets on the real paternity of her baby. While she didn't reveal who her real baby daddy was, she did reveal to the world that it wasn't Giovanni. She quickly disappeared off social media after that and I had only recently heard of her again when an announcement broke that she had given birth to a healthy baby boy. All the previous anger I had towards her slipped away the day I got Giovanni back. What was the point of hanging onto the past?

Giovanni on the other hand was less inclined to forgive her for lying.

"That was fucking torture," he corrected.

I didn't like to think back to that time without him. The back and forth was torture for both of us. I never wanted to be without him ever again. This was forever now.

"Enough about that though - should I be worried about what Reyna has planned for you for this weekend?"

I giggled. "Definitely. Even I'm a little worried. You know how wild she can be."

"I bet you she's got you a stripper."

"I tried to enforce the no stripper rule but I just know she hasn't stuck to that. She even asked me about it again just before you got here."

Giovanni laughed. "I would love to see you with a stripper."

I scrunched my face in discomfort. "I don't need another man's junk all up in my business."

"That's exactly why I'd love to see your face when that happens. I'm

58

D o m i n i q u e   W o l f

going to ask Reyna for videos."

I groaned. "This is going to be quite the weekend."

"Maybe I'll sneak into your hotel room after." He leaned down and planted a kiss on my lips, "Just to make sure you haven't run off with the stripper."

I giggled. "Never."

"I'm looking forward to the honeymoon," he said.

"Of course you are." I rolled my eyes and smiled. "Are you seriously not going to tell me where we're going to go?"

"Nope. That's the one thing I'm in charge of and since I know how much you love surprises."

I don't.

"It only makes sense to keep this one under wraps but I'll give you a hint."

I waited and he leaned closer to me out of earshot of anyone else.

"You'll be naked the whole time."

I rolled my eyes again and nudged him playfully. "You're such a tease."

He laughed and stole another kiss. "But seriously, put your trust in your fiancé, he knows what he's doing."

"I have no doubt."

He lifted his wrist to check his watch. "Okay, I have to head out but I'll come fetch you when I'm done."

"I have to lock up today so you'll have to wait for me."

"No problem." He leaned down and kissed me, this time holding it long enough for me to sink into it, "Wish me luck."

"It'll be fine." I reached up and cupped his cheek. "Call me when you're done."

With a few more kisses on my lips, my cheeks and then my forehead, Giovanni turned towards the exit and slipped outside. I stood there smiling like an idiot but my heart was so full. My phone buzzed again bringing me out of my own thoughts. Reyna had texted again.

Reyna: Penis straws. We need those, too.

I tugged at my lip to hold back a laugh. Of course, she would think that penis straws would be a good idea. I started to type my reply before another one of hers came through.

Reyna: FUCK! Isabella, that was not meant for you. You were not supposed to know about the penis straws.

This time I let my laugh out and typed back to her.

Me: Should I be concerned about the amount of penis decorations you're going to have?

A new message came through.

Reyna: Definitely!

She included an unnecessary amount of brinjal emojis. I laughed out loud again before she sent another text.

Reyna: This weekend is going to be GREAT!

I was really looking forward to it. No matter how many inappropriate and uncomfortable situations Reyna had planned, we were going to have a great time. I smiled before slipping my phone back in my pocket so I could get back to work.

CHAPTER 10:

Giovanni

I arrived at my father's office with ten minutes to spare. I had seen Alvaro's car in the basement parking lot so I already knew he was here before me. I straightened my suit jacket as I stepped into the empty elevator. I was surprised when he gave me a call and asked to meet Alvaro and me. I couldn't really think of anything he would need to speak to both of us about so I was curious about what he had to say.

The elevator doors opened and the blonde behind the reception desk battered her eyes at me the way she did the last time I was here.

"Señor, Velázquez, ¿cómo estás?"

"Estoy bien, is my father in?" I asked.

She nodded. "He just finished with a meeting so he should be in his office now. Your brother is already there."

I thanked her and made my way down the corridor leading up to his office. In the far conference room, I could see a meeting was still happening but my father wasn't there. As I turned in the direction of my father's office, I was stopped in my tracks as Nate stepped out of the other boardroom.

"Giovanni." He extended his hand politely.

That was new. Last time I saw him, he didn't even bother making eye contact with me and now he was extending his hand.

I extended my own and shook it. I was trying this thing where I tried not to be a dick if I could avoid it. This was one of those moments.

"Nathaniel," I replied, my tone as curt as ever.

"My name is Nate."

"I don't care." Trying not to be a dick didn't last very long it seems.

He ignored my comment and continued. "I believe a congratulations is in order. I heard you and Isabella got engaged."

"We did."

Nate nodded but he looked as if he wanted to say something further. Before I could give him the opportunity, I replied, "How long is your project with my father's company?"

"We're actually finalising the last of it. Should be done in the next couple of weeks."

"And then what do you plan to do?"

A flash of confusion presented itself on his face. "What do you mean?"

"Do you plan to stay in Barcelona?" I asked, slipping my hands in my pockets.

"I haven't figured that out yet," he admitted.

"Look, Nate, I don't mind if you stay. If you're good at what you do and it benefits the company then great but don't think you're going to have another opportunity to try and win Isabella back because that ship has sailed."

I watched the heat spread across his cheeks and his jaw drop slightly. I had caught him off-guard and to be quite honest, I was also surprised by my choice to call him out. It wasn't my style but I needed to make it perfectly clear that Isabella and him were in the past. I wasn't one to allow my relationship to be disrespected.

"I...I wouldn't do that," Nate said, sheepishly.

"You wouldn't do that *again* you mean," I corrected.

"If Isabella is happy then that's all that matters."

"That we can agree on."

Before anything further could be said, we were interrupted by Alvaro calling me down the hall.

"Giovanni!" he shouted and gestured for me towards my father's office.

"That's my cue." I extended my hand to Nate once more. "Nate."

He shook my hand and nodded before taking off past me. I walked over to Alvaro and greeted him as he stood back, allowing me to enter. My father was already seated behind his desk and he made no movement to shake my hand or give any other greeting than his typical nod of the head. Alvaro and I took a seat on the chairs in front of him. He had aged significantly since I had last seen him. His hair was the greyest I had seen and he looked tired. While he usually carried himself with this great powerful demeanor - that appeared to be faltering.

"Thank you two for coming on such short notice," he started to say but stopped as there was a knock at the door and the receptionist peeped her head inside. *"Perdóname, señor,* I've got Clarissa on the line about the *Maremagnum* project."

"Please hold my calls till I'm done here." He was curt in his response and she just nodded, closing the door behind her.

"I'm going to get straight to the point," he announced. "I'm retiring."

"You're what?" my jaw dropped.

Alvaro echoed my surprise with a look of confusion on his face. My father had worked his entire life and there was never any doubt that he would continue to do that until, frankly, it killed him. He chose work over family for as long as I could remember.

"Retiring," he repeated. "I wish to no longer work and given my age and financial security, I don't have to either."

"So, you're just going to step down?" Alvaro asked. "What does that mean for *Velázquez Constructa?"*

"That's what I wanted to speak to the two of you about. I have worked for far too many years and I don't want to do it anymore. Frankly, I'd like to live a little before I die and I haven't done that."

He's not wrong. He hardly ever took vacations. When we moved to Barcelona and the business continued to take off, we saw our father less and less. Even when we would go on family vacations, he would appear for a day or two and then leave again. He lived for his job.

"But I also don't want to leave the company in the hands of anyone here. None of them have shown the promise that I need to take over the company so my next resort is you two."

I rolled my eyes at his backhanded compliment. "And what exactly are you asking us?"

"Velázquez Constructa is now yours." He gestured to both of us. "I have already announced it to the board that I'll be leaving the company to the two of you."

"You're not really asking us then, you're telling us," I clarified.

"Do you have to make this difficult, Giovanni?" he snapped. "I wouldn't trust anyone else but family to continue the success of this business. I know you two have done exceptionally well with *Mala Mía* so I'm sure you'd be able to continue the same success with this company."

Exceptionally well? He was damn right but the fact those words came from his mouth was more shocking than the fact he was retiring. I wasn't even sure if I wanted to work here. I was quite happy with my focus on the expansion of our clubs. If anything I wouldn't mind overlooking some of the projects but to be in charge of the day-to-day aspects, that wasn't appealing to me.

"The two of you can discuss what roles would suit you best here but end of the month, I will be stepping down."

"That's two weeks away," Alvaro pointed out.

My father's expression remained unchanged.

"How long have you been planning to retire?" I asked, a flicker of irritation in my voice.

I didn't know what it was but a part of me was always easily set off by my father. The resentment I had towards him was still there and I had to actively push through it in moments like this. I wasn't annoyed that he was practically giving Alvaro and me his company, it was the fact he clearly thought we would drop everything to take on the opportunity. There were a lot of moving parts to this that needed to be discussed and two weeks wasn't enough lead time.

He shrugged. "Are you two interested or not?"

I looked at Alvaro, waiting on him to answer first but he looked at me and gestured for me to speak first.

"Look, Alvaro has worked here already. I know he's helped out with a lot of projects so it obviously makes more sense for him to take on the more active role," I explained. "I love running *Mala Mía* and we're doing really well with the expansion. With that being said, I have no problem taking the lead on some of the projects you have but I can't dedicate my full-time here."

"Gio's right. When Penelope had Mateo, I had already taken a step back with *Mala Mía* so that became his focus." Alvaro turned back to our father. "But you know I'd be more than happy to take on a more active role here. Given that you're okay with me stepping back from the club permanently."

Alvaro turned to me and waited for my response.

"Of course," I replied. "And I'm not saying I wouldn't want to be involved here at all but it just won't be as much of a focus for me as it will be for Alvaro."

My father leaned back in his chair. "Then it's settled. We can get started with the handover straight away."

"What are you going to do now?" I asked.

"Sleep in late. Travel. Hell, read a damn book." He shrugged. "My whole life I've been so focused on work that I had lost sight of what was really important, and now it's too late."

I could see the flicker of guilt in his eyes. Alvaro was right - he didn't look well and not in the physical sense. He looked like he was struggling emotionally and that didn't surprise me but I couldn't help but feel a little bad.

"So, I'd like to just take a break and figure out what my next step in life will be."

My father was the last person to ever allow his vulnerability to show. He clearly realized his true emotions were slipping through because he quickly caught himself and sat up straight again, the emotion leaving his eyes. He always viewed emotions as a sign of weakness. His inherent toxic masculinity would be his downfall.

"We can set up a time for next week to meet up and discuss the next steps," he said. "Leave your availability for next week with Athena at the front desk and she can put it in my schedule."

He stood up which clearly indicated that this meeting was now finished. I was still surprised by his willingness to walk away from the company he had worked so hard at but I respected his internal change. There was no doubt he carried around a great amount of regret when it came to how he had lived his life. Alvaro said his goodbyes to us as his phone started to ring. He pulled it out of his pocket and answered it as he slipped out the door. I turned to say my own goodbyes but my father opened his mouth as if he was going to say something but quickly stopped.

"What?" I asked.

"Is your mother bringing Sebastian to your wedding?"

"Not that it's really any of your business who she brings," I clarified in her defense. "But yes she is."

I watched his jaw tighten but before he could say anything else, I interrupted him. "If that's going to be an issue for you then I'd ask that you rather don't attend."

"I didn't say that would be an issue," he lied.

"No, but you didn't bother coming to Christmas for this very reason. You missed my birthday, Alvaro's birthday - you need to get over this." I could see on his face he didn't like what I was saying. "Because you started this, remember? Our family is this way now because of your mistakes so either you can man up and move on from that the way we all have or you're going to end up alone."

He remained silent. I was pretty sure he was going to crack a tooth with the way he was clenching his jaw.

"Think about that before you decide to attend or not because I am going to make sure that nothing ruins that day for us," I explained. "Isabella and I deserve a day where everyone puts their shit aside. This isn't about anyone else - it's about her and I."

I half-expected him to remain silent but instead, he opened his mouth to reply, this time his tone much calmer than before. "I haven't had a chance to offer my congratulations."

He extended his hand. I didn't expect it but that was practically extending an olive branch. I shook his hand and we said nothing more. I nodded one last time towards him before making my way out of his office.

CHAPTER 11:

Isabella

"Isabella?" I heard Giovanni shout.

"I'm in the office," I shouted back as I continued to shuffle through the pile of papers in front of me.

I had already locked up earlier when it was closing time. Savannah and Federico left a few minutes ago but I still had a couple of things to sort out. It was just me here now as I waited for Giovanni to fetch me so we could head home. I heard his footsteps getting louder until the door of the office slowly swung open. He leaned against the door frame with his hands casually in his pockets, smiling over at me. "Are you looking for something?"

I sighed and dropped onto my chair. "Yes, there is this one invoice that I've been looking for."

I continued to shuffle through the papers until I found the one I was looking for. "Ah here it is! Okay, crisis averted."

Giovanni chuckled. "Thank goodness. I was just about ready to call law enforcement."

I rolled my eyes as he closed the door behind him before walking over to me. He stopped and leaned against my desk. He had since removed his suit jacket and tie that he had earlier. His sleeves were rolled up to his elbows revealing his tattoos. I reached my one hand out and rested it against his arm.

"How did it go with your father?"

"Oh yeah, about that - so he's retiring and he's leaving *Velázquez Constructa* to Alvaro and me."

"He's leaving you the company?" I couldn't hide the surprise in my voice.

He nodded. "And not in a couple of months from now. He's retiring at the end of the month."

I dropped my arm and leaned back in my chair. "So, what does that mean? What are you going to do about *Mala Mía*?"

"Nothing's changing with that. I told them I am happy to be involved with some projects here and there but *Mala Mía* is my focus. We're doing so well with the two branches we have and with the Sevilla expansion in play, I don't want to step away from that."

"What does Alvaro say about this?"

"He's always wanted to run *Velázquez Constructa*. He was always the one that was more involved anyway so he's going to step in and take over my father's job. There are still a lot of details to iron out but that means that *Mala Mía* is officially my baby to take care of now."

"I don't know if I should congratulate you."

He shrugged. "Technically, I just became a CEO of a company so you could at least give me a round of applause."

I chuckled as I stood up to start gathering the loose papers in front of me. I placed them neatly in a file. I noticed Giovanni out of the corner of my eye, watching my every move.

"What?" I asked, eyeing him.

"Nothing." He reached for my hand, pulling me closer to him, forcing me to place the file back on the desk, "I just missed you today."

I wrapped my arms around his neck and placed myself between his legs as I leaned into him. "I missed you."

He brought his lips to meet mine and I sunk into the kiss, suddenly relaxing in his arms. He always had this calming effect on me. With his arms around me, I could conquer anything. What started out as a soft kiss quickly deepened into something more and the arousal stirred deep inside of me. His tongue forced my lips open as he flicked his tongue over mine. I leaned closer to him, feeling how he came alive against me.

I pulled away and brought my hand over him. "Someone's awake."

He leaned into my neck and started leaving a trail of kisses along it. "For you, baby. Always."

I slowly ran my fingers against the outside of his pants, teasing him with my movements. I flicked my eyes up to meet his and he was already looking at me with intense desire. His lips were parted and his eyes dropped to my lips. "You going to do something about that, Isabella, or are you just going to be a tease?"

I tugged at my lip trying to hide how much I was enjoying this little game I had started. I leaned closer to him and my lips met his cheek first before starting to move over his jaw and then down his neck. Soft kisses at first until I got to the base of his throat. I stopped and sucked on his skin a little, causing him to let out a small breath. He loved it when I did that.

"We're alone here, aren't we?" Giovanni murmured.

"Mhm-mm," I continued to kiss up his neck again towards his jaw.

"Perfect," he said before grabbing me and turning me around, lifting me up onto my desk.

We had fooled around his office at *Mala Mía* a handful of times but we had yet to christen my office. Now was the time it seemed.

"This isn't a movie - don't go tossing my papers onto the floor," I warned.

"If you can sit still then nothing will move out of place," he challenged. "But that's up to you."

My breathing picked up in anticipation. His lips found mine again with a new refound energy. I handed myself over to him, soaking in every hungry kiss. He ran his hands up my bare thighs, pushing my dress up to my waist. I was suddenly very happy with my decision to wear a dress today. Heat pooled between my legs and I was craving the release only he could give me. His one hand left my leg and reached for the spaghetti strap against my shoulder. He slowly pushed it down my arm and brought his lips to my shoulder. I leaned my head back, letting out a sigh of relief at what he was doing to my body.

Slowly his hand slid further up my inner thighs until his fingers grazed the outside of my underwear.

"Someone's ready for me," he murmured in my ear.

He reached for my underwear and I lifted myself enough for him to bring them down my legs. I pulled him closer to me, my lips finding his again. Forget the foreplay - I wanted him, now. My kiss let him know exactly how I wanted it. The small tugging at his bottom lip with my teeth caused him to release a deep throaty groan and my hands went for his belt. I started to undo it, dropping it to the floor before I popped open the button of his pants. The throbbing between my legs continued to increase with each kiss and my body needed him. I needed him. He pulled away from me and pulled his zip down before pushing his pants and underwear down enough to free himself to me. I reached for his shirt and worked my way through the buttons, opening his shirt to reveal his body to me. I loved it. I loved everything about it and I could never get enough.

He pulled me by my legs so I was closer to him. He was so close to my entrance but instead of pushing inside of me like I thought he would, he quickly pushed a finger inside, teasing me. I was already sensitive to his touch given how turned on I was. He removed his finger and edged closer as I opened myself to him. He rubbed against me, continuing the teasing and I couldn't help the groan that escaped my lips

He chuckled at my impatience. "Spread your legs for me, baby."

I happily obliged and in one swift moment, he pushed deep inside of me. Both of us let out a sigh of relief as he filled me up. The intensity of skin to skin was something we loved to experience. He started to push in and out of me, each movement reaching deeper and deeper. The pleasure was already seeping into every part of my body as he hit the back of my wall. My hand found the back of his neck and I dug my nails into him as his arms came around me, lifting me with each movement so he could hit me deeper.

"Oh, yes," I moaned and let my head fall back as I soaked in every thrust.

His lips found my neck again as he moved and I tightened around him, my orgasm already building. I tried to contain my moans but I couldn't - they rolled off my tongue along with his name.

I lifted my legs and wrapped them around his waist, forcing him deeper inside of me from an angle that had me biting down on my lip. His hair fell forward and I watched as he soaked in the euphoria of being inside of me. I couldn't hold it back - I was tightening around him again causing his own groans to escape.

"Sit," I instructed him.

He flicked his eyes to meet mine and there was no mistaking the interest in them as to what I had planned. He lifted me up, turned us around and took a seat on my chair. I was now straddling him. With my hand still hooked around the back of his neck, I started to flick my hips forwards and backward. A deep moan came from inside him which only made me increase the pace. I took the opportunity to ride him and I watched as he leaned his head back, enjoying every flick of my body. I was so close now. Each movement pushes me closer and closer to the edge.

"I'm close," I breathed.

Without warning, his hands gripped either side of my hips and he started to thrust harder and faster inside of me. I couldn't keep up with his pace and handed my body over to him, allowing him to destroy me. The moans rolled off my tongue as I found my climax, the pleasure pulsing through my veins. My body was reeling from my orgasm as he continued, the sounds of his heavy breathing causing me to roll my eyes back. I loved hearing him like this. With one last deep thrust inside of me, Giovanni came undone. He leaned his head against my chest as we both tried to get a handle on our breathing. For a moment we just sat there, soaking in our shared pleasure. I felt his heartbeat was fast and erratic like my own. I ran my fingers through his hair, pushing it back as he lifted his gaze to meet mine. He smiled, allowing that deep dimple of his to make an appearance. I leaned down and left a small kiss against it before bringing my lips to his. He tightened his arms around me and pulled me closer to him. I didn't think it was possible to love him any more than I already did but every day I was proved wrong.

"See, we managed to do that without messing up your desk." He leaned into my neck again.

"Should have done it harder then," I challenged.

He cocked an eyebrow. "Oh? Careful what you wish for."

I brought my lips down to his again and took his bottom lip between my teeth. A deep groan came from his throat.

"If you keep doing that then I'm just going to have to stay inside of you," he breathed.

I nipped his lip again, challenging him. He was still hard inside of me and with the pulsing desire in my veins, I was ready to go again which earned no protest from him as we had sex for the second time in my office.

CHAPTER 12:

Giovanni

"I'm almost ready," Isabella shouted from upstairs.

She had spent the last few hours getting ready for tonight. We both had our bachelor and bachelorette parties tonight and although they were separate occasions, we had decided to all stay at the same hotel. The plan was to meet at the hotel before going our separate ways. We were getting closer and closer to our wedding date and honestly, I just couldn't wait to marry her. I wanted to be binded to her in any way humanly possible. There was something selfish and possessive about wanting to claim her as mine but that's what I wanted.

I finished rolling up the sleeves of the well-fitted black button-up shirt I had on as the sound of her high heels against the stairs caused me to turn to face her as she made her way down.

My jaw dropped at the sight of her. "Fuck."

She stopped at the bottom of the stairs. "What?"

She ran her fingers through her dark wavy hair that spilled over her shoulder. After living with her for as long as I have, I knew the difference between her different types of hairstyles and she had definitely taken her curler through her hair for this one. Her hair and makeup weren't what caused the blood to rush straight to my groin - it was that dress she was wearing. A tight black leather dress clung to every curve of her body and reached mid-thigh. The plunging neckline accentuated her breasts and yet still left enough to the imagination.

She turned to the side and glanced back at me. "Is there something on my dress?"

"Why have I never seen this dress before?" I gawked at her.

"I was saving it for a special occasion."

I walked over to her and slipped my hand around her waist, pulling her closer to me. "Nope. You're not going out like that. I'm taking you upstairs and I'm ripping that off you."

She giggled. "No way. I did not get all this dressed up to not leave our apartment."

I slid my hand over her ass and squeezed. "But baby, look at you."

She ran her hands up my arms to then wrap around my waist. She leaned closer to me and flicked her eyes up to meet mine as she felt me hard up against her. "I take it you like what you see."

"I love what I see." I breathed.

I couldn't think of anything else but all the ways I would devour her body. She was a fucking goddess to me and I was ready to worship her. I cupped her cheek with my hand, her big hazel eyes staring up at me. She was so beautiful. It fucking blew my mind.

"I don't think I want to share you with the world." I leaned closer to her ear and nipped the top the way she loved. I knew all the ways to drive her body crazy.

She groaned and pulled away from me. "Don't do that."

I pressed my lips against her jawline just under her ear next. "Don't do what?"

"You know what you're doing, Giovanni." Her voice was laced with desire.

Her breathing had changed the way it always did when she got turned on. My own arousal was shooting through my veins. I brought my lips to meet hers and took her bottom lip between my teeth.

She couldn't hold back the small moan that escaped her lips. She broke the kiss and pulled away.

"Nope. We're already running late and here you are trying to turn me on."

"Is it working?"

I slipped a hand underneath her dress, moving in between her thighs. She didn't stop me. Her own arousal shining in her eyes. I wasn't about to let her out of here without satisfying her. I was aching to be inside of her.

"I can't let you leave here now," I murmured into her ear and slid my fingers closer to her between her thighs. I kept sliding up to meet her underwear but there wasn't any.

"Isabella," I groaned. "Are you trying to kill me here?"

She chuckled and stepped away from me, causing my hand to leave her skin. "Sorry, but there is no way I could wear underwear with this dress and this is way more fun."

She stepped back closer to me and rested her hands on my chest. "Now the whole night you'll be thinking about how I have nothing under this dress."

God, what a tease. I was already thinking about how I wanted nothing more than to lift that dress up right now and bend her over the counter again. I shifted my erection that was begging for a release. He was going to have to wait a little longer now.

"You're playing a dirty game here, baby." I leaned closer to her, our lips now inches away. "You better come and find me after this party of yours. If my blue balls have survived until then."

She burst out laughing. "You'll be fine."

"I'll be thinking of you all night."

"I promise I'll come and find you 'cause I can already tell you now that I'm guaranteed to be intoxicated and we both know how great our drunk sex is."

"And our sober sex."

"And our sober sex," she repeated with a naughty smile on her face.

Her lips met mine a lot easier now that she was taller thanks to the heels she had on. She was always surprising me. Her new refound confidence when it came to our sex life had me hanging on her every word. She loved to play games like this and I was happy to go along with them because once I got a hold of her, we'd get exactly what we needed out of each other.

"Give me a minute or two. This guy has to calm down now."

She laughed and walked over to the mirror hanging against the wall. She flicked her hair over her shoulder again and turned to check herself out, making sure her dress was fine.

"Are you ready for your last celebration as a single man?" she asked playfully.

I scoffed. "I haven't been single for long, baby."

"You know what I mean. You have to get it out of our system now, they say. Last chance to get cold feet," she teased.

I walked over to her and wrapped my arms around her waist, leaning my head against her shoulder as we looked at each other in the mirror. "I don't care about the clichés that getting married is the end of the world. You are my world, Isabella and I've never been more sure of anything."

And I meant that. She was everything to me and there was never any doubt in my mind that she was the one for me. I had known it from the first moment I met her. There was something that had me hooked and although I did everything I could to fight it in the beginning, I knew that I was never going to be able to shake her. She consumed me. I was drowning in her and I didn't want to find the surface again.

She turned to face me, her eyes brimming with tears. "You're going to make me cry again."

I chuckled and kissed her lips. And then her nose. And both of her cheeks and finally her forehead. She had the biggest smile on her face and I loved the way her eyes shone up at me. It was so clear in her eyes that she loved me and I couldn't explain what that did to me. I wish I could find the words but there were none that would be able to explain the true euphoria I felt. I had always been so terrified of falling in love. It made you feel powerless and I hated not being in control. But when it came to Isabella, I couldn't stop myself from falling even if I tried. She consumed my world in every way possible and there was no life without her.

"We need to leave now before I either ruin your makeup from crying or I rip that dress off you."

She reached up as her lips met mine. "Let me quickly grab my bag."

CHAPTER 13:

Isabella

I had gotten pretty drunk tonight.

Reyna held nothing back when it came to my bachelorette party and I had never had a celebration quite like that before. The unnecessary amount of penis decorations sent me into a laughing fit for most of the night and the over-the-top stripper really sealed the deal. We spent the night at this fancy beach bar where the music was great, the drinks kept flowing and we kept celebrating. It wasn't a large group of us but we were definitely the loudest. I didn't care - it was my bachelorette party for crying out loud. I had so much to celebrate. Even Camila came out of her shell for the evening. I had never even seen my sister drunk so by the time she was dancing on the tables with Reyna, I knew we had peaked for the evening.

It was well after two in the morning and Reyna had attempted to put me to bed in her own drunken state. She passed out next to me as soon as her head hit the pillow and I was pretty certain there was a hangover waiting for her tomorrow. I tip-toed over to the snacks we had bought earlier. I grabbed a box of Pringles and leaned against the counter attempting to stop the world from spinning. All through the night, I was celebrating the fact I was about to marry the love of my life.

I had yet to change out of my dress. Giovanni loved it so much when he saw it earlier that I knew it took all his self-control for us to walk out of our apartment. I was so close to giving in but the delayed gratification was going to be worth it. I looked back at Reyna who was now snoring and I chuckled. The alcohol was still pulsing through me but I was too awake to sleep so instead, I slowly made my way to the door and slipped out. Giovanni's room was at the end of the hall so barefoot me, with my Pringles still in hand, made my way towards his door.

I knocked lightly at his door as I used my other hand to lean against it as the world continued to spin around me. I was way past tipsy but I didn't care.

I wanted to see my man.

I knocked again before slowly opening the door.

"Sergio, I said I'm fi-," he walked into the lounge area and stopped as he noticed me and his face lit up. "Hi baby."

I smiled and threw myself into his arms. "Hi."

"You have your drunk smile on," he teased. "And what are th-" He stopped to take my Pringles from me before laughing. "Pringles?"

I nodded and giggled. "I needed something in my system cause 'm pretty sure I'm still drunk." I wasn't slurring but my sentence was definitely coming out a lot slower than it usually would. "Are you not drunk?"

"Not like you, but I'm definitely feeling the alcohol."

I wrapped my arms around his neck. "Reyna thought she put me to bed but I had to come and find you."

"Did you have fun tonight?" He asked before leaning down to give me a quick kiss.

I nodded and smiled. "A man stripped for me, it was weird."

He burst into laughter.

"Don't laugh!" I tapped his arm playfully. "He was trying to be s-sexy but nooo."

His laughter continued as he leaned down to kiss my forehead.

"Did you have a stripper?" I asked, popping the 'p's.

"Yes."

I pulled a face. "Ew, don't tell me that."

He tightened his arms around me and laughed. "You asked!"

"I know."

"That's typical bachelor party stuff." He shrugged. "You know you're the only woman to do this to me."

He took my hand and brought it down to him. I felt him hard against me and I couldn't help but smirk. The alcohol was burning in my system and that allowed my desire to push to the surface. He was all mine and soon, we would be married. I couldn't contain the way that made my heart feel.

"I haven't even done anything though," I murmured.

"You don't have to. Just look at you, *mi hermosa,* and that dress." He lifted an eyebrow and tugged at his bottom lip before smiling. "That dress is coming off."

I giggled. "You wanted to do that earlier already."

"Yup and I haven't been able to stop thinking about that since we left our apartment."

I smiled and he started to pull away to walk over to the mini-fridge but I held onto him.

"I'm just getting you some water," he laughed and I dropped down onto the couch, letting go of him as he reached for a bottle.

He handed it to me. I sat there, a smile playing on my lips. I couldn't believe that in a couple of weeks time, I would be Mrs. Isabella Velázquez. That thought alone brought the biggest smile to my face. I couldn't hold it back. I had never felt happiness quite like this before.

He dropped next to me and handed me the bottle of water. "And that smile?"

I sipped on the water before turning to face him. "We're getting married."

I emptied most of the water in the bottle before he took it from me and placed it down on the coffee table in front of us. He pulled me onto his lap, my legs draping across him as I wrapped my arms around his neck.

The happiness in his eyes mirrored my own. "We are."

He flicked his eyes up to meet mine and I could see the love in them. He was smiling, that deep dimple of his on full display and I slowly ran my thumb across his cheek. I often found myself wondering how it was possible that I found Giovanni. Someone who loved me more than I thought I could ever be loved. He was everything I needed and more.

"I can't wait to marry you," he murmured.

My heart could have burst right out of my chest, I was so overwhelmed with happiness. I ran my fingers slowly through his hair and he leaned back into my touch. "I love you."

He reached up and brought his lips to mine. "I love you, baby."

My stomach growled and I couldn't help the bubbling laughter that escaped me. Giovanni must have heard it too cause he jerked his head back playfully, eyeing my stomach. "Is there something living in there?"

I shook my head, the uncontrollable laughter still at large. "That's just my hunger talking."

He lifted me up and placed me back on the couch as he strolled over into the small kitchen, reaching for my box of Pringles that he left on the counter. "Do you want me to order room service?"

He strolled back to me and handed the box over. I reached for it and popped the lid open.

"I mean I wouldn't say no to a burger. Or pizza. Oh my God, pizza would be so good right now or fries- please can we get fries?" I begged.

He chuckled and reached for the phone on the table next to the chair. "So a burger, a pizza and fries?"

I nodded excitedly. "You can have some of it too."

"I should hope so," he laughed. "Do you think you'd be able to finish all of that?"

"Definitely," I admitted. "But I'll be a nice fiancé and let you share some of my food."

He leaned across to me and kissed my temple. "How kind of you."

I continued to eat my way through my chips as Giovanni ordered room service.

***

An hour later, I only made it through half the large fries he ordered before I tapped out.

"Okay, I may have overestimated how hungry I was," I admitted.

Giovanni laughed. "Yeah, I thought you might have, which is why I left the burger off the order."

"You said that was an accident." I slapped his arm playfully.

"Nope. I know my woman and when you're drunk, you want to eat everything but you also get full easily."

He knew me so well. There was still an intense amount of alcohol coursing through me but I had gone from drunk Isabella to just tipsy. Everything was still heightened but the world was no longer spinning and I was thankful for that. I was still counting on a major hangover to present itself later but right now, I was awake.

And so was my body.

I had done well up till now keeping my desires at bay but now I wasn't going to hold back. I glanced over at Giovanni as he dusted his hands off on his pants before leaning over to grab the bottle of water on the table. He removed the cap and brought the bottle to meet his lips. He titled his head back and I watched as the muscles on his arms displayed themselves through the black shirt he was wearing. I couldn't pull my gaze from him. The way his Adam's apple moved as he swallowed or the way he licked his bottom lip as he pulled the bottle away, closing it up before placing it down next to him. He must have noticed me staring cause he slowly turned to face me, his eyes had the same intriguing intensity they always got when he had dirty thoughts running through his mind.

"You done staring?"

I shook my head. "Never."

He smiled before reaching out for me and pulling me onto his lap again. My legs were on either side as I straddled him. I smiled and brought my lips down to his. He ran his hands up my bare legs and my body came to life. I was intoxicated which meant that everything was heightened. Every kiss, every touch - he set my body on fire. I flicked my tongue over his and grazed his bottom lip with my teeth.

"*Joder*," he breathed and pulled me closer to him.

God, I loved hearing him speak Spanish. Everything sounded better. I flicked my hips forward, rubbing myself up against him. He was hard and ready for me. I loved knowing that I had this effect on him. His lips reached mine again before moving across my jaw and down my neck. My nails dug into the back of his neck as he sucked gently on my skin. Fuck, I wanted him.

"Giovanni," I whimpered, the pressure between my legs increasing with each kiss.

His hands ran up my legs again and round the back, squeezing my ass in his hands. It was rough and electrifying. The deeper desires inside of me were pushing forward and I wanted nothing more than to be taken by this man. My man. My hands pushed into his hair as I pulled. He nipped at my neck - both of us increasing the intensity of our movements. I loved him so much and I couldn't get enough of him.

"Yes, baby," he whispered in my ear and reached for the zip at the back of my dress, pulling it down.

I slipped my dress off my arms, exposing my lace black bra. His lips moved further down my neck and started to work their way over my breasts. He grabbed one with his hand and squeezed - the throbbing between my legs pulsed with his every touch. His eyes were blazing with desire. I wanted to devour him. I wanted to run my lips over every inch of his skin, soaking him in for as long as I could. I reached for his pants and started to undo his button, needing to feel him. Before I could move any further, he lifted me up and turned around, placing me back down against the couch. He grabbed my hands and pinned them above my head, holding them in place.

"Don't move," he instructed.

He positioned himself between me and used his knees to part my thighs. "You were right about something earlier."

"And what was that?" I breathed.

"I haven't been able to stop thinking about the fact that-," He stopped and slipped his hand underneath my dress to graze his fingers over where my underwear was supposed to be. "You had nothing underneath this dress."

He slipped a finger inside. "You were such a tease earlier, baby."

I already felt myself tighten around him as he slowly moved in and out of me, his thumb finding my clit as he started to rub. The pleasure was already pulsing through my veins. I tugged at my bottom lip to keep the moans from escaping.

His lips claimed mine again, flicking his tongue with a sense of desperation. My hands came over and were headed for his hair but grabbed and pushed them back down.

His lips moved to my ear. "I thought I told you not to move."

I groaned.

Giovanni was not afraid to take charge and I loved it. It was exhilarating. I already rolled my eyes back in pleasure at just his words. They were dominant and I was happy to hand myself over to him. He had my heart, soul and body. Forever.

"Permission to rip this dress off you?" he asked as he removed his fingers, my body immediately craving his touch again.

"Yes, please."

He wasted no time before he reached for my dress and pulled it over my head, tossing it across the room. His hand ran down my stomach and further until he was running his fingers over me again. I was already sensitive to his touch and the throbbing between my legs was begging for a release.

He slipped his finger back inside and his name rolled off my tongue. I couldn't hold back the moans that escaped my lips as he moved with a rhythm that had my body pushing closer and closer to its climax. He slipped a second finger in and found his rhythm again, knowing exactly what to do. I tightened around him as his thumb circled over my clit. My body jerked and I couldn't hold back as his name left my lips.

"I love hearing you moan my name," he murmured. "You're mine, Isabella."

"I'm yours."

"Forever."

I couldn't hold back any longer. I reached up and pulled him to me, my greedy lips finding his again. We grabbed each other - squeezing, pulling at whatever we could. He removed his fingers as I ripped his shirt off him, buttons flying across the room. He quickly pulled it off him, never once breaking the kiss. It was a greedy kiss - he devoured my lips with each one. There was no holding back. I reached for his pants and started to push them down, telling him what I needed. He stopped my hands and instead of letting me undress him, he slipped his hand around my back and unclasped my bra. I pulled it off me and dropped it to the floor.

He brought his lips back to my ear. "Do you want me?"

"Yes." I breathed.

"You want me to fuck you, baby?"

Oh yes. I groaned at his words, the throbbing between my legs had intensified. I was now aching for him. I wanted more of the filth that could come out of his mouth. There was so much love between us but when it came to our sex life, I wanted him to take control of my body. I wanted the passion, the intensity, the dirty words. I wanted it all.

"More than anything."

"Hard?"

I tugged at my lip. "Hard, Giovanni."

My name rolled off his tongue and I watched the arousal intensify across his face. He didn't hold back. He quickly removed his pants and underwear, dropping them to the floor next to us. With a newfound roughness to his movements, Giovanni was ready to give me what I wanted. He pulled me by my legs, drawing me closer to him and parted my thighs. He positioned himself in between my legs and leaned closer to my entrance, teasing me with his tip.

"Please," I begged.

"Please what?"

He knew exactly what he was doing. He wanted me to beg and it was pushing my body to the edge.

"Giovanni," I moaned. "Don't make me do it myself."

His eyes flickered with interest. "Oh?"

Without warning, he pushed deep inside of me and I cried out in pleasure as he filled me up. All the arousal that had built up tightened around him as he started to thrust deeper inside of me with each movement.

"I'm sure I can do more for you than your own fingers, baby."

Of course, he could. I only said that to get what I wanted. With each movement, he pushed deeper inside of me as he increased the pace. He didn't hold back. Giovanni ripped through me as I moaned his name for the world. The pleasure pulsed through me. His greedy mouth found mine again, parting my lips with his tongue.

Suddenly, he broke away and reached for my legs and slowly bent my legs, pushing my knees closer to my chest as he continued to move in and out of me. Each movement was slow and calculated but each thrust inside was harder than the one before. He pulled my legs forward to rest over his shoulders and I cried out as he entered me from this new angle.

"Oh, God."

"No, baby. Just me."

That finished me. That one line had my body reeling from the control he had over it. He was so fucking sexy and he knew exactly what he was doing to me right now. Harder and deeper he went as I cried out, my orgasm building inside.

"I'm close." I moaned.

His hand moved up my body, over my breast until it reached the base of my throat.

"Do you trust me?" he breathed.

"I trust you."

He started to squeeze ever so slightly around my throat as he increased his pace. *Holy fuck.* My body came undone as Giovanni had his way with my body so hard, I was pretty sure I was going to break. With his hand still around my throat, I cried out as my orgasm shot through me, reaching every inch of my body. A few small moans escaped his lips and I threw my head back as I soaked in the pleasure settling over me. With one last thrust, Giovanni reached his own climax. He brought my legs down and collapsed on top of me, his head against my chest.

Both of us lay there, trying to catch our breath. I had never experienced such an intense climax before and I didn't even attempt to try and move my body. I was exhausted. Giovanni lifted his head to meet my gaze.

"I didn't hurt you, did I?" he asked.

There were two sides to Giovanni. There was the sweet Giovanni who loved me with every part of him and there was the dirty side to him. The side that had no problem fucking my brains out. And I loved every part of him.

"Not at all." I ran my fingers slowly through his hair. "Whatever you did, I'm going to need you to do that again."

He chuckled. "That's what I like to hear."

For a few moments, we just lay there in each other's arms. I listened to the sound of his breathing as I ran my fingers through his hair the way he liked it. The exhaustion from the night's activities started to creep up on me causing a yawn to escape.

"Bedtime," Giovanni said as he pulled himself up.

He reached for my hand and brought me up, keeping his hand in mine as he led me into the bedroom. I didn't know what time it was but I knew I had officially used up all my energy. We slipped into bed and he pulled my body close to his.

And with a calm mind and happy heart, I slowly drifted off to sleep.

CHAPTER 14:

Giovanni

I woke to the sound of Isabella throwing up. Or at least trying to. I jumped out of bed and made my way to the bathroom, knocking on the door.

"Isabella? Are you alright?"

"Don't come in here."

I ignored that request and pushed open the door. She was hunched over the toilet, her one arm leaning against it as she held her head. She doubled over and tried to throw up again but nothing came.

"I told you not to come in," she groaned. "I don't want you to see this."

I rolled my eyes and walked over, hunching down next to her as I slowly pushed her hair back. She had lost all the colour in her face and her eyes were droopy.

"I know we're not married yet but I'm sure you're aware that the vows say, 'in sickness and health' right?"

She groaned and leaned her head over the toilet again.

"This is sickness and health, baby." I started to slowly rub her back.

"I keep feeling like I'm going to throw up but nothing happens."

"Do you want me to stick my finger down your throat?"

"No!" she objected.

"Hey, it'll probably help."

She lifted her head and eyed me. "You'd really stick your finger down my throat?"

"Of course I would. If that's what will make you throw up and ultimately feel better."

"That's weirdly romantic."

"I keep telling you I'm a romantic guy."

"I was expecting like flowers and romantic messages, not offering to stick your finger down my throat."

I shrugged. "Romance is romance, babe."

She started to laugh but another rush of nausea caused her to lean over the toilet again. I kept waiting for something to come out of her but nothing did and she was starting to get frustrated. She leaned back against the bathtub next to her. "Remind me never to drink alcohol ever again."

I chuckled. "You party animal, you. Look at what you've done now."

She smiled but I could see the exhaustion in her eyes. She looked sick. I had seen her hungover before and it wasn't anything like this so either she drank more than I thought last night or she had a bug or something. I reached for the towel on the rack and slowly started to dab the sweat by her hair. She closed her eyes and leaned into my touch as I cupped her face.

"You don't look well, baby," I murmured. "I think we should get you home so you can spend the day recovering."

"Why am I so weak?" she complained and slowly opened her eyes. "I should be able to handle my alcohol."

I placed the towel down on the counter and extended my hands to her. She brought them up, her movements slower than usual and I wrapped my arm around her waist as she leaned her head against my arm.

"It happens. I just think you need to sleep it off."

"Could you let everyone know? I don't have the energy to meet for breakfast."

"Of course." I leaned down and kissed her hair. "You get back into bed while I go get your stuff. I'll wake you when it's time to leave."

I walked with her to the bed and opened the duvet for her. She dropped down and her head immediately found the pillow. I tucked the duvet over her as she closed her eyes. I leaned down and kissed her forehead that was warm against my lips. *Did she have a fever?* I'd have to check that as soon as we get home.

"I'll be right back, okay?" I said softly to her.

She grabbed my hand and her eyes fluttered open. "I'm sorry."

"You're apologizing for being sick?"

She nodded.

I shook my head and smiled. "You don't need to apologize for anything, *mi hermosa*. We're going to get you home and once you've got some food in your system and rested up a little, you'll feel a whole lot better."

She sighed and closed her eyes again. "I love you."

I leaned over and kissed her. "I love you. I'll be right back."

I let go of her hand and she made herself comfortable in bed. Her eyes remained closed and I hoped that when she opened them up again, that she would be feeling better. Hangovers can be unforgiving if you had enough alcohol in your system. I knew all about that from back in the day when I used to party till I blacked out. The next day I would wake up and feel like absolute trash. Definitely didn't miss that.

I left Isabella sleeping and slowly slipped outside our hotel room. I turned down the hall in the direction of where she and Reyna were supposed to have slept last night. As I looked up, Reyna stepped outside the room with a pair of huge sunglasses on. She was still wearing her dress from last night and her hair was all over the place.

"Don't you dare say a word," she warned. "I feel as bad as I look."

I tried to hold my laughter in. "I wasn't going to say anything."

"I woke up in a panic this morning 'cause I couldn't find your *fiancé*."

"She snuck over to my room last night."

She peered over her glasses. "I figured as much. You two can't even spend one night apart."

"Nope, but I actually came to tell you that she and I aren't going to make the breakfast I know you and Sergio had planned. Isabella's not doing so well."

"What's wrong with her?" her voice laced with concern.

"Pretty sure she's just hungover." I shrugged. "But she's man down so I want to get her home so she can sleep it off. You really did a number on her last night with that party."

Reyna snickered. "Trust me, she had a great time. Dancing on tables, taking body shots off the stripper."

My jaw fell. "She did not."

Reyna burst out laughing. "No, she didn't but your reaction was priceless."

I started clapping loudly causing her to flinch at the loud noise that was definitely not helping her hangover in any way. "Joke of the day."

She shoved me playfully. "You're such a dick."

I couldn't help but laugh. She was clearly struggling with her hangover this morning so I was pretty sure that's all that had Isabella down right now. My priority now was getting her home, hydrated and fed.

"I need to grab Isabella's bag," I explained. "Do you mind letting the others know?"

"No problem."

She unlocked the door to their room, stepping back so I could head inside.

"Her stuff is in the corner. You might need to pack in her shoes - they should be by the bed."

"Thanks, Rey."

I slipped into the room as she stayed in the doorway, keeping the door open. She leaned her head back up against the door. I couldn't help but chuckle at how hungover she was. I wondered how the rest of the party was doing this morning. I couldn't picture Camila getting drunk but I also couldn't see Reyna allowing anyone to remain sober. What I would have given to be a fly on the wall at that party.

I grabbed Isabella's bag in the corner and placed it on the bed, looking around to see if I was missing anything of hers. By the side of the bed lay the high heels she had on yesterday. I grabbed them and shoved them in the bag before reaching for her cellphone on the bedside table. It was dead so I made a mental note to put it on charge when we got back home. After a final scan of the room, I was sure I had everything of hers. If I forgot anything, Reyna could bring it.

I made my way back to the door where I found Reyna still leaning against it. She was looking down at her phone but lifted her head as she heard me.

"I need to go meet Katrina at the restaurant. She's with Camila in the lobby."

"Will you mak-"

She cut me off, already knowing what I was going to ask. "Yes, I'll make sure Camila gets to the airport safely."

I smiled. Reyna was a good friend to both Isabella and I. I never thought I would have been thankful for her friendship but she had grown on me. I had always known her as the loud party animal who would get drunk every weekend at my club. One thing about Reyna was that she knew how to have a good time but I had also come to know the Reyna beneath that and I was thankful Isabella had someone like her in her life.

"Thank you."

"Let me know how she's doing later."

"I will."

We said our goodbyes and I headed back down to my room. I unlocked the door and slipped inside, dropping Isabella's bag at the entrance. I walked back into the bedroom and found her tossing and turning. She turned over to face me.

"I can't sleep. I keep feeling like I'm going to throw up."

I walked over and dropped down on the bed, reaching out to cup her face.

"I think we need to get some food in your system."

She reached out and grabbed my hand, looking up at me with those big hazel eyes of hers.

"Promise you'll never let me drink again?"

I laughed and brought her hand up to my lips. "Sorry, baby. Can't do that. You know we're big wine drinkers now."

She groaned at just the mention of alcohol.

"You know what the best hangover cure is?" I asked.

She looked up at me waiting for an answer.

"Keep drinking."

"God, no."

I leaned down and kissed her forehead as I laughed. She looked exhausted. The colour had yet to return to her face. I just needed to get her home.

"Just kidding. No more alcohol for you today." I said. "I think we should head home, are you ready?"

"I need to get my bag."

"Already got it."

She smiled up at me. "Thank you. Could you help me sit up? The world is spinning again."

I grabbed her hands and slowly started to pull her up. She closed her eyes as she swung her legs down the side of the bed. She took a deep breath in and

I hovered around her, waiting to see what she would do next.

"You okay, baby? Do you need me to carry you?"

A small laugh escaped her lips. "I'm okay but I do think I should eat something."

"I think some greasy fries would do."

"Oh, definitely."

CHAPTER 15:

Isabella

Hours later my eyes slowly fluttered open and I was greeted by darkness. The only light visible was from the faint street light peeking underneath the curtains in our room. I took a deep breath in and rolled over, facing Giovanni's side of the bed which I found empty.

I felt like trash.

After Giovanni brought me home from the hotel and made sure I forced some greasy fries down, he put me right to bed. The nausea was still there - constantly hovering over me but never quite consuming me enough to force anything out. I couldn't really be surprised at how I was feeling. I had lost track of how many shots we had throughout the night - it was all a blur but I knew I had consumed enough alcohol to be suffering like this. I turned back and reached for my phone that was usually on my bedside table. *What time was it?* I had clearly slept through most of the day. I reached for the switch of the lamp and turned it on, illuminating the room. I didn't find my phone but I did find a full bottle of water, two headache tablets and an orange juice.

I couldn't help but smile at Giovanni's thoughtfulness.

I pulled myself up and leaned against the headboard, careful to make my movements as slow as possible to stop the world from spinning again. I reached for the tablets and the bottle of water. I twisted the cap off, popped the tablets in my mouth and downed them. I forced more water down knowing I needed to hydrate my body again. After a few more forced sips, I placed the bottle back down and closed my eyes.

The sound of footsteps getting louder outside the door caused me to open my eyes up again as the door creaked open. Giovanni popped his head inside and his eyes lit up as he saw me.

"You're awake."

He walked over my side of the bed and dropped down, reaching for my hand.

"How are you feeling?" he asked.

"Fine - better, I think. I just took those tablets you left here for me. Thank you for that."

He brought my hand up to his lips. "Of course. I figured you might need them."

"I feel so bad right now," I admitted.

"Why?"

"I completely derailed our plans. We were supposed to have breakfast with our friends an-"

He cut me off. "Isabella, hey, you don't have to feel bad. You had fun last night and today you need to recover - it happens."

I still felt bad.

He leaned down against the bed, propping an elbow up to lean his head against it. "Seriously, baby. Everyone was cool with it. I think Reyna was secretly happy about it 'cause she was just as hungover as you."

I chuckled. "Well, I should hope so. She did not go easy on me last night."

"She told me all about the dancing on the tables."

I brought my hand over my mouth. "That was fun before the manager came to tell us to get off."

"And she told me about the body shots you took off the stripper."

"She what?" My jaw dropped. "I didn't do any shots off any stripper!"

Giovanni tried to keep a serious face but his lips pulled in amusement before he started laughing.

"I could never picture you doing that anyway," he chuckled.

"Hey, I could if I wanted to."

He cocked an eyebrow playfully. "You think you could take body shots?"

"Totally. Definitely not off a stripper but I wouldn't object to trying it on you."

He was intrigued. His eyes lit up at the sound of what I was suggesting. He was right - I was definitely not one to do body shots off a random stripper but I would totally try them off his body. No need to ask me twice to do that.

Just not now when I was this hungover.

"You've piqued my interest, *mi hermosa.*"

I smiled and tilted my head towards him. "You can add that to the list of things we need to do on our honeymoon," I suggested.

"Hell yes. What else would you like to add to that list?"

I was thankful for the distraction from how bad I was feeling. I was able to focus on him and the conversation at hand instead of whether my body was going to work against me or not.

"How can I make any suggestions if I don't know where we're going?" I challenged playfully.

He rolled his eyes and smiled. "Easy. We're talking about things to try out in the bedroom and we're definitely going to be staying in one of those - doesn't matter yet where that is."

He was insufferable. He was seriously hanging onto this honeymoon surprise and I had to admit it was exciting me. I trusted his judgment and I knew whatever he had planned for us, it was going to be memorable.

"So back to your list - what else do you want to add?" he asked. "I'd love to know what dirty things you have in mind."

I thought for a moment. "Sex in public?"

He burst out laughing. "I tell you to think of bedroom things for our honeymoon and your first suggestion is one that doesn't require the bedroom at all."

I couldn't help but giggle. "It was the first thing to come to mind."

He leaned back against the bed, smiling as he looked back over to me. "You realize we've already done that right? That time in my car in the parking lot by *Paradiso.*"

Oh, how could I forget? That was intense. I had never been fuelled by desire and anger before and that night I had both pulsing through me.

"Well, we can do it again," I smiled. "What do you want to try?" I was intrigued by what he could have in mind.

"Handcuffs."

I cocked an eyebrow. "Handcuffs? You want to use them on me?"

"I'd like to use them to handcuff you to the bed."

I tugged at my bottom lip at just the thought of what he had in mind. I may have a lingering nausea over me but my body could still react to what he was suggesting.

"That way you'd be leaving your body completely in my control," he explained. "You think that would be something you'd want to do?"

Hell fucking yes.

"Absolutely," I answered eagerly, which earned me a chuckle from Giovanni.

I loved hearing him laugh. It was so carefree. He pulled himself up, shifting closer to me. He was casually dressed in a pair of black sweatpants and a navy t-shirt sitting comfortably around his muscles. I would never get tired of looking at him. Whether he was dressed casually or suited up - I loved all his looks. I reached up and cupped his face, caressing his cheek with my thumb, his facial hair rough against my touch. He smiled and his dimple appeared which caused a smile on my lips. That was one of my favourite features of his.

"So, we have body shots, sex in public and handcuffs," he recalled. "A good start to the list, I'd say."

"I'll definitely have some more ideas when I'm not feeling so bad."

I dropped my hand and reached for the bottle of water again.

"Let's try to get some food in your system then you can have a quick shower and bring yourself back to bed," he instructed. "You'll feel as good as new tomorrow."

"You're right." I sighed. "This is just my body punishing me for poisoning it."

He rolled his eyes and smiled. "It'll be fine, baby. I spoke to Camila earlier, by the way, she wants you to give her a call when you're feeling better."

"Shit. I forgot all about my sister." I groaned.

"Don't worry, Reyna made sure she got to the airport in time and she's back safely in London." He reached for my hand again, taking it in his. "I wanted to ask what your sister was like last night? I'm sure Reyna was a shock to her system."

I chuckled. "I was worried about the two of them interacting again but once they were both drunk dancing on the table together, I figured they were getting along just fine."

"Careful, your sister is going to steal your bestie," he teased.

I scoffed. "Sober Camila and Reyna would never work. I love Camila but you and I both know what a tight ass she can still be."

My relationship with my sister had come a long way from what it once was. We got along now and I even kind of enjoyed her company every now and then. She was still a splitting image of my mother but if she had any judgment lately, she made sure to keep it to herself and that was a win for me.

Giovanni stood up and extended his hand for me. "Okay, time to get some food in your system."

I sighed and lifted both my hands to him. He took one hand in each and slowly pulled me up. My feet touched the cold floor and I stopped, waiting for the world to stop spinning before standing up.

A wave of nausea washed over me and I felt my stomach turn. I rushed past Giovanni into our bathroom and found the toilet just in time to double over and finally let out whatever was causing me to feel this way. My stomach heaved and another rush made its way out of my system. I dropped to the floor and reached for the toilet paper but Giovanni beat me to it. He broke some off and handed it to me as his other hand went to my back.

"Well, at least you're managing to throw up now."

I closed my eyes and took a deep breath in, relieved that the nausea had now alleviated itself.

"Good thing I didn't eat anything or that would have been a waste," I commented.

Giovanni smiled and reached over to flush the toilet. I remained on the floor, keeping my eyes closed as I focused on my breathing.

"I'm going to run you a bath. We can get you food after."

CHAPTER 16:

Giovanni

"**A**re you sure you have the rings?" I asked Alvaro over the phone as I strolled back towards my car, "Isabella is running through her list a million times."

Alvaro laughed through the phone. "I got the rings, *hermano*. Sounds like Isabella needs a shot or two."

"At this point, she could do with a joint."

I said my goodbyes to him as I unlocked my car and slipped into the driver's seat. My phone buzzed in my hand and I glanced down to see a text from Isabella.

Isabella: I'm sorry if I'm freaking out but our wedding is two days away! I just want to make sure everything is perfect.

I couldn't help my smile. She had been working through her final checklist today which meant my phone was buzzing the whole time with questions from her making sure of every little detail she could.

Two days away.

In two days' time, I got to marry the love of my life and I couldn't be more excited. I used to think happiness was found in materialistic things or ongoing success but I had learned that I had never felt true happiness until Isabella walked into my life.

I typed a reply back to her.

Me: Everything will be perfect. As long as we're both up at that altar, baby.

I placed my phone on my lap and turned the car on, pulling out of the parking lot and heading down the street back towards her shop. I had finished up with a final meeting with Pedro about the Sevilla expansion. We were set to head over there when I was back from my honeymoon. He would handle the logistics of it while I was gone and I was actually looking forward to seeing the progress. My phone buzzed again and I glanced down to see another text from Isabella.

Isabella: I can't wait to marry you.

It felt just like yesterday that we were getting engaged. Time had passed so quickly and even quicker since the weekend of our bachelor and bachelorette parties a few weeks ago. Isabella was sick for a couple days after that but she eventually came around again. She had yet to touch alcohol since then but I was just thankful that everything was back to normal. After she closed up the shop tomorrow, we were headed to the venue. While our wedding was on Saturday, we had the villa booked out for our guests for the whole weekend. When deciding on a venue, we had found a stunning villa in the Costa Brava coastal region. Perched up on a large hill, the venue overlooked the deep blue of the Mediterranean sea and Isabella was sold. If there was one thing she loved, it was beautiful views and with the one this place had, no other venue measured up.

I stopped at a red traffic light and quickly typed back a reply to her.

Me: Neither can I, baby.

I popped her another text.

Me: Down the road. I'll see you in a bit.

Even though it was late afternoon, the summer sun was shining as bright as it would when it had reached its peak in the sky. Summertime meant that the sun only set well into the evening which suddenly created the illusion that one had so many more hours in the day. I turned down the street and found my usual parking spot across from *Aroma*. I slipped outside, closed the door and locked the car behind me before making my way across the street. The last of the customers were making their way out as I reached the entrance. I held the door open for an older couple before slipping inside behind them.

Federico lifted his head as I approached the counter. *"Hola, Giovanni. ¿cómo estás?"*

We shook hands and briefly exchanged polite pleasantries. He had surprised me these last few weeks with the way he took initiative. Isabella was happy with him as an employee and I was happy to see that. Whenever I got to see her in her element here, it was like she was floating. She was always smiling and chatting it up with customers as best as she could with the language barrier. She was starting to pick up on more Spanish the more as she interacted with it on a daily basis. I tried to teach her some at home too. It was so cute watching her try. *Aroma* was exactly what she needed. She was always happy to help behind the counter or unpack the boxes of new stock being delivered. I could tell she loved this place and I loved to see how happy it made her.

"Isabella's in her office," Federico said as he removed his apron and hung it on the hook on the wall behind the counter. "I'm heading out now and I know I won't see you again before your wedding so congratulations in advance."

"*Gracias, Federico.*"

He nodded and grabbed his bag, heading for the door. I strolled through the bookshelves as I made my way to the back. Isabella's office door was open slightly and I could hear her in conversation with someone. I tapped lightly on the door and pushed it open to see her and Savannah hunched over by her desk, shuffling through some papers. Isabella lifted her head and smiled as she noticed me.

"Hi, baby," I said, leaning against the door frame.

"Hi," she sighed. "Perfect timing. I just had to take Savannah through the order list for next week when I'm not here."

Isabella handed her a file and she placed it under her arm.

"Your fiancé stresses too much," she commented playfully.

"Trust me, you're not the first person to tell me that."

Isabella dropped onto her chair, smiling as she rolled her eyes at us. She paused for a moment, dropping her hand against her lower stomach. A confused look spread on her face which caused a flicker of concern inside of me.

"You okay?" I asked, walking over to her desk.

She looked up at me and shook the confused look away. She reached for my arm and smiled. "Yeah, sorry. I think I just need to eat."

Savannah said her goodbyes to us before slipping out. Isabella leaned back against her chair, stretching her body which caused a pained look on her face. I brought myself onto my haunches in front of her.

"What's going on?" I asked.

She shook her head. "I don't know. Just got this weird pain."

She must have noticed the concerned look on my face cause she reached out and cupped my cheek, rubbing her thumb over my facial hair, reassuring me she was fine.

"You don't need to worry. I'm pretty sure it's cause I haven't eaten today. This place was crazy busy."

There was a nagging feeling in my stomach that had presented itself and I couldn't quite place the reason for it. Isabella assured me she was fine and stood up. I straightened up and pulled her closer to me, placing my lips against hers. I felt her relax against me.

"Let's order in tonight," I suggested.

"Sounds good. You can decide what to get."

CHAPTER 17:

Isabella

I had this constant aching in my stomach the entire day. I brushed it off as nothing more than stress and lack of food in my system but it was starting to annoy me now. It was persistent and I didn't know how to get rid of it. Giovanni and I had worked through the pizza we had ordered and we were still seated at our kitchen counter. I stretched to the side trying to alleviate the annoying ache but nothing would give.

See, Isabella this is what happens when you stress too much.

I ignored that little voice in my head because I knew she was right. As organized as I always was, I couldn't help the ongoing anxiety when it came to making sure everything went the way it was supposed to and this time around, I was planning my freaking wedding. Of course, I wanted everything to go off without a hitch.

I ignored the pulsing ache and turned to Giovanni, reaching for his hand across the counter.

"Sorry, what were you saying about Sevilla?" I asked.

He rubbed his thumb over my hand. "When we get back from our honeymoon, we're going to have to take that weekend up there that I mentioned. I need to take a look at the progress of the venue."

"Sounds good to me. We can go on a weekend when Reyna is working at *Aroma*."

He nodded and reached for his whiskey glass, bringing it up to his lips.

"I'm also going to be getting involved in this new project that Alvaro said *Velázquez Constructa* is working on. I don't need to worry about it now obviously but it's on the list for when we get back."

"We've got a lot waiting for us when we get back," I commented.

He shifted his barstool closer to mine and rested his hand on my thigh. "Yup, so we better relax as much as we can while we're away."

I smiled and leaned my elbow against the counter, resting my head against it as he slowly ran his fingers up and down my thigh.

"And I have plenty of ways to destress you," he murmured.

"Oh?"

He nodded. "We don't even have to wait for the honeymoon to start either."

The pulsing ache in my stomach increased in pressure making it difficult to ignore. I shifted in the barstool, trying to find a comfortable way to sit but nothing was working. I couldn't even focus on the conversation at hand.

"Sorry, babe. Could you give me a minute?" I asked.

"Of course." He couldn't hide his confusion but quickly brushed it off. "I'll clean up in the meantime."

I leaned over and kissed his cheek before disappearing upstairs. What the hell was going on? I pushed through our bedroom door as the pain started to shoot through me, causing me to hunch over. I couldn't hold back from vocalizing my discomfort. I reached over to lean against the counter but was forced to hunch over again. This was a different kind of pain. I had never felt anything quite like it before. Suddenly it felt like the pain was tearing through me and I dropped onto the toilet seat, trying to get a handle on what was happening. I suddenly regretted coming upstairs alone. Something was wrong and I was starting to think it was more than just stress. My breathing started to become short. A rush of nausea came over me and my world started to spin.

"Ahhh!" I screamed out as the pain in my stomach worsened.

It felt like my insides were on fire and the aching in my stomach started to spread through me as I screamed for Giovanni. I closed my eyes and hunched over, holding my stomach. I heard Giovanni rush into the bathroom, knocking the door against the wall as he stepped inside.

"What happened?" his voice was thick with concern, "Baby, wha-"

I interrupted him. "I don't know. Something's wrong."

A lump had formed in my throat as I tried to hold back the tears that were now forming from the pain.

"Isabella," he hunched down in front of me and I met his gaze. "You're scari-"

He stopped as his eyes dropped down, looking at my legs. I followed his eye line and my breath caught in my throat. He wasn't looking at my legs but at the blood that had soaked my jeans between my legs. I didn't even feel that happen, I was too preoccupied with the piercing pain in my stomach.

"Did you just start your period?" he asked gently.

I tried to do the math in my head, but it didn't add up. This couldn't have been that.

I shook my head. "It's not my period."

Now I could feel the way my jeans were soaked from the blood. Just the sight of it made me feel lightheaded. There was so much blood.

"Hospital. Now," Giovanni said, his voice almost hollow as he tried to hide the fact he was as scared as I was.

I didn't know what was happening but the tears finally escaped my eyes. He reached for me and helped me stand up. I couldn't stand up straight, the pain kept causing me to hunch over.

"I need to change," I managed to get out.

Giovanni reached for a towel and wrapped it around my waist, covering the blood.

"No time, baby. I'm sorry but I'm taking you to a hospital right now. You can change there once they've checked you out."

"What's wrong with me?" I cried.

He wrapped his arms around my shoulders and started to guide me out of the bathroom. "I don't know, baby, but you're going to be fine."

I didn't know what to say. Something definitely didn't feel right and I felt foolish for how long I had tried to ignore the pain. He pulled away from me long enough to grab a small bag of mine from my cupboard. I watched as he shoved underwear and a pair of sweatpants into it before closing it and swinging it over his shoulder. He reached me again and wrapped his arm around my waist, helping me as we made our way down the stairs. I could focus on nothing but the pain in my stomach. I didn't even realize how much I was crying until Giovanni tried to console me.

"You're going to be just fine, my baby," he reassured me.

I could hear the concern in his voice and I knew he was trying his best to hide it from me. He kept reassuring me that everything was okay as we made it to the basement parking and finally, over to his car.

"I'm going to mess your seats up," I whimpered.

"I don't give a shit about my seats. I care about getting you to the hospital."

He opened the door for me and I dropped onto the seat, hunching forward as I wrapped my arms around my stomach. I closed my eyes and tried to get a handle on my breathing. Giovanni started the car and I felt it speed off.

"In and out." He rubbed my back. "Everything's going to be okay. You're going to be okay."

God, I hope so.

***

Hours later I was lying in a hospital ward as Giovanni and I waited on the results from the tests they had to run. Thankfully, they had provided me with enough pain medication that the pain in my stomach had started to subside. I was feeling disorientated and disconnected from reality as I lay in that bed. Time moved so slowly when I had nothing else to focus on but my own worry. Giovanni sat next to the bed, holding my hand the entire time. He tried to hide his own fear but he couldn't - it was spread across his face. I wanted to reassure him that everything would be fine but the nagging pit in my stomach was making it difficult for me to believe that myself.

After what felt like forever, the female OB-GYN they had on call finally pushed through the doors of my room, a yellow folder in hand.

"Señora Avery, ¿cómo estamos hoy? she asked.

I looked to Giovanni for a translation. He quickly explained to her that I couldn't speak Spanish and she switched to English for me.

"Sorry about that. I'm Doctor Gavina. I saw you briefly earlier before they ran tests." She turned to Giovanni. "And are you her boyfriend?"

"Fiancé." He corrected and tightened his grip on my hand.

She nodded and turned back to me, her neutral expression now giving anything away as she opened her file onto the table at the end of my bed.

"Miss Avery," she started, her tone gentle. "Did you know that you were pregnant?"

My heart stopped. Pregnant? I was pregnant?

Wait a minute.

"Were?" Giovanni repeated, reading my mind.

I lifted my eyes to reach hers and she couldn't hide the brief flash of sadness over the news she was delivering.

No. Don't say it. Please don't.

"I'm sorry, Miss Avery, but unfortunately, you lost the baby."

She was still talking but my world suddenly stopped. I couldn't focus on anything but her words replaying over and over again in my mind.

I'm sorry, Miss Avery, but you lost the baby.

This wasn't happening. All the pain I was feeling earlier. All the blood. That was all me losing the baby I didn't even know I had.

"I didn't even know she was pregnant."

Giovanni's voice brought me back to my reality as he turned to me. "Baby, did you know?"

I could do nothing but shake my head. Of course, I didn't know I was pregnant. He would have been the first person I told. He turned back to the doctor.

"How did we not know? What happened?" he asked.

His hand tightened around mine and I felt his emotions radiating off of him. I wanted to comfort him. I wanted to do something but I couldn't even move. I just stared at Dr. Gavina as she continued to explain.

"Unfortunately, you suffered a miscarriage. These are quite common but there were many complications. Based on your scans and test results, we found that you have what is known as Polycystic Ovary Syndrome."

My mouth went dry, and I couldn't form any words so she continued.

"One of the most common symptoms is finding small cysts on the ovaries. Sometimes these tend to rupture and can be incredibly painful. One of the smaller cysts burst, which caused the miscarriage. With your current condition, it was clear that the environment was less than hospitable for the baby in the first place."

The tears that were building escaped my eyes and I bit down in my bottom lip to try and stop the choking sound building in my throat.

Giovanni turned to me, squeezing my hand in his. "Hey, baby. It's okay."

I allowed myself a moment to feel the sudden rush of sadness over me. I had so many questions. How was it possible that I didn't know? I had my period - didn't I? With everything going on with the wedding plan, I couldn't even place something as simple as the last time I had my period. It had always been so irregular anyway but I didn't think too much about that. There was so much I wanted to say but I couldn't form the words so I was thankful when Giovanni continued to ask for us.

"So, what does this mean now? Is she going to be okay?"

"She's fine for now. There are various treatments we can discuss but I do need to warn you that should you want to conceive, there are foreseeable complications ahead of you."

"Look, Dr. Gavina, could you please just say it as it is? Not in your doctor's terms." He couldn't hide the frustration in his voice.

She sighed and closed the file in front of her. "At this point, your fiancé being able to fall pregnant again is highly unlikely. Not with her current condition. It was a miracle she was able to have fallen pregnant at all."

I zoned out. I couldn't accept what she was telling me. There is just no way this was happening. *Being able to fall pregnant is highly unlikely.* What was happening? I was supposed to be getting married in two days' time and now I'm being told that I had a miscarriage and the chances of falling pregnant again are highly likely. *What the actual fuck?* I kept replaying it over and over again.

My heart shattered as the tears streamed down my face.

"It's going to be okay." Giovanni's arms wrapped around me.

"I'll give you guys a minute before we discuss your options, but we are going to need to keep you here for a couple of days. You lost a lot of blood and we don't want to take any chances."

She was talking to me but I couldn't move. I couldn't answer her. What is going to happen with our wedding now? I was supposed to be getting married.

She left the ward and closed the door behind her. I burst into tears and let out the gut-wrenching cry I was holding back.

"How is this happening?" I cried. "I didn't even know I was pregnant."

"I know, baby."

"How could I not know? I should have known. And now it doesn't even matter because it's gone - our baby is gone and we didn't even get a chance."

I was crying over the baby I didn't even know I had but just knowing that Giovanni and I had managed to conceive a little one was enough to break my heart at the loss of that, now, out-of-reach dream. That's what I had wanted. I had wanted a family with him and now that was slipping further and further from reach.

"Isabella, everything is going to be okay." He kissed my hair. "I promise, baby, we are going to be through this."

"We have to postpone our wedding," I whimpered.

His hands cupped my face, forcing me to look up at him. "Don't worry about that. I just care about you being okay, *mi hermosa*."

"I can't have children," I choked.

"She said it's unlikely - not impossible," he corrected, trying to downplay the emotion in his voice. "That means there's still hope."

"And what if there isn't?" I asked him. "What if I can never have children? What are we going to do then? You want children."

All these thoughts were bubbling over in my head now. Something I never thought I had to think about was now my reality and it was making me sick to my stomach.

"I want you, Isabella. No matter what," he reassured me. "We are going to get through this together."

I hung my head in my hands and allowed the tears to flow with nothing but the sound of my breaking heart surrounding me.

CHAPTER 18:

Giovanni

I slowly closed the door to Isabella's ward behind me. After the doctor left, it took a while before I was able to calm Isabella down. She wouldn't stop crying and I felt fucking helpless. I consoled her as best as I could. I brought myself onto the bed with her and let her cry against my chest until it exhausted her. Her eyes slowly closed, the tear stains still around it but it wasn't long after that when all I heard was her soft breathing. I had spent that time trying to reassure her that everything would be fine but I didn't even have time to really process what Doctor Gavina had said.

I leaned against the wall and closed my eyes, trying to work through what just happened. One minute we were at home finishing off our dinner and the next Isabella was crying out in pain, her pants soaked in blood. It was fucking terrifying seeing that. Just the sight of her like that caused a fear to burn inside of me in a way that I had never experienced before. I was afraid for her but I never thought that bringing her here would reveal to us that she had a miscarriage.

A miscarriage of a baby we didn't know we had.

A flicker of grief awoke inside of me. A deep hollow pain over the loss of something I didn't even know was a possibility right now. I didn't think of Isabella falling pregnant. We were so focused on the wedding and planning our life together that we failed to see the plan that had already unfolded. Isabella was devastated - it was written all over her face and I couldn't find the right words to console her. And not just about the miscarriage but about the cysts or possible infertility - everything. I watched her heart break and I could do nothing but stand by as it happened.

A lump started to form in my throat as I ran my fingers through my hair. I took a deep breath in and tried to compile a list in my head of everything I needed to deal with now. I needed to tell Alvaro and Reyna since they were going to have to help me cancel our wedding. We were supposed to be getting married. Both Isabella and I had been looking forward to our day. All the effort that was put into this for everything to be brought to a halt. We were supposed to be at home getting ready for this weekend. I wanted to drive her up to that villa as my fiancé and come back with my wife. That was what was supposed to happen. Not this. We didn't deserve this. Isabella didn't deserve this.

I pulled my phone from my back pocket, dialing Alvaro's number before bringing the phone to my ear. After the second ring, his voice appeared on the other side.

"Giovanni, ¿cómo estás?, hermano?"

An unexpected rush of tears pooled in my eyes and I tried hard to keep it together.

"Alvaro, something's happened," I managed to choke out. "Do you think you could meet me at St. Maria's hospital?"

"Hospital? Giovanni? What's going on?" My brother's voice was full of concern.

"Isabella had a miscarriage," my voice cracked.

I heard Alvaro suck in a breath as he processed my news.

"I didn't even know she was pregnant," he said.

"We didn't know either, but she was and she lost the baby. They have to keep her here for a couple days so we have to postpone the wedding."

The more I said all of this out loud, the more a rush of emotion washed over me.

"I'm walking out my front door now, I'll be right there, Giovanni."

We said our goodbyes just in time for the first tear to escape my eyes. It took me by surprise. I was usually very good at keeping my emotions intact but I couldn't when it came to Isabella. She made me vulnerable. A part of my heart was walking outside of me wrapped up in the body of Isabella Avery. Her pain was my pain. I had to be strong for her now. Isabella felt everything so much stronger than your average person. She was the soft-hearted one who practiced sympathy and empathy on a daily basis. She was the person who would cry because of sad movies or books. She would be moved by a random video she saw online of an older man visiting his wife in hospital or a dog with three legs. She felt everything so strongly that I was terrified that this grief was going to consume her.

Grief over the baby we were supposed to have. Grief over the life that would have come with bringing our child into the world. I knew that because I was feeling it, too. I was feeling grief over that loss and the loss of the future we were meant to have.

Doctor Gavina's voice brought me back to reality as she stopped in front of me, extending her hand to rest on my arm.

"*Lo siento, señor.* I know how difficult something like this is." She had a comforting sincerity to her voice. "She's going to need you now more than ever."

I nodded. "I already feel like I don't know how to help her."

"There are plenty of options and treatments for us to still discuss but all you can do for now is remind her that she isn't alone in this."

"*Gracias.* She's sleeping right now so we'll have to discuss all of that later."

She nodded. "No problem. She needs her rest."

Before she could continue, my phone started ringing in my hand. Doctor Gavina smiled and turned down the hallway, leaving me to answer the call. I glanced down and Reyna's name lit up my screen.

"Alvaro," I muttered, knowing he would have told her what happened.

I sighed and brought the phone to my ear.

"*Hola, Rey-*" I started to say but she cut me off.

"Is Isabella okay?" Her voice was frantic. "Alvaro told me what happened."

"She's fine. She's sleeping now but things don't look good, Rey."

"Listen, I'm at Diego's place about ten minutes away. I'm leaving now to come meet you."

I could hear a pair of keys in her hand. I slid down the wall onto the floor, leaning my hand against my forehead.

"Are you alright?" Reyna asked gently.

"I don't know. I didn't even know she was pregnant." My voice cracked again. "And you could see the devastation in her eyes. It fucking killed me."

"Isabella couldn't have known either. You know her, she's terrible at keeping secrets so she would have told us."

"I know. I know she didn't know."

"I'm so sorry that this happened, Gio." Her voice was sincere. "What are you guys going to do about the wedding?"

"We need to postpone. She lost a lot of blood so they're keeping her here for a few days."

"Listen, you don't worry about any of the wedding stuff, okay? Leave that to Alvaro and me. We will cancel everything. You just need to be there for Isabella."

I took a deep breath in. She's right. My fiancé needed me right now. I needed to be strong for both of us.

"Thank you."

"No problem. I'll see you now. Text me if you need anything while I'm out."

We disconnected the call and for a moment I just stared down the blank screen trying to process what I was supposed to do next. I just wanted Isabella to be okay. She was in so much pain and with the blood she lost, she needed these next few days to recover fully. I was not about to take any chances with her. I allowed myself a few more moments of processing before pulling myself up again and making my way back into her ward.

CHAPTER 19:

Isabella

Their voices started out as just a soft murmur in the distance, but as I slipped further and further from sleep, I was forced to hone in on them around me. They were much louder now, trying to talk in a hushed tone so as to not wake me. The memories of what had happened came flooding back to me and I didn't want to open my eyes and face reality. I wasn't ready for it. I felt an ache in my chest and the tears started to pool in my eyes again. I took a deep breath in, trying to hold them back. I didn't want to cry again. I needed to try and be strong.

"Do you want me to call her parents?" I heard Reyna say.

Reyna? When did she get here?

"No, that's okay. I think I should do it," Giovanni said.

"Penelope's just told Ma now. She wants to come to the hospital," Alvaro said.

Alvaro's here too?

"I don't want too many people here. Isabella and I need time to process this."

A tear managed to escape my eye and I used all my strength to hold back the cry that was building in my throat. I hadn't even said a thing but Giovanni knew what I needed. I didn't need people to be hovering around me now. I needed to come to terms with what had happened. I felt so stupid for not knowing I was pregnant. Shouldn't I have known that? How did I have a human growing inside of me and I didn't notice any indication of that? I should have been able to tell. I was sick with guilt. I didn't know I had cysts. I brushed my pains off as nothing more than stress. I used to get the same pains in high school right before a test so I didn't think anything of it. The pain would come and go. It wasn't meant to be a problem I had to deal with. It wasn't supposed to have caused such a drastic change in my life.

I was so high on the ecstasy of planning our wedding that I didn't notice anything. I couldn't even remember the last time I had my period - it was never anything very memorable. I have always had such a light flow but I didn't think anything of it. Was that a problem in itself? Should I have picked up on this earlier? Giovanni and I have had so much unprotected sex lately but I didn't think it was unusual that we didn't have a pregnancy scare. I never thought that having children was going to be so out of reach for me.

This time I wasn't able to hold my cry back again longer and a whimper escaped from my throat. I heard Giovanni rush over to me, his voice louder as he slipped his hand in mine.

"Isabella? Baby, hey, I'm here."

I opened my eyes as the tears spilled over. My gaze landed on his deep brown eyes that were filled with worry. Seeing his own concern made me cry even harder. I turned and buried my head in my arms as I heard Reyna on the other side of me.

"Izzy, we're here for you. I'm so sorry that this happened," she consoled.

I didn't respond. I tried to get control of my tears. I forced myself to take a deep breath in and turned to lie on my back, keeping my eyes still closed. The tears ran down my face as I focused on the hollow feeling inside of me. I needed to just pull myself together.

I took another deep breath in before opening my eyes again, staring up at the ceiling.

"I need to phone your parents and tell them what's happened," Giovanni said softly, I felt his lips against the back of my hand. "I'll be right back but Reyna is here."

Giovanni slipped out with Alvaro following closely behind him. I kept my gaze on the ceiling as I nodded, a few more tears slipping out of my eyes. I felt his hand leave mine but felt Reyna next to me. I slowly turned to face her.

"Hey," she said softly.

I tried to force a smile but all I managed to do was allow a couple more tears to slide down my cheeks. She reached for my hand, careful not to squeeze too tight on the drip that was in it.

"How you feeling?" she asked.

"Tired. Still a bit sore but they have me on some good pain meds." I tried to lighten the mood but I was just forcing it.

She smiled bleakly. "I'm going to be honest with you, Izzy, I don't even know what to say right now. I'm just so sorry that this happened."

I squeezed her hand in response. I didn't know what to say. She couldn't tell me what I needed to hear. I needed to hear that everything was going to be okay and this was all just a misunderstanding. A case of mistaken identity of patients. Anything that would stop this from being my reality.

"I didn't even know I was pregnant," I said softly. "I feel like I should have known."

"You can't think of that now. You didn't know - it happens, Izzy."

"I feel so stupid," I admitted.

"Why?"

"I'm crying over a baby I didn't even know I had. How can I be sad over something I didn't know about?"

"You have every right to be sad about this. It didn't matter that you didn't know - you know now and it's okay to be affected by that."

I turned back to focus my attention on the ceiling above me. I didn't want to be affected by this. I didn't want to have the grief that was settling over me. I didn't want to have to mourn the child I was never going to have. I couldn't. So instead I focused on the ceiling above me. I counted how many dots there were against the white ceiling. Six. Seven. Oh, look there's another two - nine. I focused my attention on anything else but what was really going on here. Reyna didn't push for further conversation, she just kept her hand in mine. I couldn't give in to the hovering pain that was waiting for me to drown in. I wouldn't. I wasn't strong enough to pull myself out of it.

My attention turned to the door opening and Giovanni walked in with Alvaro right behind him. He came to my other side and pulled the chair closer to my bed as Alvaro leaned on the overhead table at the end of my bed. Giovanni slipped his warm hand in mine again.

"You okay?" he murmured, leaning his elbows on the bed as he brought my hand to his lips again

I nodded.

"Your father sends his love. He wanted to get on the first flight out of London but I assured him you were fine and that you were going to need a few days. Is that alright?"

I nodded and attempted a smile. The last thing I needed was more people to hover over me. All looking at me with the same pitiful look. They would mean well - of course, they would - but it would just make me feel like there was something wrong with me.

The reality was that I already felt like that.

Doctor Gavina basically told me my body wasn't fit for a baby. Everything she said mulled over in my mind again and again. I didn't know what all this meant for us moving forward and a part of me was terrified of it.

"Someone needs to call the caterers," I murmured.

"We'll do that," Reyna assured me. "And everyone else that needs to be told."

"I don't want you to worry about the wedding stuff, *mi hermosa,*" Giovanni said softly. "You just need to focus on getting better."

Better? How was I supposed to get better? Sure, my physical pain would stop but the emotional stuff? I was already attempting to close my mind off from that. If I let it in then I would be accepting it and I wasn't ready for that.

"When can I go home?" I asked.

"Doctor Gavina needs to still speak to us about our -" he paused for a split second. "Our options but they want to just monitor you."

"Are you going to go home?"

He shook his head. "I'm not leaving your side."

A lump formed in my throat again. God, I love this man so much. More than I ever thought I could love anyone. I was so ready to marry him and start our life together. I was ready for it all and that included starting a family now.

My heart ached for that dream which was now slipping further from my reach. I knew he wanted that too and I couldn't help the bubbling fear inside of me over what our future would look like now. I couldn't allow myself to give in to those thoughts. *You need to still hear from the doctor.* I tried to focus on the hopeful voice in the back of my mind. I could do with a bit of hope right now.

CHAPTER 20:

Isabella

The elevator doors opened and I slowly made my way through our apartment with Giovanni by my side. He kept his arm around me the entire way up and constantly made sure I was doing alright. Physically, I was fine for now. Nausea still hovered over me and there was a possibility of bleeding for the next two weeks that I had to monitor but thankfully, there were no aching pains in my stomach anymore.

But emotionally I was a mess.

Giovanni let go of my waist as we reached the kitchen counter. He dropped the bag of mine he was holding onto the floor.

"Can I get you something? Maybe some water or coffee?"

"Water, please."

He nodded and made his way over to the fridge, pulling it open to grab a bottle for me. He turned back and handed it over before leaning against the counter, looking up at me. The concern in his eyes had yet to falter.

"I think we should talk about what happened," he said softly.

I turned my attention to the bottle of water in my hands. I opened the cap and slowly brought it to my lips, allowing the cold liquid into my system. He was right. We should talk about what happened but just the thought of it brought tears to my eyes. I took a deep breath in, making sure I kept the tears at bay. I was so tired of crying.

"We were supposed to be getting married today," I said, my voice almost a whisper.

He reached for my hand. "I know, bab-"

I cut him off. "This wasn't supposed to happen. Today was supposed to be the happiest day of our lives. I was ready to marry you, Giovanni."

"I was ready to marry you, *mi hermosa*. You know that but these things happen and we just have to get through this together."

I shook my head. "Everything feels different now."

I heard him suck in a small breath and he let go of my hand. I kept my eyes firmly on the bottle in my hand but felt his presence as he came around to stand next to me. He reached for my hand and turned me to face him. I didn't want to. I was wrapped up in guilt over what happened. I couldn't help it. I should have known I was pregnant. I should have paid attention but I didn't. Maybe if I had known, I would have made better choices. I would have taken better care of myself. I would have done something that would have stopped this from happening.

"Yes, things are different. They are different because now we have to find the right treatment and we have to deal with the fact that we -" he stopped as his voice cracked, causing me to look up and meet his sad eyes, "We lost a baby, Isabella, but nothing else has changed. I love you just as much as I did - if not more now and I would marry you in a heartbeat."

Tears spilled down my cheek. He lifted his hands to cup my face, using his thumbs to wipe away the tears.

"And I am going to marry you, *mi hermosa*. I can promise you that." There was clear determination in his voice. "But all I care about right now is being there for you, whatever you need and for however long you need."

I wanted to tell him how much I love him. I wanted to tell him that I couldn't wait to marry him and that I know that will happen in the future but I couldn't form the words. There was an unwanted, nagging voice in the back of my head.

Everything is different now.

And everything was different. My body was not equipped to bear children. The one thing I never thought would be an issue was now my reality. We spoke about having children. Giovanni was so excited about that possibility - as was I. I had seen him with Mateo and I knew in my heart that he was going to be an incredible dad.

And now we didn't know if that was ever going to happen.

There was so much uncertainty. So much that was out of my control that it was starting to drive me crazy. My mind wouldn't stop with all that I had now lost. It wasn't just the baby. It was the future that I had wanted with Giovanni. Our future was supposed to be different and it pained me that now it was all a blur. I couldn't see our future now.

"Please say something."

"I'm scared," I admitted.

"Scared? What are you scared of?"

"Losing you."

"Baby, no." He pulled me into his arms, his hand coming up to rest against my head as he held me close to his chest. "That's never going to happen."

I tried to believe that. I know how much Giovanni loves me but a part of me felt...

Broken.

And I didn't know where to begin to start putting myself back together.

"Isabella, listen to me." He pulled away enough for his gaze to meet mine. "You are never going to lose me. Not even a possibility. You and I are meant to be together and I know you know that too. This is just a small hurdle that we have to get through and we will, I just need you to believe that."

He spoke with such conviction and surety in his voice that I almost felt a flicker of hope inside. It was momentary before the dark thoughts settled in my mind again but I had a feeling I was going to have to actively push through those. My mind was ready to swallow me whole. I wrapped my arms around his waist and rested my head against his chest again. Being in his arms made me feel calm, even if it was just for a moment.

"Technically, we still have these next two weeks off and I think you should take them and use this time to rest. We can pick up the wedding planning and all of that at a later stage. There's no rush for us to get married."

"What about the honeymoon?"

"I'll handle canceling that," he murmured and left a kiss against my hair. "Unless you still want to go on it."

I thought for a moment but shook my head. "I want our honeymoon to be just that so I'll wait."

"You're not going to ask me again what I had planned?"

I pulled away and shook my head. "I don't want to ruin anything else."

His finger rested under my chin as he tilted it up, forcing my gaze to meet his.

"You haven't ruined anything. I need you to believe that," he murmured. "None of this is your fault. It's just the universe's way of testing us."

"I'd really rather us not have to go through any more tests."

A small smile played on his lips. "I know, baby, but this is nothing, okay? In a few years time, this is just going to be that thing that happened."

He was trying his best to be encouraging and I loved him even more for that. I tried to fake the enthusiasm that I believed him but deep down inside, I was terrified of what was going to happen next. I reached up and placed a small kiss on his lips before pulling away.

"I'm still feeling quite exhausted so if it's alright, I'm going to just go take a nap."

"Of course." He leaned down and left a kiss on my forehead. "Do you want to sleep down here? I'm just going to be getting some work done."

I shook my head. "I'll sleep much better in bed."

"Okay, I'll bring my laptop to be-"

"You don't have to do that. You can work down here."

"But what if you need something?"

"Then I'll call for you." I placed another kiss on his lips.

He looked apprehensive but he didn't push any further. "I'll bring your bag upstairs now."

I managed a smile before turning and making my way upstairs. I reached the top floor and instead of heading towards our bedroom, I turned in the opposite direction towards the guest room we had. That room had been off-limits to Giovanni since I had my wedding dress there. I had found it quite quickly after starting my 'say yes to the dress' journey. I pushed the door open, stepped inside and closed it behind me. The room was dark so I flipped the switch, allowing the light to spill over the room. I walked over to the cupboard and opened the door. Hanging perfectly was my wedding dress and the tears pooled in my eyes at the sight of it. I was so angry that this had happened. I was supposed to have worn this today. I was supposed to have met Giovanni up at that altar and we were supposed to start our lives together.

How many more tests did we need?

I reached out and rubbed the soft material between my fingers. I leaned against the cupboard door that was still closed and shut my eyes, trying to stop the tears from falling but I was unsuccessful. The spilled over and the dull ache in my chest intensified as I replayed everything that had happened. I didn't want to feel like this. I just wanted to accept and move on but I couldn't. I was going to have to go through the pain in order to come out the other side.

I was not prepared for that.

CHAPTER 21:

Giovanni

B y the time the following Thursday rolled around, Isabella was up early and ready to head to work. I had just slipped on my suit jacket when she came waltzing down the stairs, dressed and ready to go.

"Where do you think you're going?" I asked, surprised.

"Work."

She strolled around the counter and picked up the kettle that had recently been boiled. She placed her other hand around it, testing if it was still hot or not.

This last week has been difficult. The more I tried to be there for her, the more I could sense her pulling away from me. I often found her staring off into the distance, lost in thought. She still had a sadness in her eyes that I wished I could just take away. I just wanted to see her happy again. And I tried everything I could. I tried to distract her in any way possible. I even went as far as trying to make her dinner. That earned me a smile and a small laugh when my attempt to make *paella* failed horribly. I held her hand and used every chance I could to remind her that she wasn't alone in this.

"Are you sure you should be going back to work already?" I asked softly. "You technically don't have to go back yet."

"Yes, but if I stay in this apartment any longer, I'm going to go crazy."

I didn't push. I could have argued that she still needed time to process but every time I tried to bring it up, she dismissed the conversation and started to talk about something else.

"Maybe you need a change of scenery," I suggested. "We can go to Sevilla if you'd like?"

She turned to face me, her travel mug in her hand. Even from here, I could notice the bags under her eyes. She wasn't sleeping much either and that kept me up at night too. I couldn't sleep knowing she was tossing and turning. I was always on edge, waiting to see if she was going to turn to me.

"When are you meant to go up there?" she asked.

"Whenever. It might be a good way to get away and give us some time to - uh -" I paused trying to figure out how to word this without her dismissing it again. "To spend time together outside of the apartment."

She brought her mug to her lips and nodded. "I'd really like that."

A breakthrough - finally! I've been dying to just hold her in my arms. I craved being close to her but I also didn't want to push her for anything. I watched how her mind took control of her and I was doing my best to try and pull her out of it. Maybe a weekend away would help.

"You let me know when you'd like to go and we'll go."

I walked around the counter over to where she stood. I reached for her hand and pulled her into my arms. She didn't resist. She wrapped her arms around my waist and let out a sigh.

"You guys didn't tell all our guests what happened right?" she asked softly.

"No, baby." I left a kiss against her hair. "We said we had to postpone due to a medical emergency but we didn't elaborate. Only your family and mine know what happened."

"I don't want to tell people."

"You don't have to."

She didn't say anything further but she kept her arms around me. I held her close to me, soaking in how much better I felt just by having her in my arms. Loving her was like leaving my heart exposed where I was susceptible to her pain and right now, I just wanted to take it all way. I was adamant that a weekend in Sevilla would be good for us to reconnect. Or at least to remind her of how loved she is.

"Could you drop me on your way out?" she asked.

"Of course."

I pulled away and leaned down, my lips meeting hers. She kissed me back. Soft and first until she used her tongue to part my lips. *God, I had missed her.* I matched her energy, my kiss suddenly becoming hungry as the desire inside of me awoke at her touch. I pulled her close to me, deepening the kiss before she pulled away.

"We should get going - don't want to be late."

I glanced up at the clock on the wall behind her. *Aroma* didn't open for another hour but I didn't push the subject. She wasn't ready yet. I understood that.

I leaned down and left a kiss against her forehead. "You got everything you need?"

She nodded.

I slipped my hand in hers, reached for my phone on the counter, and made our way to the elevator. She kissed me. That was already progress. We had kissed over the last few days but it was always a quick hello or goodbye kiss - nothing deeper than that. But today it was different - I could feel her desire. She wanted me like I wanted her but she wasn't emotionally ready yet and I would never push her. She needed time and I would give that to her. I would wait as long as she needed. I slipped my hand in hers, reached for my phone on the counter, and made our way to the elevator.

I kept my hand in hers all the way to the car.

***

"How's Isabella doing?" Alvaro asked.

We sat in Alvaro's, now, office which he took over from our father when he retired. There were a couple of new projects that we discussed but I knew this conversation was going to come up.

I sighed. "I don't know."

I leaned back against the chair and ran my fingers through my hair. Ever since we got back from the hospital, something felt different between us and I didn't know how to make it better.

"I feel helpless," I admitted. "Since we got back home, she's just been so sad and no matter what I try to do to help, I just don't think anything is working."

"You just have to continue to be there for her. She's probably working through all this in her head."

"I know. I just wish she would talk to me about it though. I don't want her to have to go through this alone but I can feel she's been pulling away from me."

"And how are you dealing with all of this?"

"What do you mean?"

"You lost a baby, too. You were also affected by what happened."

I thought for a moment. I hadn't stopped to think about how all of this could have affected me cause I was so concerned about Isabella. She was the one that I needed to be there for - no matter what. I hadn't even had time to fully process this myself and I felt almost selfish for feeling that I should. She was the one who went through the pain, not me.

"I don't know," I admitted. "I don't know how I'm supposed to feel. I feel stupid even saying this out loud because I didn't even know she was pregnant and now we don't even know if that's something that's going to happen for us."

"What did the doctor say?"

"She went through some of the treatments. She put Isabella on this other pill - something about regulating her flow. I don't know. She also has to monitor the cysts because they don't want another one to rupture, but those cysts are the issues."

"Is she going to get them removed?"

I shrugged my shoulders. "Isabella said she needed time to think about all this and I haven't brought it up again. Every time I do, it's like watching her heart break all over again and I just can't do that to her."

Alvaro got up from his chair and walked over to the wooden table against the right wall. He leaned down and opened the cupboard just below it before pulling out a bottle of whiskey and two glasses. Perfect timing. I could really use something right now. He brought it over to his desk and took a seat again as he started to pour for us.

"I'm sorry this happened, Gio. Honestly, I am. You and Isabella don't deserve to be going through this."

"I know but the universe doesn't owe anyone anything apparently."

He leaned forward and handed me the glass. I took it from him before leaning back against the chair. I brought it up to my lips and sipped on the bitter taste.

"I'm planning on taking her to Sevilla for a weekend and I spoke to her father on the way here. Her parents want to come to Barcelona for the day so

I'm hoping that will help."

Alvaro nodded. "Have you guys chatted about setting a new wedding date?"

I brought the glass to my lips again and shook my head. "She doesn't want to talk about the wedding, either. I'm hoping that's still something she wants."

"Of course she does. Isabella loves you."

I knew that was true. Of course, she loves me but I couldn't ignore the nagging pit in my stomach that something was off between us. *She's grieving and processing what happened.* I chastised myself for even thinking that this had something to do with our relationship but it did. The ripple effect of what happened had direct effects on her and I. We lost a baby. We lost the idea of what we thought our lives were going to be. Would she be able to have children? Would it bother me if she couldn't? What do we do next? There were so many unanswered questions I had and instead of trying to answer them, I pushed them out of my mind and looked for the answers at the bottom of my glass.

Before I could respond, there was a tap at Alvaro's door and Athena popped her head in.

"*Lo siento*, Hernandez is on the line for you, *señor*."

Alvaro nodded and turned his attention back to me. "Do you mind if I take this?"

I shook my head. "Go ahead. I'm actually going to head out. I need to get some files from the *Mala Mía* office."

"I'll call you later."

We said our goodbyes and he reached for the phone as I slipped out of the office. I followed the hallway that led back to reception and waved goodbye to Athena before stepping into the elevator. The doors closed and I tried to find a moment of calm within the chaos of my thoughts. I pulled my phone from my pocket and opened my chat with Isabella. I stepped out of the elevator and walked over to my car. I unlocked it and slipped inside. I turned my attention back to my phone and sent her a message.

Me: Just want to remind you that I love you.

I sent the message and dropped my phone onto my lap.

By the time I arrived at *Mala Mía*, I still hadn't heard anything from her and I hated the disappointment that presented itself at that. She had such a hold over me and I would do anything for her. I checked my phone again as I pulled into an open parking spot outside. I needed to fetch Isabella after work so I didn't bother parking in my usual spot in the basement. I stepped outside the car and shut the door, locking it before dropping my keys into my pocket. I glanced back down at my phone in my hand, getting ready to type another message but was stopped in my tracks as I heard a voice calling my name

I lifted my head to the figure approaching me on the street.

My breath caught in my throat.

"Maya?"

CHAPTER 22:

Isabella

I thought I could go back to the way things were. I went back to work today as a distraction from my own thoughts but I felt worse. I was bombarded with questions about the wedding being postponed and I wasn't ready to explain. I lied through my teeth and brushed it off as an unfortunate emergency. I lied and said I had severe food poisoning and they had to keep me for days to monitor. It was a fickle lie and I could see Savannah and Federico didn't believe me. They looked at me with that look of pity. The one people don't realize they're giving you. With the way it looked and no real explanation being given, it made sense that they would think one of us got cold feet. I couldn't entertain it any longer. I sat in the office for most of the day, trying to sort through the mundane admin but by the time afternoon rolled around, I needed to get out of there. I asked Savannah to lock up and slipped out of the shop, heading for the beach.

I removed my sandals and stepped onto the rough sand. It was warm against my feet as I walked towards the ocean. I didn't want to focus on anything but breathing in the fresh ocean air. There was something about the smell of the ocean that washed a sense of calm over me. I took in another deep breath as I stepped onto the wet sand, the tide pulling the water towards the ocean before releasing it over my feet. I gasped at the cold feeling against my feet but I loved it. For a few moments, I just stood there with my eyes closed and focused on nothing but the water at my ankles and the fresh air surrounding me. The sun was still shining down but I kept my eyes closed and leaned my head back. It was the first time in days that I felt like I was okay. I had been so emotionally erratic lately that I reveled in this new calm. There were no tears, no sadness, no anger - there was actually nothing and I welcomed it.

I opened my eyes and focused on the reflection of the sun against the water. The water was calm but never still. I resonated with that. I turned my attention to the buzzing of my phone in my back pocket. I pulled it out and glanced down at the text from Giovanni.

Just want to remind you that I love you.

I smiled at my phone. I didn't deserve this man. He was too good for the world and I was angry at myself for the distance I was putting between the two of us. It wasn't intentional but I couldn't shake the guilty feeling that I got whenever I looked at him. I locked my phone and held it to my chest as the tears started to pool in my eyes again. I had never loved anyone like I loved Giovanni and all I wanted was for us to start our lives together. I wanted to marry him. I wanted to be his forever. I wanted a family.

There was that dull ache again.

I couldn't escape it. Every time I thought about wanting to start a family, the pain presented itself and reminded me of how out of reach that was. I was put on another pill to assist with regulating my period better and I was meant to decide what to do about the cysts. She wasn't too worried about them now as none of them seemed to be life-threatening but with them on my ovaries, having a baby was less than likely. It's not like I wanted to have a baby right now. That wasn't part of our plan originally anyway but now that it might never be part of the plan, I didn't know what that meant for Giovanni and me. I was too scared to have that conversation with him. I was terrified of losing him. All I wanted to do was throw myself at him and remind him how much I loved him but I just couldn't. With each drowning thought, I pulled further and further away from him. I didn't want to but I knew it was happening.

A new wave of cold water washed over my feet, bringing me out of my thoughts. *Time to snap out of it, Isabella.* Even if it was momentarily, I needed to make an effort here before I was consumed by my own thoughts. I slipped my phone back into my pocket and made my way back to the walkway. I stopped on the concrete and dusted the sand off my feet before slipping my shoes back on. Giovanni was meant to fetch me in a couple of hours' time but I decided to head out to meet him. I pulled my phone out and dialed his number. I brought it to my ear as it rang. It kept ringing until eventually, it reached his voice mail. *Maybe he was still with Alvaro?* I dialed Alvaro's number next and was greeted by his friendly voice.

"*Hola,* Isabella. *¿cómo estás?*"

"I'm fine thanks, I'm just looking for your brother. Is he still with you?"

"No, he left a while ago. He said he needed to get some files from *Mala Mía* so you should find him there."

"Oh perfect - thanks Alvaro."

We said our goodbyes and I kept my phone in my hand. If he was already at *Mala Mía* then it makes sense for me to make my own way home. I swiped up and opened Giovanni's chat.

I love you, Gio.

I sent a second text.

Tried to call but you must be busy. Don't worry about fetching me from Aroma. I'm already on my way home. See you soon.

I slipped my phone back into my pocket and headed in the direction of the metro.

CHAPTER 23:

Giovanni

"You haven't changed." She smiled as she pulled her handbag over her shoulder.

What are the chances? I didn't expect to bump into Maya of all people. I hadn't seen her since the night I decided to end it. All our sneaking around was a ticking time-bomb and ending our relationship was inevitable. She was the last person I would have expected to see today. Or ever.

"Neither have you."

Maya was still the fresh-faced beauty I had once known. Objectively, I could acknowledge that she had attractive features. Her dark curls were still bouncing from her head the way they always did. Her blue eyes were always a jarring contrast against her darker skin. She looked much older than the girl I once knew but she was still the same old Maya.

"What are you doing here?" I asked. "I didn't know you were still in Barcelona."

"I never left but I've been job hunting lately and I just came from an interview up the road. I saw you get out of the car and thought there was no way that it was you."

I chuckled. "Yeah it does feel like we've opened the door to the past all of a sudden."

She tucked a piece of stray hair behind her ear. "You look good, Gio."

I didn't know what to say. She was looking at me with a flicker of interest behind her eyes. I recognized that same look from back when we had our brief relationship. I couldn't even categorize it as a relationship but I couldn't think of another word for it.

"I heard you were getting married." She glanced down at my hand. "When's the big day?"

"Uh, we haven't picked a date yet."

"Oh? Well, I guess a congratulation is in order anyway." She smiled. "She's a very lucky lady."

"And you?" I glanced down at her hand but noticed her ring finger was empty.

"I'm not married if that's what you're asking. Not engaged either. Actually, I've been single for a while."

Interesting. Maya and Paulo had been a toxic pairing that I got caught in the middle of. When I ended it with her that one night, I never looked back and I hadn't seen either of them since. I didn't seek her out. I cut off all ties.

"You and Paulo finally broke up?"

She flicked her eyes up to meet mine and there was something new in them. Guilt? Longing? Sadness? I couldn't quite place it.

"Yes. Turns out we weren't good for each other," she murmured. "But you already knew that."

"Everyone knew that."

Anyone that had seen the two of them together could see how bad they were together. They fueled each other's fires and the toxicity of their relationship was just something they had both gotten used to. No matter how many times someone tried to make them aware of their clear red flags, if they didn't see it for themselves then it didn't change anything.

"Well, at least you can say I told you so," she said.

"I would never do that, Maya."

She sighed. "I know. You were always a much better person and I didn't see that soon enough."

"Everything happens for a reason." I shrugged.

"You're right. I actually think that's why we bu-". I cut her off with an apology as my phone buzzed in my pocket. I pulled it out and noticed a missed call from Isabella. *Shit.* She had sent a text message too.

"Sorry, I have to just check this," I said.

I swiped up and saw it was sent just a few minutes ago.

Tried to call but you must be busy. Don't worry about fetching me from

Aroma. I'm already on my way home. See you soon.

"What's your fiancé's name?" she asked.

"Isabella." I glanced up from my phone. "That was actually her. She tried to call."

"Oh - sorry, let me not keep you."

I dialed Isabella's number and waited to press call. I turned back to Maya. "I hope you're happy, Maya."

"I was, once."

There it was again. That look in her eyes that I now identified as guilt and almost a sense of longing laced in it too. Her reply was simple and yet, loaded with so much that was unspoken between us. I didn't feel a flicker of anything inside when I looked at her. She was just someone that I used to know. Someone that was part of my past. There were no lingering feelings or regret. I looked at her and all I got was confirmation that I never loved her. Isabella taught me what real love was.

My phone started to ring again, this time Pedro's name popping up.

"I'll see you around, Giovanni," she said as she noticed the call coming through.

"*Adiós*, Maya."

She turned and took off down the street. It was strange to see her again. A part of me had always wondered what it would have been like. Would I feel anything? Would I miss her? But there was nothing. She and I weren't meant to be and I had known that from the first moment I got involved with her.

I should probably tell Isabella though.

But not on the phone. I'd tell her when I saw her. I turned back to my phone that had stopped ringing now. I went back to dial Isabella's number as I started to make my way across the road, slipping through the entrance of *Mala Mía*.

CHAPTER 24:

Isabella

"**G**iovanni?" I shouted as I walked down the stairs of *Mala Mía*. "You here?"

He popped up from behind the bar. "Over here, baby."

I strolled through the dance floor over to the bar. It was weird to see this place so empty. I was so used to the blaring music and crowds of people scattered throughout. Seeing it like this was almost eerie. The lights by the bar were on keeping the area illuminated but nothing like when the dance floor lights were on. I stopped by the bar and placed my handbag on it, leaning over to get a kiss from him. He leaned forward and placed his lips on mine. My time at the beach helped with this new refound calmness that I needed. It still lingered so I was planning to hold onto it for as long as I could.

"Where's everyone else?" I asked.

"Just me here. Ali just left. We were going through the last minute things for tomorrow's event happening here."

Ali had worked as the manager for *Mala Mía* for almost a year now. My first impression of her wasn't great since I thought Giovanni was sleeping with her when we were broken up at the time but that was a brief misjudgment. I had grown to really like her and she was great at her job. Giovanni trusted her and this place had continued to grow under her supervision.

"Are you guys not opening tonight?"

He shook his head. "She needed to finalize the installation of the new sound system and the guy can only come tomorrow morning so we decided it's best to keep it closed tonight."

I nodded and leaned against the counter. He turned around and reached for two glasses - one whiskey glass and one gin glass. He placed it down in front of me.

"Gin?" he asked.

"Are you any good at making them?" I eyed him playfully.

"I guess we're about to find out," he snickered.

He dropped down and reached for the tonic in the small fridge underneath the bar. Before turning to place it on the bar, he reached for the bottle of whiskey on the shelf against the wall. He turned back and grabbed the gin that was already on the counter. He started to pour some into my glass.

"How come you left work early? You know I was going to come fetch you right?"

"I know but I had kind of had enough of the day and Alvaro already told me you were here."

"Alvaro?"

"Yeah, I called him when I couldn't get a hold of you. Just wanted to see where you were."

He reached for the tonic and clicked open the can before emptying it into my glass.

"Did you not have a good day?" he asked, eyeing me carefully.

He had been looking at me like that for the last few days. Almost as if he was treading carefully, just waiting to see how I was going to react. I couldn't blame him. My emotions had been quite erratic lately and he had done his best to be there for me. I haven't made it easy for him but after my one-on-one by the beach today, I wanted to make an effort with him.

I shrugged. "Just need time to get back into the swing of things."

I didn't want to tell him that I felt broken. The pitied looks and ongoing questions made me feel like there was something wrong with me. He knew all of that already so I didn't feel the need to repeat myself. I was trying to work past everything that had happened, not bring it up every time.

He handed me my drink. "I may have been a little heavy handed with the Gin."

I smiled and picked the glass up, bringing it to my lips. It was surprisingly refreshing but he was right, the alcohol was strong. He poured himself a whiskey as I placed the glass back down on the bar.

"I hate to break it to you but your mix-drinking skills are not up to standard."

"Mix drinking?" he chuckled. "I believe the correct term for that profession is mixologists."

"Well, either way, that career is not for you."

I continued to sip on my drink, allowing the alcohol to work its way over me. I hadn't had alcohol since the night of my bachelorette party and my last meal was a small muffin at lunch so my body was already latching onto the alcohol. It warmed me up and I let out a sigh of relief. I didn't want to think right now. I focused my attention on Giovanni standing casually on the other side of the bar. He had his sleeves rolled up to his elbows and I allowed my gaze to wander to the markings on his skin. There was always something about them that got me flushed. I found them just as attractive as I did the first time. His shirt was hugging his muscles and it had been so long since I had felt his hands on my body. His beard had grown out a bit but it suited him. I could still make out his jawline underneath it and I wanted to run my fingers over it. I wanted to run my fingers over his body. My dormant desire pushed through to the surface and there was nothing else for me to focus on but that.

"So today I actually ra-" Giovanni started to say but he stopped as I pulled myself onto the bar, swinging my legs over to hang on either side of where he was standing.

"Sorry, I hope you don't mind me sitting here." I reached for my drink and brought it to my lips again.

"Not at all. Perks of owning the place." He winked.

I placed my glass back down and reached for the glass that was in his hand. I took it from him and placed it down next to us. He looked surprised but also intrigued. I was focusing on nothing but him. I ignored everything else running through my mind. I didn't want to focus on the sadness or the dull ache in my chest. I wanted to focus on the building desire coursing through my veins. I reached for his hand and slowly started to run my nails up his forearm.

"Isabella," he breathed as I extended my legs to wrap around his waist, pulling him closer to me, "What are you doing?"

"There's no one here," I murmured.

We were so close now that I could feel his breath on me. I moved my hand up to cup the back of his neck, his skin hot against my touch. He was holding back. I could feel it and I didn't want that right now. I needed him. I let my legs hang on either side of him.

"Do you not want me anymore?" I asked softly, afraid of the answer.

He flicked his eyes to meet mine. "Of course I want you, baby."

He grabbed my legs and pulled me closer to him. I was up against his body, his erection making an appearance that caused a stir of excitement inside of me. His hand went up to slide into my hair.

"I always want you," he breathed. "But I know how ha-"

"No, Giovanni, don't." I lifted my finger. "I don't want to talk right now."

I dropped my hand and leaned closer to his neck, leaving kisses against it. I moved up and down, stopping to suck his skin. A deep groan escaped his lips and he gripped my thighs.

"I need to know you still want me," I murmured in his ear.

He pulled away and a look of pure hunger settled over his face. His eyebrow was cocked the way it always goes when he hears something that intrigues him. He leaned closer to me, just inches away from my body.

"Let me show you how much I want you, baby."

CHAPTER 25:

Giovanni

She needed me right now. I could see it in her eyes. They were blazing with a deep desire that I hadn't seen in a while. She was open for business and she wasn't about to let anything ruin it. There were so many things I wanted to say to her but now that the heat had rushed to my groin, there was only one thing I was focused on and that was giving her what she wanted. She needed to feel desired and I had never wanted her more. I wasn't expecting anyone to be coming to the club tonight so I was ready to have my way with her right on the bar counter.

"Should we go upstairs?" she asked.

I shook my head. "No way, I want you right here."

"What if someone comes?"

"The only person that's going to be coming is you, Isabella."

Her head fell back as she groaned at my words. She tightened her legs around me and I knew she loved what I had just said. She loved my dirty words and I had no problem telling her exactly what I had in mind. Isabella was sweet and innocent but not when it comes to this.

Without warning, I brought my lips against hers. My greedy tongue parting her lips as I didn't hold back. I had been craving her. My body was ready to tear her apart. I wanted to spend hours working my way across every inch of her, reminding her how much I want her. How much I need her. I grazed her bottom lip with my teeth causing a moan to leave her lips. *Fuck, I loved that sound.* Hearing her vocalize what she was feeling made me so hard. I wasted no time moving my lips from hers over to her jaw and then down her neck. I took pleasure in kissing and sucking on her skin, never once stopping to give her a moment to catch her breath. I ran my fingers up her thighs. I was dying to feel her and the only thing between us was the underwear she was wearing. I pulled her to the edge of the counter with enough space to spread her legs. I pushed her dress up exposing her to me. I had full access to her now.

Running my hands up her bare skin, her touch burned against me. I slowly moved my fingers closer and closer to her, brushing over her underwear, feeling how ready she was already for me.

"You're so wet," I breathed against her lips before kissing her again, using my tongue to part her lips. She moaned against my lips causing the heat to rush to my groin again. I was already about to fucking burst. I needed to be inside her but not before I had given her what I knew she enjoyed.

I pulled away and used my other hand to squeeze on either side of her chin.

"You're mine, you understand that?"

"I'm yours." She breathed.

I slowly ran my finger up and down the outside of her underwear. She pulled at her bottom lip as she soaked in my touch. I brought her hand against my erection.

"Do you see what you do to me?"

She flicked her eyes to meet mine.

"This is all because of you, Isabella. I would spend my life inside of you if I could."

"Please, Giovanni," she begged.

"Please, what?"

"I need you inside me."

I leaned closer to her ear. "Patience, baby."

I nipped at it before pulling away, pushing her dress up to her hips, exposing her to me. She was so ready for me. I gripped the lace thong she was wearing and didn't even bother sliding it off her. Instead, I gripped it with both hands and tore it off. She gasped as the material split in two but her eyes lit up like fireworks. Isabella loved it rough. She was a delicate, soft soul but she knew how she wanted to be fucked.

"I liked that underwear," she protested.

"I'll buy you more."

Without hesitation, I slid a finger inside of her. Wet up against me, I pushed in and out of her as her hand gripped the back of my neck, her nails digging into my skin. I wanted to rip her apart. There was no stopping me as I slipped another finger in, increasing the pace as I hit the back of her. She threw her head back, small moans escaping her lips. I needed to hear her. I needed her screaming my name.

I removed my fingers from her and positioned myself between her legs. Leaning my arms on the counter, I hooked them around her and pulled her closer to me. She smelled of sex and it was intoxicating. I brought my tongue over her, sliding up her opening. She jerked forward and her hand found my hair. The harder I went against her, the harder she pulled on my hair so I held nothing back. I found my rhythm against her, working my way up and down her, stopping at the top of her opening to suck against her clit.

"Giovanni," she moaned.

That's what I wanted to hear. Her encouragement had me quickening my pace over her before bringing a finger back inside of her as I continued. I did everything I could. I licked and sucked every part of her I could manage. It wasn't long before her orgasm rolled through her as she screamed my name. I could feel her release against my lips. I didn't want to stop there but I pulled away, her legs shaking from her pulsing orgasm. I reached for the button of my pants and undid it, my zip following before I pushed them down along with my underwear, freeing myself to her.

She brought her head forward, eyeing my erection. I grabbed her by the ankles and pulled her closer to the edge of the bar again, positioning her with enough space for me to push deep inside of her. We both let out a breath of relief as I filled her up. She already tightened around me, causing me to roll my eyes back. I loved this feeling. I loved being inside of her. Filling her up every way that I could. Skin to skin, we were the closest we could ever be and there was something different about the way that felt. I wrapped my arms around her and lifted her hips so I could push deeper inside of her. I was consumed by her. My own pleasure pulsed through me as I increased my pace. She held nothing back. Her moans filled the room and I leaned my head back, soaking in the beautiful sound. Between the sounds of our bodies colliding and her screaming my name, my own climax was starting to build.

"Harder!" she moaned.

I almost came undone at what she was asking me. I pushed deeper inside of her, each thrust harder than before. I was pretty sure I was ripping her open but I didn't stop. She wanted harder and I gave her exactly what she wanted.

"I'm close," she cried.

So was I. She wrapped her arm around my neck and flicked her hips forward, meeting my movement. We moved as one and I was consumed by the euphoria. She screamed my name one more time to the night as she found her climax again. My hand gripped her hair, forcing her head back as I spilled inside of her. There was nothing but the sound of our heavy breathing surrounding us. I held her to me. I didn't want to let her go. I could feel her heart beating against my body. She leaned her head forward, a satisfied look had settled over her face. She was so breathtakingly beautiful. With her flushed cheeks and sweat spots along her hair. Her hair was a mess and that was all my fault. I loved to see it.

I leaned forward and brought my lips to meet hers. She sunk into the kiss, leaning her body against mine.

"I've missed you, baby," I murmured in between our kisses.

"I've missed you."

CHAPTER 26:

Isabella

Pulling into an opening parking spot along the street, I pulled the handbrake up and reached for my phone in the compartment between the seats. I typed out a text to Giovanni.

Me: I've just arrived at Reyna's. Call me later after the event. I love you.

Dropping my phone on my lap, I unclipped my seatbelt and took a deep breath in. Reyna had been asking me for days to come over. I kept putting it off. I did that with everyone. I wasn't ready to immerse myself in the world yet but I couldn't put it off any longer. Giovanni had convinced me that a night with Reyna would be good for me. She was my best friend and I could always count on her to be there for me. I just didn't want to say a lot of what I was thinking out loud. Then I'd have to face what has happened and I didn't know if I was strong enough for that.

My phone buzzed, bringing me out of my thoughts.

Giovanni: I'm glad you're safe, baby. Enjoy your time with Rey. I love you so much.

I smiled at the text. Every time Giovanni told me he loved me, it was like hearing it for the first time. The same warmth spread across my chest. He was so good to me. I often felt undeserving of his love. Especially lately when I had been pulling away from him. I was so happy that we had managed to reconnect again - even if it was just for that moment on the bar. I didn't want to keep pulling away from him - that was the last thing I wanted but I was awful at dealing with my emotions. You're supposed to be the one in control of your emotions but I often found them controlling me.

One thing I was adamant to change. I didn't want to focus on that.

Tonight I just wanted to enjoy my night with my best friend. I grabbed my phone and reached over for my bag on the passenger seat before stepping outside. Closing the door behind me, I locked it and made my way into the apartment building. Nostalgia washed over me. I remembered when I first arrived in Barcelona and Reyna brought me home. I had never felt more like a fish out of water. I had just run away from home and I remembered being racked with fear over if I had made the right decision. I had no idea of knowing what the future would bring but I had never been more thankful for what came next. If I never came to Barcelona, I never would have met Giovanni and I couldn't think of anything worse.

I made it to her apartment door and knocked lightly before pushing it open, peeping my head around the door.

"Rey?"

"Did you seriously just knock like you haven't lived here before?" Reyna gaped at me from behind the counter.

"Of course I did," I chuckled. "Wanted to make sure I wasn't interrupting you and Diego."

Reyna rolled her eyes before skipping over, throwing her arms around me. "I know you've moved out but this will always be your home, too."

I tightened my arms around her. I could already feel the tears building in my eyes but I shook them away. I didn't want to deal with my emotions right now.

Reyna pulled away and reached for my bag. "And Diego isn't here. He's with his brother tonight. I told him I needed the apartment for girl's night."

"You kicked your boyfriend out of his apartment?" I couldn't hold back the amused laugh on my lips.

"Of course I did. He's allowed back here tomorrow. Tonight, it's just us girls."

She placed my bag by the couch as I strolled over to the counter. We always sat there together. The open plan design allowed for free range of the kitchen and living room.

"What's Giovanni doing tonight?" she asked, strolling past me towards the fridge.

"There's an event at *Mala Mía* so he's overlooking it tonight. I think Sergio, Jose, and Alonso are joining him too so it seems like a guys night out."

"Oh that reminds me, Kat will be here soon. I sent her out to get some burgers."

My stomach reacted at the mention of food. "From *Castellos*?"

"You know it." She flashed me her brilliant smile.

Castellos was one of our favorite restaurants close to the apartment. Famous for their stacked burgers, Reyna and I had helped ourselves to that place after a night out on a couple of occasions when I had tagged along. And sometimes even just for a midnight snack. They were open 24 hours a day and that worked in our favor.

Reyna passed me a glass of red wine and leaned against the counter in front of me with hers in hand.

"I'm actually thinking of taking my parents there on Sunday when they arrive. I know my dad is going to love their food."

"Papa Avery is coming to Barcelona?" Reyna couldn't hide her surprise.

I nodded. "And my mother."

"Well, I'll be damned."

I chuckled. "Right? I didn't expect Gloria Avery to ever set foot here but they insisted so they're coming for the day."

"How are things with your mother? I know your relationship with Camila is better but what about good 'ol Gloria?"

"Well, she hasn't questioned my decisions or tried to take control of my life in months so I think we're in the clear."

"That's a good sign."

I nodded. "I actually think this is the best our relationship has ever been. I still won't call her up to talk when I've had a bad day or anything like that but we talk a lot more than we did before."

"I'm glad. As long as she stays in her lane then there are no issues."

I couldn't help but laugh. She was right. If my mother respected the boundaries, then I was happy.

"Have you and Diego picked a wedding date yet?"

She shook her head and brought her glass to her lips. "We've discussed a few options but to be honest, we're not in a rush. I'm happy with how things are right now."

"Do you think you'll ever make it down the aisle?" I teased.

She rolled her eyes and laughed. "At this rate, who knows? Maybe we'll be that couple that just stays engaged forever. I don't mind that."

I brought my glass to my lips, allowing the bitter taste to soak against my palate.

"My mother is the one who might not let that happen," Reyna continued. "You know she still makes comments about the fact we are living together, unmarried. As if we aren't already having sex."

I couldn't help but laugh. "Your mother has always tried to stay old-school."

"Don't remind me." She rolled her eyes. "I love her to bits but sometimes she is just delusional."

Reyna lifted her glass but stopped halfway. "And she's totally on the grandch-"

She stopped herself before finishing her sentence but I already knew she was going to say, grandchildren.

"You can say the word children, Rey, I'm not going to break."

Her hand slipped across the counter, finding mine. "I know. I'm sorry - I didn't mean it like that. We just haven't really had a chance to speak about that and I want you to know that I am here for you, Izzy. Whatever you need."

I sighed and placed my glass back down on the counter. Propping my elbow up, I leaned against my hand. "I don't even know where to begin. To be honest, the whole situation caught me completely off-guard."

Before I knew it, I couldn't stop the words from slipping from my mouth as I started to divulge more to Reyna about how I was feeling.

"I'm angry. I'm angry at myself because I didn't know but how was I supposed to? I was pretty sure I didn't have any symptoms that I was pregnant. Or maybe I did and I was just completely oblivious to them which is so wrong. I should have paid attention. I should have known I was pregnant."

"Izzy." Reyna reached for my hand. "Breathe."

I stopped myself from saying anything more and instead did as I was told. I took a deep breath in through my nose, filling my lungs and allowing the simmering emotions inside of me to settle.

"Sorry," I said sheepishly.

"You can keep going," Reyna teased. "I just don't want you to pass out from lack of air."

I smiled and took in another deep breath.

"I'm just really angry at myself and a part of me feels really guilty about what happened." My throat constricted as the emotion made its way there, forcing me to hold back my tears.

"You didn't know you were pregnant. Every woman is different and our bodies react differently too. Some have hectic morning sickness and every symptom in the book and others don't. You know that if you had known, things would have been different but you can't blame yourself for something that was completely out of your control."

"You know I made a joke once to Giovanni about not knowing if I should be scared or thankful that we had never had a pregnancy scare - I never imagined that it was going to be an issue for us."

My lip quivered but I quickly pulled it between my teeth, trying to stop it. "I feel so guilty. You know I've always wanted children."

"You have nothing to feel guilty about." She leaned over, forcing me to look at her. "I need you to believe that, Izzy. These things are completely out of our control."

I knew she was right but a part of me still couldn't accept that. I still felt like there was something wrong with me. I was the broken one whose body doesn't function the way it was supposed to. I was supposed to be able to have children. At least that had always been drilled into my mind. Growing up, that's what you learn - go to school, get a degree, get married, have children. That's how it works. There was no need to follow that blueprint, I knew that but having children was something I had actually always wanted. No matter how unclear my future had been at times, children would be what I wanted down the line. I reached for my wine and brought it up to my lips, taking a big sip this time. The hovering tightness in my chest was starting to settle and I hated it. I didn't want to feel like this. I just wanted to forget. Tilting my head back, I washed what was left of my wine down. Bringing it back down to the counter, Reyna was already looking at me.

"Okay. Message received. Lots of alcohol will be needed for tonight."

I nodded. "Yes, please. I don't want to keep talking about this. I just want to drink and do anything else that will take my mind off this fuck up."

Reyna said nothing further. Instead, she turned to the cupboard door above her stove and opened it. I didn't see what she grabbed until after she closed it and turned to face me.

"We're going to need this." She lifted the bottle of tequila.

Any other day, I would have rejected the idea of having shots of tequila but not tonight. Tonight I was going to take full advantage of that bottle.

CHAPTER 27:

Giovanni

"**Y**ou've done a great job, Ali," I shouted over the music booming through the speakers, filling the club.

Mala Mía was packed. Ali had decided to host an event that included trying out some DJs of different genres. She wanted to test it out and see if it would bring new people to the club and she was right. People were stacked together throughout the club. There was not a single space open on the dance floor and given the cheering coming from downstairs whenever the song changed, people were having a good time. I was pleased with the outcome.

"Thank you," she smiled. "We should try this at least once a month or so. We don't want to lose the essence of this place but changing it up like this every now and then seems to work."

"You have my full support to run this whenever you see fit." I lifted my glass to meet hers.

I felt a hand on my shoulder and turned to find Sergio had returned with his own drink from the bar.

"Where's Alonso?"

"Stuck at the bar. Some pretty lady battered her eyelashes at him and he was gone."

I snickered and brought my glass to my lips. "We won't be seeing him the rest of the night."

"Nope."

One of the bouncers signaled for Ali and she politely excused herself before slipping past us and downstairs. Sergio leaned against the railing, his drink in hand.

"How's the Sevilla branch coming along?"

"We're getting there. I wanted to head up there this weekend but Isabella's parents are coming to visit."

"Oh?"

I nodded. "I think with everything that happened with her, they wanted to come down and spend some time with her."

"Do you think that's going to help?" He lifted his drink to his lips.

I shrugged. "I'm really hoping. I feel pretty fucking useless lately so I'm hoping that spending some time with them will get her mind off everything."

"How are you handling everything?"

"One day at a time. I'm just doing what I can to remind her that she's not alone in this." I leaned against the railing. "Sometimes I think she forgets that."

"Katrina does the same. It's like they think they believe they have to be strong all the time."

"Right? Anyway, I'm going to take her to Sevilla with me. We just need some time to deal with all this and then we can focus on moving past it."

Sergio straightened up and rested his hand on my shoulder. "Well listen, *hombre,* if you want to head down to the gym for a few rounds in the ring, you know I'm always down for that."

"I'll take you up on that, thanks."

I brought my drink to my lips again and allowed my eyes to travel across the crowd. They stopped as I watched Alonso pull into the woman that Sergio mentioned. I nudged him and pointed. "We definitely won't be seeing him again."

Sergio chuckled. "Good for him. Hopefully, he doesn't fall on this one."

"Oh shit, I completely forgot about that." I couldn't hold back my laughter.

Back in our university days, we all drank way too much all the time. One night Alonso pretty much out-drank us and we had him leaning up against a wall as we tried to scramble some water for him. By the time we came back to find him, he was making out with some women, and the next thing we knew they were both on the floor.

"And we didn't even help them." Sergio threw his head back in laughter.

"I was far too fucked to help them up."

"I couldn't stop laughing," I recalled. "I remember trying to pick him up but I just couldn't keep it together."

"That was a crazy night."

"Feels like a lifetime ago."

Sergio turned to say something but stopped as his eyes landed past me just as I felt a light tap on my shoulder. I turned to meet those familiar blue eyes.

"Fancy seeing you here," Maya said, smiling up at me.

I straightened up, leaning with my back against the railing. I hadn't seen Maya in years and now it was twice in one week? What are the chances?

"*Hola,* Maya. What are you doing here?"

"Came with some friends." She flicked her gaze past me and over to Sergio. "I remember you."

He looked to me for help as I could see the confusion on his face.

"You studied with Gio, didn't you?" she asked.

He nodded and extended his hand to greet her. "I did. Have we met before?"

"Briefly." She flicked her eyes back to me before landing on Sergio again. "I'm Maya."

"Nice to meet you again, Maya."

Her attention turned back to me, her blue eyes peering from behind her thick eyelashes. "I had heard you owned this club."

"How'd you hear that?"

"I may have asked around about you."

I was unsure how to reply so instead I just brought my drink to my lips. Seeing Maya again wasn't something that even crossed my mind and I felt nothing short of uncomfortable. I needed to tell Isabella that I had run into her. *Shit, I should have told her already.* I had every intention of doing that but when Isabella brought herself onto the bar and offered herself to me, I didn't think of anything else but worshipping her body the way she deserved. The feeling of her hand in my hair, tugging at it as I enter-

"It's a great place," Maya said, bringing me out of my thoughts.

A flicker of irritation presented itself. I was quite happy reminiscing on the way in which I had taken Isabella on the bar before Maya's interruption.

She stepped forward and leaned her hip against the railing. I turned back to the dance floor.

"You want another drink?" Sergio asked.

I nodded and handed him my empty glass. He looked over to offer one to Maya. I tried to eye him to not extend this reunion longer than it needed to be.

"I'll have one, thanks." She smiled at him.

He nodded and started to make his way through the crowd towards the bar in the VIP area we were in. I couldn't blame Sergio. He was just being the nice guy that he was and he wasn't aware of our history. No one was. Maya and I had always been a secret.

"I remember your friend. He almost caught us once," she commented. "Remember that time in the lecture ha-"

"Maya." I turned to her. "I don't feel like walking down memory lane with you. Especially not about that."

She rolled her eyes. "Someone's uptight tonight. Maybe you do need that drink your friend is getting for you."

"Don't start with me," I warned.

She cocked an eyebrow. "Or what?"

"I'm not playing this game with you," I huffed. "I'm engaged."

"Where is your fiancé?"

She was like a dog with a bone. I was trying to think of a polite way of telling her to fuck off but somehow, nothing came to mind and I wasn't in the mood to be a dick. I didn't trust her. That was the thing with Maya - you never could.

"Girls night out."

"And what is this then? A guy's night out?"

"Something like that."

Her lips pulled up in amusement. "Those can be dangerous sometimes."

I brushed her comment off and scanned the room for Sergio. Or Jose. Or Ali. Anyone that could break this interaction but instead of someone I knew interrupting, a ditzy black-haired woman threw her arms around Maya.

"*Nena! Ahí estas! Te llevo buscando.*" I could smell the alcohol on her as she positioned herself between us. She extended her hand to me. "*¿y tú eres?*

"Giovanni." I shook her hand politely.

Her eyes widened as she turned back to Maya, obviously recognizing my name.

"*Aquí no, Clara,*" Maya said to her, her eyes full of warning.

Okay, that's my cue. I had entertained this conversation for far too long and I didn't want to get sucked up in whatever Maya was doing. I had no time or patience for childish antics.

"If you'll excuse me," I said politely as I turned to make my way to the bar. I felt Maya's hand on my arm, stopping me. Turning back to her, her eyes were filled with so much she wanted to say. I pulled my arm from her touch. Nothing but pure irritation filled me at the mere sight of her.

"Come have a shot with us."

"No thanks."

"There's nothing wrong with a friendly drink, Gio."

Friendly drink? That was never the case with Maya.

"*Adiós,* Maya."

And with that, I turned and made my way over to where Sergio stood by the bar. The bartender placed our drinks on the bar just as I arrived.

"Why does she look so familiar?" Sergio asked, glancing back at where Maya and her friend still stood.

"She studied where we studied," I answered casually.

Sergio wasn't buying my answer as he looked over at me with an unimpressed look on his face.

"What?" I asked.

"There's got to be more to that story. She pretty much eye-fucked you that entire conversation."

"Jesus, Sergio," I mumbled and reached for my drink, suddenly needing some alcohol in my system.

"*No me mientas,* Gio. How do *you* know her?"

I sighed and leaned my elbow on the bar, turning to face him. "We may have hooked up back in the day."

"Oh? I don't remember that."

"Yeah, that's because she was kind of in a relationship at the time."

Sergio gaped at me, his drink pausing halfway to his lips, "*Joder.*"

I shrugged and sipped on my whiskey..

"How come you never told me?" Sergio asked.

"It's not something I was proud of," I admitted, "And then I ended things and moved on with my life. It's not like I still give a fuck about what happened. I don't even think about it."

I watched Sergio glance over at Maya again before turning back to me. "Watch out for that one. She seems like trouble."

"Trust me, she will not be a problem."

"Good."

I felt my phone buzz in my back pocket. Pulling it out, I noticed Isabella's name flashing across the screen. She was trying to facetime me and that couldn't have come at a better time. My heart warmed at the sight of it. I placed my drink down on the bar.

"Izzy's calling. I'll be right back."

Sergio nodded and I started to push my way through the crowd. I swiped up and her beautiful smile greeted me. I saw her mouth moving but I couldn't make out anything she was saying.

"Baby, hold on. I'm just trying to get to my office."

The music surrounded me as I pushed my way downstairs. I picked up my pace as I made my way to the back.

CHAPTER 28:

Isabella

I couldn't stop laughing. Reyna even had me snorting and I couldn't even remember what the joke was.

"What in the world are you laughing at?" Giovanni asked, his face finally coming up on the screen. The music that had surrounded him had become background noise as I noticed him stepping into his office.

"I don't even know!" I exclaimed, causing another bubble of laughter from my lips. Reyna and Katrina stood by the counter in the kitchen, both doubled over in laughter. Katrina wasn't drinking tonight as she was meant to fetch Sergio so she was enjoying our little show. Reyna and I had already downed a significant amount of shots tonight which had caused me to drunk-dial my fiancé.

"You seem like you're having a good time," Giovanni said, smiling at me.

I nodded, a goofy smile setting on my lips. "We have been having lots of this." I reached for the bottle of tequila on the coffee table and showed it on screen. "Look! Itss almost empty,"

Giovanni chuckled, flashing that gorgeous smile of his. Fuck, how was he so attractive?

"So what you're telling me is that this is a drunk dial?"

"It-s it is," I mumbled, swallowing as the alcohol continued to work its way over my body. I was all warm and fuzzy inside already. Not a single thought in my mind.

"I was telling them how often you watch the Twilight movies with me." I giggled as I glanced over at Reyna again. "Reyna said it's cause you secretly love them. Do you? Do you secretly love them?"

"Of course I do. Who doesn't love a sparkling vampire?"

I burst out laughing. It didn't actually matter what was being said, at this point everything was funny to me.

"Tell him about the bed!" Reyna shouted.

"Oh oh oh!" I exclaimed and turned back to my fiancé. "Wait, I don't want you guysss to hear,"

I could hear I was slurring, no matter how hard I focused on being serious. Giovanni was looking at me with such amusement.

"You already said it to us!" Katrina shouted.

I flung my arms at them, gesturing for them to get lost as I made my way through the door onto the balcony. The cold air brushed over my skin but I welcomed it.

"Are you standing outside in the cold with no jersey?" Giovanni asked, a hint of playfulness to his voice.

"Maybe." I leaned with my back against the railing as I lifted my phone to see him. "Maybe you should come and bring me one."

"Are you missing me already?" he chuckled.

"-course I am,"

"What's this about the bed? You've piqued my interest now, *mi hermosa.*"

I giggled uncontrollably but reprimanded myself to focus. "I was saying that you know in Breaking Dawn when Edward and Bella do the deed?"

He snickered. "Yes?"

"He broke the bed."

"He did."

"We should break a bed."

This time he burst out laughing. "You want us to break a bed? How would we do that?"

"By doing it really really really hard."

I listened to the sound of his laughter through the phone and I was hypnotized by the sound. It was the most perfect sound in the world. It was the sound that could make you forget about all your problems.

"I think that sounds like a challenge Miss Avery."

I scrunched my face. "I don't like that name. I want your surname."

"It's yours when you want it, baby. You know I'd marry you in a heartbeat."

"Pinky promise?"

"Lift your left hand," he instructed.

I did as I was told and lifted it up, displaying the beautiful engagement ring that lived on my finger.

"That ring on your finger is my promise, *mi hermosa.*"

My heart warmed at his words. I had been stuck in my own head for the past few weeks that it often clouded how in love I was with this man. He made my heart feel like it could burst out of my chest at any moment.

"Let's get married now," I said.

"Right now?"

I nodded, pulling my bottom lip between my teeth as I tried to hold back my smile.

"I'm wearing one of Reyna's old shirts though. I don't think that's as nice as a wedding dress."

"I don't know hey babe, you're looking pretty good to me right now."

"You're lying!" I giggled.

"I am not. I think this is the best you've ever looked," he teased playfully. "An old graphic tee, your messy bun - you've never looked more beautiful."

"Giovanni." Sudden tears swelled in my eyes. "You're too good to me."

He chuckled. "That's how it's supposed to be."

"I know but sometimes I feel like I don't deserve you."

"No such thing," he dismissed. "You're making me want to get into my car and come and get you. I don't like you being away from me."

"It's just for one evening." I smiled.

"That's too long."

"We can meet for brunch tomorrow," I suggested. "I think I'm going to need something greasy."

"I think so too." He smiled. "I'm glad you're having a good time."

"I am. It's nice not to think sometimes."

"I know."

I took a deep breath in and filled my lungs with the cool nighttime air. Glancing up at the dark sky, I was somehow comforted by the sight. Everything was calm and as it should be. I clung to that moment.

"How's your night been?"

"Fine. I actually wanted to tell you I ra-,"

Before he could continue, I heard Reyna call for me from inside, forcing my attention away from him. I was too intoxicated to focus on two conversations.

"Sounds like Reyna needs you," Giovanni said.

I turned back to him. "Sorry, I think I have to go back inside."

"No problem, baby. Let me not keep you. We can chat tomorrow. Put a jersey on okay?"

I smiled. "I love you."

"I love you, baby. See you in the morning,"

With one last smile from him, we disconnected the call. My heart was warm and for the first time in days, my mind was still. There was no overthinking. No unfiltered thoughts. Nothing.

And I loved it.

CHAPTER 29:

Isabella

By the time Sunday rolled around, I was finally hangover free and I couldn't be more thankful. Between Reyna and myself, we had managed to finish an entire bottle of tequila and I spent the next day paying for it. My raging headache lingered behind my eyes and once again, I swore off alcohol so when Giovanni asked if I wanted some wine with lunch, I declined straight away.

"Your daughter suffered with quite the hangover yesterday," Giovanni told my dad who was sitting across from us.

My dad chuckled, glancing over at me. "I always told you alcohol was poison."

He said that and proceeded to order himself a whiskey along with Giovanni. My mother shifted in her seat and politely ordered a glass of water for herself. For as long as I could remember, I had never seen my mother with any alcoholic beverage. Our waiter took our order and turned to make his way back inside. We sat at one of the tables outside *Castellos* on the street with the warm Barcelona sun beating down on us. We had fetched my parents from the airport and after showing them a bit of our city, we stopped for some lunch. I was nervous about having them here. Whenever it came to my mother, I was never entirely calm. It was just my default setting around her but she had been surprisingly pleasant. Quiet but pleasant nonetheless.

I found that being around people helped. It was when I had a moment to allow my thoughts to consume me that I got sucked into the sadness. It constantly hovered around me and instead of dealing with it head-on like I know I should, I just didn't have it in me so I continued to push it away. A war continued in my mind with my thoughts and it drained my mental strength to try and fight them off. I didn't want to be the sad one all the time. I didn't want to continuously mope around about what happened but it felt so out of my control. It was as if I was trying to grip onto my emotions but they kept slipping through my fingers.

I felt Giovanni's hand on my thigh, squeezing me back to reality. He always had this sense of when I needed him and that was the perfect moment. Right before I was about to become a hostage to my overthinking, he pulled me out of it.

"Your mother and I can't wait to see *Aroma*, my Bella," my dad said.

"We'll head there after this," I said. "It's open so you'll see it in full swing."

"How is it doing?" my mother asked.

"Not bad."

"Don't be modest, *mi hermosa,*" Giovanni said from beside me. "People love that place."

I smiled, a small amount of heat spreading across my cheeks. "Maybe they do."

Giovanni turned back to my parents. "They do."

I allowed him to be my personal hype-man since I wasn't able to do it myself. I felt silly doing that. I'd rather let my success speak for itself than have to tell people about it. There's nothing worse than needing to try to convince people that you were good at what you did. The proof was in the pudding.

"Did you see the latest transfer news?" Giovanni asked my dad. "I never thought I would see the day when Messi left Barcelona."

"Me neither. I was almost certain he was going to stay there until he retired," my father said.

I looked over at my mother. "I don't think you and I can contribute to this."

She smiled and shook her head. "Definitely not. Although your father has been going on about the transfer news for days now so I'm sure I probably know more than I realize."

I couldn't help but laugh. Giovanni and my father were engrossed in their conversation about which players had left their clubs and the shocking changes. I allowed them to have their fun.

My mother pointed past me. "Do you think that place sells souvenirs?"

I turned to where she pointed. A tiny tourist shop stood across the street. Turning back to her I said, "Definitely. You looking for something specific?"

"Just a keyring. Do you mind walking with me?"

I swallowed, my stomach already feeling the nerves but I pushed that away. "Of course."

"I don't mean to interrupt," I said to Giovanni and my dad as I did just that. "But we're just going across the road quickly."

They acknowledged me before jumping right back into their conversation. I slipped off my chair, my mother following my lead.

We walked side by side as we strolled across the cobblestone road. There was an awkward silence between us before she finally spoke.

"I'm sorry for what happened to you, Isabella."

Out of all the things I expected her to say, it definitely wasn't that. I didn't think she would bring this conversation up at all.

"It's okay, mom."

"I know exactly what you're going through."

I stopped and turned to her. "You do?"

She nodded, a brief flash of sadness appearing in her eyes. "After Camila, your father and I tried for years to have another baby. You asked me once why there were so many years between you and Camila, and the truth is that it was out of our control."

We continued to walk up the street, our steps becoming smaller as we were in no rush now to get to the little shop. I didn't expect my mother to show such vulnerability but I resonated with what she was saying down to my very core. It was the first time we had ever been able to relate to each other.

"We tried for three years before I finally fell pregnant again," she explained. "We were so happy. It's draining to try for a baby and to have to remain hopeful but it finally paid off until one night I woke up with a terrible pain in my stomach."

I swallowed, forcing myself to keep my emotions in tact. I could already feel the tears starting to build which caused the ache in my throat as I held them back.

"It was the worst night of my life." Her voice was hollow now. "So I completely understand how you must be feeling. I wasn't the same for a long time. It took me years before I was ready to put my hope in having another baby which is why we were so happy when you came around."

I gave her a small smile as we started to approach the entrance of the tourist shop. We were in no rush to get inside so I stopped by a sign on the curb, leaning against it as I looked over at her. She was staring out in the distance. I could still see the pain in her eyes as she recalled what she went through. I had never seen her like this before.

"I just want you to know that you're not alone." She looked over at me, reaching for my hand. "It may not seem like it now but you won't always feel like this."

My lip quivered and I looked down, not wanting to cry in public. "I feel so lost right now," I admitted. "I just never expected this to happen and I'm not sure how I'm supposed to deal with it."

"You just have to take it one day at a time," she said softly. "And if I can give you some advice, Isabella, don't push Giovanni away."

I looked up to reach her eyes. They were kind and comforting and this was the first time I had ever seen my mother like this.

"I did that to your father. I thought I could deal with it on my own and I pushed him away. I don't want you to make the same mistakes I made."

I didn't know what to say. I didn't want to push Giovanni away but I knew I had been doing that. We had good and bad days and I knew I was the catalyst for deciding what it was going to be.

"He's a good man and I can see how much he loves you." she said.

"He is a good man. He's the best man I've ever known, which is why I feel so inadequate now."

"Inadequate?" she repeated.

I nodded. "My doctor said that it's unlikely I will ever be able to fall pregnant. That thought alone has been tearing me apart inside. I don't want that to be true."

I leaned my head back, trying to keep the tears from falling but I was unsuccessful. A few managed to escape and I closed my eyes, trying to focus on my breathing.

"Bella," my mother murmured. She never called me that which only made me want to cry more. "The world is full of surprises sometimes. You never know what could happen but what you shouldn't do is allow this to come between you two. You have something good here. Something not a lot of people are lucky enough to find."

"I know."

She squeezed my hand. "One day at a time. That's all you have to do and eventually, you'll see it won't hurt so bad anymore."

It was a bittersweet moment. I had always wanted this kind of moment with my mother. The heart to heart I had never experienced growing up. For the first time in my life, I felt loved by my mother and it took me having to go through this to experience this with her.

I reached out and pulled her in for a hug. I needed this. We needed this. Her arms tightened around me and I felt like a little girl again. Sometimes all you need is your mother and now I knew what it feels like to have that.

She pulled away and cupped my face with her hands. "You are stronger than you think."

"Thank you, Mom."

Dropping her hands, she smiled at me. "Now, let me quickly get that key ring and then we can make it back to the football pundits at our table."

I chuckled and followed her inside.

CHAPTER 30:

Isabella

"This place is beautiful," I gasped, taking in my surroundings as we walked along the pathway.

Sevilla was slowly becoming my new favourite place. It was breathtakingly beautiful. Giovanni had become my self-appointed tour guide and had spent most of the day showing me all the city had to offer.

"It's one of my favourite places," Giovanni said, slipping his hand in mine.

Giovanni was right about getting away for the weekend. After my parent's left last week, I was working hard to try and make things feel normal again. We fell back into our routine and I started to feel calmer again. The sadness still hovered over me - just waiting for its chance to strike but I was using all my strength to push it away. Things were better now and I didn't want to do anything to ruin that. He suggested we head to Sevilla for the weekend and I was more than happy to take him up on that offer. I was happy, walking hand-in-hand with the love of my life. I could see he was still hesitant in many ways. He would take a moment longer before bringing something up or quickly change the subject when it was headed in a direction that I didn't want to go in. I know he wanted me to open up and talk to him about what happened but I just couldn't bring myself to do that. I couldn't bring myself to face the reality of our situation. As naive as that may be, ignorance is bliss.

"There's this great rooftop bar that we should go to," he started to explain. "I was thinking we could get dressed up and head over there tonight. We'll take a taxi so we can both drink. I think we could use a night out, what do you say?"

"That sounds great," I said, a flicker of excitement in my voice.

"It's a date then."

We stopped at a bench across from the *Cathedral de Sevilla* and took a seat. It was an absolute masterpiece to look at. This gothic cathedral was unmatched in its size and you can't help but stare at it. There was so much to see. Giovanni shifted closer to me, our legs brushing up against each other as he placed his arm behind me, leaning against the back of the bench. I took a deep breath in, soaking in the fresh breeze as the sun continued to beat down on us. It wasn't uncomfortable though - it was just the right amount of warmth that we needed.

"Thank you for bringing me here," I turned to face him.

He leaned down and rested his lips against my temple. "You're welcome. You know I'd do anything for you."

I smiled and leaned my head to rest on his shoulder. We were silent for a few moments, just soaking in our surroundings.

"I hope that coming here has helped in some way," he said softly.

I kept my eyes forward. Even just a subtle hint at what happened was already enough to push the hovering sadness and fear to the front of my mind. I didn't want to elaborate further - I just didn't want to ruin this moment.

"It did," I answered quickly and shifted the topic. "Are we going to stop by the new *Mala Mía*?"

I half-expected him to shift the conversation back but instead, he went with my subject change

"There's not much to see yet," he admitted. "But yes, I want to show you the new space. It's smaller than the one in Barcelona but the spot is quite central and easily accessible so we're happy with the location of it."

He continued to explain more and I just watched him speak. The sun hit perfectly against his side profile, washing over his tan skin. The sunshine lightened his features - his dark beard was a rich chestnut colour in the sun as was his hair. His eyes remained the deep dark brown they always were. They were my weakness - there was something about those eyes that I couldn't help but become hypnotised by.

We sat on that bench for hours, chatting about whatever came to mind. There was no pressure, no awkward silences - nothing. I could have sat on that bench with him forever. Our debate about what we should have for lunch was interrupted by a phone call coming through from Pedro. Giovanni excused himself and stood up, pacing up and down while he answered the call. He was incapable of sitting still when he was on the phone.

I closed my eyes and leaned my head back, soaking in the sun beating against my face. My calm thoughts were interrupted by the sudden crying of a baby. I opened my eyes and turned to the mother that had taken a seat at the end of the bench, trying to console the baby in her arms. I couldn't drag my eyes away from them. I watched as she murmured small affirmations and slowly lifted the baby against her chest, swaying side to side. The baby's cries subsided as she continued to rub its back. The longing that presented itself in my chest was unexpected and I had never felt that before. I had seen babies in the past but now it was different. I had seen happy parents with their children but I had never longed for that. I had thought about my future and how I was looking forward to that when the time was right but now that it seemed so out of reach, that was all I could think about.

You always want what you can't have.

"Isabella?" Giovanni's voice broke me out of my trance and I turned to look up at him, noticing for the first time the tears that had built up in my eyes.

"Baby," he breathed and sat down next to me. "Talk to me, please."

I stared down at my hands in my lap, unable to form the words on my tongue. I tried. I really tried to explain to him the sadness that lived inside of me. I tried to form the words to explain how consumed with guilt I was and how I couldn't see light at the end of this tunnel but nothing happened. I just couldn't do it.

"I wish you would let me in," he admitted softly, reaching for my hand. "I wish you would realize that you're not alone in this."

"I know," I said, my voice almost a whisper. "I just don't know what to say."

"Anything. Everything. What you went through wasn't easy." he rubbed his thumb over my hand, "And I just wish I could make everything better. I wish I could help."

"You are helping. Everything you've done has been helping me, Giovanni. I don't want to think about what happened. I just want to forget. I wish I could forget."

He lifted my hand to his lips. "I know, baby but I just want you to know that nothing that happened has changed anything for me. I love you, Isabella. I want to marry you. I want a life with you. Nothing will ever change that fact."

"Even if it means not having children?"

I was terrified of the answer. It was all good and well that he loved me but could I give him what he truly wanted out of life now?

He turned his body towards me, leaning his elbow against the back of the bench to lean his head against it.

"We don't know that it will never happen," he said softly.

"You didn't answer my question."

He lifted his eyes to meet mine. "I want you, Isabella. For the rest of my life, I want to wake up next to you. I want to share my life with you and if that means that it's just you and I, then I'll take it."

I believed that he meant that but I could hear a brief flash of apprehension in his voice. It was ever-so-slight but it was there. He wanted me and I knew he loved me but I couldn't help the nagging feeling that that might not be enough for him.

"Come with me," he stood up and extended his hand. "We should get going."

I slipped my hand in his and followed him.

CHAPTER 31:

Giovanni

S he was pulling away from me again. I watched how her energy shifted as she watched the mother with her baby. These last couple of days, things felt fairly normal. She was laughing again, flirting again - even making love to me again but now? Now, that vacant look in her eyes had reappeared and I wanted nothing more than to pull her out of that dark place she had just gone into.

Just when I think we're making progress, she shuts me out and I feel helpless again but I was adamant to keep trying. She needed to know everything was going to be fine with us but for now, she needed a distraction. We had made it to the city center where the vacant space stood, waiting to have our vision brought to life.

Isabella looked around, a look of confusion on her face.

"And now?" I asked.

"Is this where it is?"

I nodded and pointed in the direction we were headed. "There."

"But the street looks so..." she paused for a moment. "Old."

I chuckled. "Welcome to Spain, baby, the buildings are all old here."

"I know that but you wouldn't expect a club to be in this building."

"Wait till you see inside, there's a lot of potential," I explained. "And you can't deny that you can already feel the atmosphere of the area."

She glanced around and smiled. "You're right. Seems like everyone here is looking for a good time."

"Which is exactly what we need."

We had crossed the city center, passing the crowds of people that had formed. These buildings were situated around us in a square formation, trapping the energy of the area in it. There were restaurants and bars scattered at the bottom of the buildings. The only thing missing from this area was a nightclub. As you glanced up, there were small balconies that were lined two floors up. I noticed a couple of people standing, leaning against the metal railings. One was smoking. One was glancing down at the people on the streets. I found myself wondering how anyone could live in this area. The entire vibe of it was the reason we had decided on this building. I highly doubted anyone would be able to get a good night's sleep living here.

I had gotten the keys from Pedro when we first arrived so I pulled them out of my back pocket. We stopped in front of the large wooden double door on the corner and I let go of her hand to unlock it. I opened the door towards us and stepped back, letting her go in first. It was dark as we stepped inside. I walked over to the nearest wall, feeling against it until I found the light switch. I flipped it on, light spilling over the room.

"Oh wow," Isabella gasped.

I turned and she had walked ahead, looking over the balcony.

"I would never have known that this went further down," she said.

"That's what we loved about it."

I was surprised when Pedro had decided to bring me to this location. I had the same reaction Isabella did. I just couldn't see what was behind those double doors. It was empty so our footsteps echoed as we followed the stairs down to what would be the dance floor. It was a large open space for now with high ceilings.

I pointed to the opposite side. "So, we're thinking of putting a bar there."

Isabella followed my gaze as we strolled across the area. It was much larger than you would expect but it was perfect for a nightclub. You wanted to feel like you were in a world like no other and that was exactly what we wanted to bring to life.

"We're going to replicate the chandelier we have at the Barcelona branch. It would be perfect hanging from here." I pointed up as we made it to the middle.

"I love that," she said. "That's my favorite thing about *Mala Mía*. You wouldn't expect something so fancy in a club."

"Exactly and that's because it's a sophisticated club."

"That it is," She smiled.

I continued to show her around, explaining what Pedro and I had discussed. A lot of it would follow the same blueprint of the Barcelona version but with the layout being different, it wouldn't be an exact replica.

"And are you on schedule with the progress?" she asked as we made it back to the staircase.

I nodded. "If everything goes as planned, we'll launch this just before New Year's Eve."

"So we'll be spending New Year's Eve here?" she smiled.

"We can spend it wherever you want."

She reached out and slipped her hand in mine. "I wouldn't mind here. I thought Valencia was my favourite place but Sevilla is stealing my heart."

We made it upstairs and slipped outside the door. I pulled it closed behind us and locked up, slipping the keys back into my pocket. I reached for her hand and we started to walk across the square again, the sun starting to set behind the building.

"Would you want to live here?"

She turned to me. "In Sevilla?"

I nodded.

She thought for a moment. "Would you want to leave Barcelona?"

This time it was my turn to think. I loved Barcelona. My family was there, my work was there - I didn't have any complaints about it but something about it felt almost tainted now. With everything that had happened, I couldn't shake the feeling that maybe Isabella and I needed a clean slate. We needed a new place to start our life together.

"I wouldn't mind. If that was something you want."

"I couldn't leave *Aroma*."

"You can open up another one," I suggested.

She glanced up at me, a small smile on her lips. "I can't just open up another one. The one I have is only just finding its feet."

"Firstly, that's a lie. You know people love that place. Secondly, we can open up a new one where we go. We just have to find the right location."

She shook her head and smiled. "Maybe."

"I'd happily buy you a building if that's what you wanted."

This time she laughed and I was so happy to hear it. I loved that sound.

"You wouldn't." She nudged me playfully.

"I would." I leaned down and kissed her hair. "If you told me you wanted to live here, I'd do whatever you needed me to do to make that happen."

"Giovanni." She breathed.

"I'm serious. I just want to make you happy, *mi hermosa,* whatever that takes."

"I just need you."

I lifted her hand to my lips. "And you have me, baby. I'm not going anywhere."

CHAPTER 32:

Giovanni

We continued the rest of the weekend as best as we could but I couldn't ignore the looming elephant in the room. Every time I tried to speak to her about it, she deflected or changed the subject so eventually, I stopped trying. When I asked if she had thought about a new date for our wedding, she just shrugged and said she had to think about it. I didn't push her. I would never but I kept hoping for something from her. Some kind of indication that she still thought about our future the way that I did. When I mentioned moving again as a real possibility she could think about, she just nodded along. There was no indication that she was thinking the same. We didn't need to move. We could stay put. All I was looking for was some kind of sign that there would be light at the end of this tunnel.

This continued for days, even after we got back from Sevilla. The time away was good but once we got back into our usual routine, it was as if nothing had changed. I tried my hardest to be there for her. Constantly reassuring her how much I love her and couldn't wait to marry her. I didn't care what our future brought - as long as it was one with her.

She had decided to take the day off and I was at *Velázquez Constructa* today. Alvaro allocated me an office in the corner next to the boardroom for when I was here. We were starting the new upgrades to the *Maremagnum Mall* and this would be my first role as a project manager under the company. We had been stuck in meetings all day with the team to finalize the timelines. One of the younger interns, Xavi, had been assigned to shadow me for the project. I didn't mind. He was quiet at first but once he started to relax into the project, I could see his potential. He had a great eye for these things and his ideas were welcomed.

"If we start from the bottom and work our way up, that would minimize the disruption to the retail outlets during the hours," he explained as he pointed to the blueprints in front of us. "This area is a no go. They want to take this entire parking area out and replace it with an easier way to access the metro on the other side."

"Okay, add that to the timeline," I instructed. "We'll probably need a new team for that."

"I was thinking the same."

"And I want to see the suggested designs for that before we send it to Alvaro."

Xavi nodded and leaned forward to write that down. I closed up the file and handed it to him. I glanced at the clock on the wall in front of me. I was set to fetch Isabella in the next hour but I had already finished earlier than I expected. We had a doctor's appointment for her checkup. It had been over a month since she was admitted to hospital and her doctor was adamant to keep an eye on her. Isabella had said she would go alone but I refused to allow that to happen. I was going to hold her hand through all of this.

Xavi excused himself as my phone started to ring. I glanced down and saw Reyna's name flashing on the screen.

"*Hola, Reyna,*" I greeted and put the phone on loudspeaker.

"Giovanni, *¿cómo estás?*"

"Good, are you looking for Isabella?"

"No, I actually just got off a call with her. Just wanted to check in on how she's doing and find out if you guys are coming to Sergio's birthday this weekend but she said that she'd let me know."

"I'll chat to her and see if she's up for it. She's probably not in the right space cause we're meant to head to an appointment with her OB-GYN."

A month ago I didn't even think that word was in my vocabulary.

"She didn't even mention that to me," There was a flicker of sadness in Reyna's voice.

"She doesn't really want to mention things to anyone." I tried to comfort her.

"But I'm her best friend, she should be letting me in."

"Rey, I'm her fiancé and she hasn't been letting me in either so I wouldn't take it personally."

She sighed. "You're right. I'm sorry. I just feel so helpless."

"Join the club."

"I also just wanted to phone to give you a heads up that Camila has been trying to get a hold of Isabella. She phoned me to see if I'd chatted to her but she might try to call you next."

"I'm surprised she didn't call me first considering I live with Isabella."

Reyna chuckled. "Don't take it personally. Camila and I have actually been keeping in touch."

"Are you swapping besties now?"

"Hell no," Reyna laughed. "But we're all worried about Isabella so..."

"I understand," I sighed and picked up my phone. "I'll give Camila a call and chat to Isabella. I'll update you later on what the doctor says."

"Thanks, Gio. I just want to make sure she's okay."

"You and me both."

We said our goodbyes and I ended the call. I grabbed my jacket hanging over the chair and reached for my car keys in the pocket. I placed my jacket over my arm, car keys and phone in hand and I headed out of my office.

I got to the basement parking and clicked the button to unlock my car. As I reached the door, I heard someone call my name. I turned to see Maya's bouncing curls walking over to me.

Not again.

"You're here!" she exclaimed and leaned forward to greet me.

"What are you doing here?" I asked, not bothering to hide my confusion.

"Well, I just finished with a job interview actually. Your dad's company was hiring but when I got here I was told that he's not the boss anymore and that you and your brother own it. I had no idea."

I stopped, confused. *A job interview? Here?*

"Another interview?" I asked.

"Yeah, that other one didn't go very well," she admitted. "I thought you just owned that fancy club. I didn't know you worked here as well."

"I do own the club, but I work on some projects here," I answered quickly. "Wait, so you're going to work here?"

She shrugged and smiled. "I hope so. The interview seemed to go well but Alvaro said he wo-,"

I interrupted her. "You did your interview with Alvaro?"

She nodded. "And don't worry, it's not like he knew who I was. You and I were never very…" She paused for a moment. "Uh visible."

"Maya, what are you really doing?" I sighed. "I haven't seen you in years and now all of a sudden you're trying to work for my family's company?"

"That wasn't intentional, Gio. I got retrenched from my previous job and I've been struggling to find something since. I'm kind of taking anything I can get right now."

She had a sadness in her eyes. I could admit that I felt a bit bad but I couldn't have her working here. *Right?* That would be weird. I doubt Isabella would be happy with that.

Fuck, I still needed to tell her that I bumped into Maya at all.

"I'm not trying to disrupt your life here. I just really need this job." A flicker of desperation appeared in her voice. "You wouldn't have a problem with me working here, would you?"

I thought for a moment but before I could answer, she continued.

"Our relationship was years ago," she said in a hushed voice. "And I'm not here to come and ruin yours. I know you're getting married."

I was reluctant. It wouldn't bother me that Maya worked here - it's not like I had any unresolved feelings or anything but I highly doubted Isabella would be thrilled with the idea. How would I tell her? How could I tell her now that she's dealing with all these other things? I didn't want to add to her plate in any way. Would this even be a problem for her? I had no idea.

Maya reached out and rested her hand on my arm. "Seriously, Gio, it's been how long? There isn't anything still between us."

She paused for a moment and flicked her eyes up to meet mine. "Is there?"

I pulled away from her touch. "Not at all."

Her face fell for a moment but it was long enough that there was no way I could have missed that. She regained her composure but I didn't trust her. There was something about her intentions that I couldn't help but doubt. That didn't matter though. Maya was not my problem - whether she worked here or not.

"Then everything will be fine." She smiled. "And I'd love to meet your fiancé."

Like hell that would happen.

"Speaking of, I need to head out." I yanked my door open. "*Adiós,* Maya."

"See you soon."

CHAPTER 33:

Isabella

Seated in Doctor Gavina's office, I stared down at my hands in my lap. My leg was shaking the way it always did when I was starting to feel anxious. I didn't know what to expect. This was just a catch-up for her to see how I was doing and make some treatment suggestions based on my progress. In an ideal world, I would be expecting that all those cysts had magically disappeared and I would be all good to go.

Realistically, I knew that wasn't going to happen.

Giovanni reached for my hand and slipped his hand in mine. "You okay?"

I nodded.

He squeezed my hands. "Everything is going to be fine."

He said that a lot. I knew he was just trying to be there for me but I was less inclined to have a positive outlook on the situation. That probably wasn't helping but I was at war with my own emotions here. I always felt everything so intensely - I hated it in situations like this. With love, I became overwhelmed by it. I felt it right down to my core. The problem was that happened with every emotion and right now I was feeling so many at once. Hence, the overwhelming feeling.

Doctor Gavina strolled in and took a seat across from us by her desk. She leaned forward, interlinking her fingers and smiled at me. "You're looking much better, Miss Avery."

"I do feel better. No pain or bleeding or anything like that."

"That's good." She turned to the file on her desk and opened it. "Okay, let's get right into it. So the cysts are still there but the good news is that the pill I put you on has helped stop the growth of any new ones. A few of them appear to be inflamed but if you're not in pain or anything then that's a good sign. They tend to flair up in moments but there is nothing to be concerned about at this point. If they rupture or appear to be cancerous, then we definitely have something to worry about."

"But they're not cancerous right?" Giovanni asked, a flicker of worry in his voice.

Doctor Gavina shook her head. "Not cancerous."

A wave of relief washed over me. I hadn't given much thought to that, but I was thankful I didn't need to entertain it.

"How will I know if another one ruptures?" I asked.

"Unfortunately that's all symptom based so you'll just have to monitor yourself. There is no way of knowing why they would rupture either or if they'll rupture at all. Sometimes it happens and there are no symptoms at all and other times there are more severe cases. All you have to do is continue with what I have prescribed you - the new pill and some of the pain medication if needed. That's just in case but life can pretty much go back to normal except that you'll need to schedule these check-ups more regularly."

I nodded. Things can go back to normal. That was a good sign but there was still the looming question at hand - will I be able to have children?

"And fertility-wise...?" I let my question trail off - she knew what I wanted to know about.

She slowly closed my file and sighed, turning her attention back to me. "Are you trying for children now?"

I looked over to Giovanni for an answer. He turned back to her. "Not actively but it is something that we would want in the future."

"With your current condition, there's no way of knowing for sure," she explained. "Unfortunately, as it stands, it looks less than likely but you never know. We can discuss a possible surgery to have the cysts removed but that's really only recommended in severe cases and I don't categorize your condition like that."

"But it would help if I was trying for children?"

"It's one of the many options that can be explored. A lot of my patients like this don't stop trying and I would recommend you continue as you have been, however, I do need to inform you that a journey like this - one with fertility complications - can be incredibly trying on a couple. I believe in preparing you for the worst-case scenario as I would hate to get your hopes up for something that might not happen."

My stomach dropped in disappointment. I knew it was silly to expect anything other than what she was telling me but a tiny part of me had hope. I wasn't even trying to fall pregnant. That wasn't something we had in our plan for right now but it's the fact that it might not be a possibility at all that devastated me.

"You can also consider adopting or looking at a surrogate"" she continued. "But I really wouldn't worry about that until you're at the point where you're actively trying for a baby."

Giovanni squeezed my hand before turning back to Doctor Gavina. "Thank you, doctor. We'll keep all that in mind."

She smiled and nodded before reaching behind her for a pile of pamphlets she had. She turned back and handed them over to me.

"Here are a few support groups that you can think of joining. They're full of other women dealing with similar situations. You might find it helpful."

I took the pamphlets. "Thank you."

"I know it's difficult, but you shouldn't stop trying. You don't know what life has in store for you," she comforted.

I smiled and nodded before we said our goodbyes and slipped out of her office. Giovanni kept his hand in mine as we strolled through the hallway towards the exit. He opened the door and waited for me to go first. We stepped onto the street and headed down the road to where we had parked.

"How do you feel?" he asked.

"I don't know."

"I think it's great that we don't have anything to worry about. You're all good now."

"Except for the cysts," I pointed out.

"Yes, but thankfully, they're nothing to be concerned about. They're just sort of…" he paused trying to find the right word. "There."

"I know you're right," I sighed. "I just can't get it out of my head that we may not be able to have children."

He stopped and turned to me, cupping my face with his hands. "I understand but like she said, we just need to get back to normal and keep trying. We're not trying to have a baby now, are we?"

I shook my head.

"So, we can continue to live our lives together and cross that bridge when we get there."

I wasn't sold but I didn't share that with him. It just seemed like we were putting off the inevitable but I appreciated how positive he had been for me during this time. I honestly don't know how I would have made it without him.

"That means we can keep having unprotected sex," he attempted to joke.

"Too soon, babe." A small laugh escaped my lips. "But you know that's my favourite anyway."

He smiled before leaning down, his lips finding mine. It was a soft kiss but there was so much behind it. I sunk into the kiss, allowing my heart to become consumed by him. Was it wrong of me to be afraid that I would lose him? I had never loved anyone like I love him. My heart was his and all I wanted was the future that he and I had spoken about.

Was that too much to ask for?

He pulled away and we continued towards the car. "Now, I know Reyna called you about Sergio's birthday this weekend. I know you haven't been up to going out and I will totally support you if you don't want to g-"

I cut him off. "We need to go. Reyna caught me right before this appointment so I was in a different mind about things earlier."

"I thought so." He unlocked his car. "I'll tell Sergio we'll be there."

CHAPTER 34:

Isabella

S ergio's birthday was just what Giovanni and I needed. We needed a day to just be distracted from everything we had been dealing with and to get back to what felt normal. Spending the day with our friends was exactly that. Sergio's family was huge and when you added Katrina's to the mix, it was easy to lose track of the number of people at their house. Married life suited them. Katrina walked with happy confidence that I loved to see on her. Shortly after their wedding, they started house hunting and ended up finding one in a beautiful neighborhood outside of the city. I stood on their patio overlooking their garden where most of their families were scattered throughout. Music was playing in the background and the sound of indistinct chatter surrounded me. I watched as Giovanni stood across the lawn, standing in a group with Sergio, Diego and a few other friends. He was deep in conversation and would throw his head back in laughter every now and then. I loved to see it. It was so nice to see him this relaxed. It had been a while and I felt bad for my part in it. I hadn't made this time easier for him but he had been so patient with me. I often found myself thinking I didn't deserve his kindness.

Reyna and Katrina were walking towards the patio, empty food trays in their hands.

"Can I help?" I asked.

Katrina smiled and shook her head. "We were just clearing the last of these on the tables."

"Walk with us," Reyna suggested.

I followed closely behind them as we made our way into their kitchen. It was a beautiful open-plan arrangement. A large granite counter stood in the middle as the centerpiece for the room. There was still food and drinks scattered on top of it. Katrina walked to the nearest door in the corner that led to their cleaning area. She dropped the empty trays in the trash before making her way back to where we stood by the counter. I leaned against it and Reyna pulled herself onto it, swinging her legs on the side.

"I think Dad found his new bestie," Reyna said to Katrina as she continued to clear things off the counter. "He and Sergio's dad have been attached at the hip today."

Katrina chuckled. "I was saying the exact same thing to Sergio. They bonded at the wedding and now even keep in touch so I think half of the reason why Dad was happy to come down for this was so he could see his friend again."

I smiled. It was nice to see how easily those two families had become one. There was no doubt about Katrina and Sergio's union - everything worked with the two of them.

Reyna snorted. "Keep giving them whiskey and they'll be stuck in conversation for hours."

"When do you go back to work?" I asked Katrina.

She was a third-grade teacher at one of the private schools in the area which means she had the Summer off. When they were looking for a place to live, it made sense for Katrina to find something close and there was a fancy private school a couple blocks away from here that she ended up finding a job at.

"Monday," she said. "We have to go back before the kids to, you know, get everything ready for them and all that."

We continued our conversation as Reyna and I joined in to help Katrina clear up the kitchen. It was so nice to catch up with them. I had been so disconnected from everyone that I hadn't realized how much I needed this normality in my life. As Katrina was wiping down the counter in the last step of our clean-up, Reyna strolled over to the drinks table.

"Izzy? A drink?"

"Yes, please. Wine if there's still some left."

She nodded and turned back to attend to our drinks. I turned to Katrina. You want something to drink, Kat?"

"No, thanks," she said and quickly disappeared to the back.

Reyna handed me my wine glass as their mother, Genevive, wandered into the kitchen. A lot of Katrina and Reyna's facial features they had gotten from their mother. They all had the same striking blue eyes and although Genevive held her age in her face with the wrinkles that had started to form around her eyes, she still had a youthful beauty to her.

"Ah Isabella!" She opened her arms and pulled me in for a hug. "I've hardly gotten to chat with you. It's so nice to see you again."

"It's nice to see you too, Mrs. Cazarez." I hugged her back. "Have you been enjoying your time in Barcelona?"

"Oh yes!" she exclaimed, "You know how much I miss my girls so I was more than happy to come and visit them."

The Cazarez family was still as close-knit as ever. I brought my glass to my lips as Reyna disappeared to the back where Katrina was.

"I was chatting to Giovanni outside," Genevive continued. "What a nice boy you have there."

I couldn't help but laugh. "He's the best."

"I was sorry to hear that you had to postpone your wedding." She reached out and squeezed my arm.

I knew that Reyna hadn't told people what the real reason was as per my request. I still felt quite guilty about how everything went down and I was still too ashamed to share what really happened. *Not now, Isabella.* I refused to allow those thoughts to consume me so instead I pushed them as far back as I could manage and turned my attention to Genevive.

"Your wedding is still going to be so beautiful. I'm looking forward to it," she continued. "Have you picked a new date?"

I shook my head. "We're still figuring that out."

"Well, you're definitely going to have to alter Katrina's bridesmaid dress. I'm sure by the time you get married, her tummy is going to be well on display."

My stomach dropped. "What?"

"With her pregnancy!" she exclaimed. "I cannot tell you how excited I am to be a grandmother an…"

The rest of her sentence trailed off as I processed what she was telling me. Katrina was pregnant and I didn't know? I know she and I were never as close as Reyna and I are but we were still close. We had lived together and shared everything. Genevive obviously thought I would have known too so I didn't give her any indication of anything different.

"It's all so exciting!" Genevive exclaimed.

"It really is." I forced a smile. "Could you excuse me for a moment? I need to quickly get something from Reyna."

"Of course! I'll see you outside."

Genevive turned to head towards the garden and I placed my glass down before making my way to the back room where Reyna and Katrina were. Katrina was rinsing off the dishes and Reyna was placing them in the dishwasher. I stepped inside and closed the door behind me, just to make sure no one could overhear us since this was a secret. Katrina turned towards me and Reyna lifted her head as she placed another dish down.

"You okay?" Reyna asked.

I shook my head. "Kat, I didn't know you were pregnant."

My voice was almost a whisper and I couldn't help the disappointed feeling I had over not knowing. I wished she would have felt comfortable enough to have shared that kind of news with me.

Katrina's jaw dropped and her eyes widened. "Who told you?"

"Your mother. She thought I knew."

Katrina turned her attention to Reyna. "You were supposed to tell her it was a secret."

"I did," Reyna retorted.

"She didn't spill that intentionally," I clarified. "She honestly just thought I knew and I guess a part of me thought that with something like this, I would have known."

Katrina sighed and reached for a cloth, wiping her hands down.

"I wanted to tell you, Izzy. Of course, I wanted to tell you but with everything that you went through, I didn't think that would be the kind of news you wanted to hear right now."

My face fell and there was a pit in my stomach. I'm the reason she didn't tell me. She had this exciting, life-changing thing happening to her and I had allowed my own sadness to get in the way of that for her.

Reyna reached for my hand. "We know how hard things have been for you. We didn't know how you would take the news and we didn't want to make things worse."

Tears swelled in my eyes and a lump started to form in my throat as I tried to hold them back. I felt awful. I felt like a terrible friend. This was a light-bulb moment for me. I had allowed my own sadness to get in the way of something so exciting for someone so close to me. That wasn't fair.

I shook my head. "That could never have made things worse. I'm so sorry. I never wanted you to feel that way. This is amazing news, Kat! You have to know that I couldn't be happier for you."

A few tears escaped my eyes and continued. "I'm sorry. I didn't mean to be so selfish lately. I don't want you guys to not tell me something like this. Of course, I'm happy for you!"

I saw the tears forming in Katrina's eyes. "You mean it?"

"Of course, Kat." I reached out and wrapped my arms around her. "I'm sorry you felt like you couldn't tell me this. This is a beautiful thing that's happened for you and Sergio."

I pulled away and cupped her face with my hands. "I mean it. You guys deserve this."

She smiled, a tear falling from her eye as she pulled me in for a hug again.

"I'm so sorry," I repeated.

"You don't need to apologize, Izzy," Katrina reassured me. "What happened to you wasn't easy and we understand."

"I know but I don't want to not be part of what happens in your life because of it." I pulled away and reached for Reyna's hand. "You too, Rey. You two have been so amazing to me during this time. I don't want to lose you guys."

"Never going to happen," Reyna said confidently.

At that moment, I truly saw what my own sadness had done. It had isolated me even further and I didn't want that to happen any longer. I didn't want to wallow in what had happened. Everyone around me tried to continue to be positive for me. They tried to show me solutions and the light at the end of the tunnel but I didn't want to see it.

That is over now.

I didn't want to allow it to consume my life. There had to be a solution and I wasn't going to allow this to come between anything else in my life.

"How far along are you?" I asked Katrina.

"Just over six weeks. It's still early days but I just got so excited, I had to share the news," she said smiling. "We're not telling everyone just yet so it's only close family."

She reached for my hand and squeezed. "And you're part of our family, Izzy."

I couldn't stop the few tears that escaped. They were my family. They had been for years and I loved them like my own flesh and blood - if not more.

"You're going to be an aunt." I nudged Reyna playfully.

"I know! God, I can't wait to spoil that child."

We continued to chat further about the baby before Sergio's voice echoed through the kitchen as he looked for Katrina. He pushed the door open and Giovanni followed closely behind him.

"Is this a cult meeting?" Sergio eyed us.

We burst out laughing.

"We'll never tell," Reyna jokes.

I slipped past Sergio to Giovanni who opened his arms for me. I wrapped my arms around his waist and leaned my chin against his chest so I could look up at him. He leaned down and kissed my forehead. "You okay?"

"Never better." I smiled. "I was actually thinking that maybe we should decide on a new wedding date."

His eyes lit up. "You serious?"

I nodded.

"You know there's no rush. We can get marri-"

I jumped in to stop him. "I know but I want to marry you, Giovanni. It's all I've ever wanted. I've allowed what happened to get in the way of our future and I don't want to do that anymore. I love you and I want to be your wife."

I paused for a moment. "If you'll still have me."

"Oh, baby." He breathed and leaned down, pressing his lips against mine. "Of course. I'd marry you in a heartbeat."

I smiled and leaned up, my lips meeting his again. This kiss was full of love and hope for our future. A future I wanted more than anything.

He slipped his hand into my hair as he cupped my cheek. He pulled away, smiling. "Does this mean we have to do the bachelor and bachelorette party again?"

I giggled. "Absolutely not. I think the ones we had will suffice."

"You're probably right. Can't have you taking body shots off another stripper."

"I told you I never did that!" I exclaimed.

He threw his head back, laughing at my reaction. The happiness had returned to his deep brown eyes and I couldn't help but mirror it. Things felt better. A sense of hopefulness settled around me and I wanted to hang onto that for as long as I could.

CHAPTER 35:

Isabella

S ince most of the wedding planning was already done, all we had to do now was rearrange everything for our new date. We had to shuffle some suggested dates around according to the availability of the venue but we finally landed on one.

The fifth of March.

We were both happy with a spring wedding. Giovanni was so close to giving in to a winter wedding but this was our wedding - we both had to be happy and springtime was the perfect middle ground for us. I threw myself back into organizing everything for our new date and I couldn't contain the bubbling excitement inside of me. Finally, things were back on track and I was ready to marry the love of my life.

Reyna was at *Aroma* today so I could spend the day finalizing some of the finer details. Our caterers were all set and I was trying to finalize the booking of the rooms by the villa for our families again. The venue was well out of the city and we wanted to minimize the number of people needing to drive back. We wanted everyone to have a great time and not have to worry about that so having them all booked into the rooms on the property was important to us. Giovanni was spending the morning finishing off a meeting with his brother for the new project he was heading up. We had agreed to meet at home before heading out for a little lunch date. I felt at ease as we slipped back into our normal routine.

I had finished up some last-minute shopping for a few things for the apartment when I turned around the corner and saw a woman banging on the door of *Mala Mía*. Her dark curls bounced off her head as she continued at the door.

"*Hola?*" she shouted. "*¿Hay alguien ahí?*

There was a hint of frustration in her voice as she tried to pull at the handle. I didn't recognize her. She was quite a striking beauty. Tall and slender, a head full of dark curls that started at the roots. Striking blue eyes up against her darker skin. I would have remembered a face like that.

I started to approach her. "Hi. Sorry, are you looking for someone?"

She turned to me and huffed. "Yes! I thought this place would be open."

"It's a nightclub," I pointed out. "And it only opens from Thursday to Sunday."

"Great," she mumbled and ran her fingers through her hair. "I tried to find him at his other office but he wasn't there so I thought I'd try here."

Him?

"Who did you say you were looking for?" I asked.

"Giovanni Velázquez," she muttered. "I've been trying to find him all morning."

She knew Giovanni? Now, I am confused. I didn't recognize her but she certainly didn't seem like a stranger to him. A disgruntled employee maybe? I wasn't sure how to place her. All I knew was that she was pissed off.

"I'd like to give him a piece of my mind," she continued, her anger rising. "Don't you hate when you think you're on the same page with someone but you're clearly not?"

What the hell was going on?

"Uh...:" I didn't know what to say and she noticed.

She stopped and took a deep breath in. "I'm sorry. Here I am rambling to a stranger. You must think I'm crazy."

"Not crazy but you're clearly upset." Curiosity got the better of me and I was dying to know what went down between them.

"I am," she admitted. "I just really need to speak to him. I've seen him a few times now and I thought we were both on the same page about where we stood with each other but clearly not."

Okay, now I was starting to think she was a little crazy.

"Sorry, I didn't even ask what your name was," I said, interrupting her rambling.

She extended her hand. "Where are my manners? *Lo siento!* I'm Maya, nice to meet you."

Maya? Why did that name sound so famil-

No.

Could it be?

Maya who Giovanni had a relationship with?

Are you fucking kidding me?

I shook her hand as the anger started to bubble inside of me. They had seen each other recently and he didn't think that would be something I should know about? My stomach dropped.

Now I was pissed off.

I opened my mouth to say something but his voice boomed behind me. "Maya?"

I turned and his gaze landed on me, his eyes widening as he realized it was me.

"Giovanni, *¡gracias a Dios!* I've been looking for you everywhere," Maya huffed, "Did you seriously stop me from getting hired at your company? I thought we were on the same pag-"

He lifted his hand to cut her off and turned to me. "Isabella."

He stepped closer to me and I heard Maya gasp as she must have realized who I was.

"Maya's been trying to get a hold of you," I said, my voice emotionless. "Seems like you two have a lot to talk about."

I didn't wait for a response before turning towards the door that led to our basement parking. Giovanni ran after me, grabbing my arm to stop me in my tracks.

"Baby, I-"

"I'd rather not do this in front of your ex." I kept my voice calm and low. "Deal with her and I'll see you upstairs."

And without waiting to hear what else he had to say, I made my way towards the door.

CHAPTER 36:

Giovanni

Well, that was a fuck up.

I needed to head upstairs and make things right with Isabella but Maya wouldn't stop whining in my ear. What the fuck was she even doing here in the first place?

"I had no idea that was Isabella," Maya said, reaching for my arm. "Giovanni, serio-,"

I pulled away from her touch and lifted my hand to cut her off again. "What the hell are you doing here?"

"I've been trying to find you all morning. How could you stop me from getting the job at your company? I thought we were clear about where we stood."

"What are you going on about?" I didn't bother hiding the irritation in my voice.

"I didn't get the job and all I could think about was because you were worried about me working there."

"May-,"

This time she cut me off. "I know we have a history, Giovanni, but I needed this job. For you to get in the way of that tells me that there's still something between us."

What the fuck was she going on about?

"May-" I tried to speak but again, she cut me off. *Oh God, would she stop doing that and let me speak already?!*

"And if there is, I need you to tell me now because I know I made a mistake letting you go."

"You what?" I was taken aback.

"I should never have chosen Paulo over you. I should have left him when I said I would. You were who I was supposed to be with."

"Maya, what the hell are you doing?" I huffed. "First you come here, unannounced, accusing me of interfering with your job application - which, just to clarify, I had fuck all to do with - and now you're telling me all this shit like it's going to make a difference now?"

"How can it not?" her face dropped. "When we kept bumping into each other, I knew that could have only meant one thing. I was meant to run into you again."

"No, Maya, it doesn't mean anything. It means we happened to be on the same street at the same time by sheer coincidence. There's no deeper meaning here."

"I-"

"What did you think was going to happen?" I snapped. "Just because you were happy to step out on your significant other doesn't mean I would. Isabella is my fiancé and I only want her. I'm only ever going to want her."

She looked as if she had been slapped. *Was she delusional?* Did she really think this would work? I haven't thought about her in years. When I found out what real love was, I knew what she and I shared was mere infatuation, if that. It didn't surprise me that she would do something like this. Maya always had a certain selfishness to her. Pure narcissism. She never stopped to think about how it would affect anyone else and clearly that hadn't changed.

"That's why you really tried to get a job at my father's company, isn't it? You thought you could somehow weasel your way back into my life."

"I had to try," she admitted. "I've been living with this guilt over letting you go."

"I walked away from you, Maya. You and I were toxic. It was fucking messy. You strung me along for months, making me believe that you loved me and wanted to be with me but that just wasn't true. I could never have trusted you - if you could do that to Paulo, you could do that to me. I don't know how I didn't see it before but once I met Isabella I realized that nothing I felt for you was love."

"Gio-" she choked.

"I shouldn't have to even explain this to you," I muttered. "You don't get to just show up here and try to interfere in my life."

"I'm no-"

I cut her off. "All I care about now is going upstairs to my fiancé. I had nothing to do with why you didn't get the job but I'm glad 'cause I wouldn't want to work with you knowing your true intentions. Stay away from Isabella and me."

I turned and rushed to make my way upstairs. Isabella was pissed. She had every right to be but I needed to save the situation before it became something it wasn't.

"Isabella!" I shouted as the elevator doors opened up to our apartment. "Why did you just walk away like that?"

She was standing behind the kitchen counter, a glass of wine in front of her. She had a hard look on her face as she flicked her gaze up to meet mine.

"You know exactly why, Giovanni," she snapped. "When were you going to tell me you had seen Maya?"

I huffed and pulled at the tie I was wearing. I pulled it over my head and dropped it on the kitchen counter. This definitely wasn't how I thought my day was going to go.

"I was going to tell you."

"My question was *when* were you going to tell me? Or better yet, why haven't you told me already? When did you first bump into her?"

"A few weeks ago."

She scoffed. "A few weeks? And you didn't think that would be something I should know."

"Baby, I was goi- "

She cut me off. "You had plenty of opportunities to tell me, Giovanni. Clearly, you didn't want me to know."

"What the hell is that supposed to mean?"

I was hurt that she would even insinuate such a thing. Her mind went to the worst possible conclusion. She was maddening when she did that.

"Is there something I should know about the two of yo-"

This time I cut her off. "Don't do that, Isabella."

"Don't do what?"

I walked around to where she stood, closing in the proximity between us.

"Don't make this something it isn't. I should have told you about Maya, I know that but I just didn't know how."

"What do you mean?" She flung her arms, exasperation in her voice. "It's quite simple to be like, 'hey, I bumped into my ex'."

Sarcastic Isabella had come out to play. She was sharp-tongued and infuriating at times.

I sighed and leaned against the counter. "Isabella, please just stop for a moment."

She opened her mouth to say something but quickly closed it. I knew I should have told her but with everything going on, that was the least of my worries.

"I tried to tell you but something always came up and if I'm being honest, I just didn't know how to talk to you, lately," I admitted. "Sometimes I still don't. Ever since we went through…" I paused for a brief second. "What happened - Fuck, we can't even say the words," I sighed. "We tiptoed around it all and I didn't know how to handle it. You've been so sad. It broke my heart to see you like that and I didn't want to upset you even more."

Her face fell and I saw the sadness return to her eyes. That was the last thing I wanted but I had to be honest with her. I had to tell her the truth about why I didn't say anything and prove to her that it was the furthest thing from what she had assumed it was.

I reached for her hand. "I'm sorry, baby. I should have told you - I know that but I don't want you to think it's because I have something to hide." I pulled her closer to me and cupped her face with my hands. "You're the only one for me, *mi hermosa*, I would never do anything like that to you - you know that."

Tears escaped from her eyes.

"I just feel helpless." I couldn't hide the emotion in my voice as I finally admitted to her what had been racking my brain. "I wanted to be there for you but you kept shutting me out. I tried my best to make you happy again. I didn't want to do anything to upset you."

She leaned her head against my chest and cried. I hated hearing her cry. It always brought on a rush of emotion over me. I wrapped my arms around her and leaned my hand against the back of her head, pulling her closer to me. I just wanted her to be happy again. She was getting there. These last few days had felt normal again and the last thing I wanted to do was ruin that.

"I've just felt so ashamed," she cried.

"Ashamed?" I reached for her face and tilted her chin to look up at me.

She nodded. "I keep feeling like there was something wrong with me. I'm supposed to be able to have kids, Giovanni. I'm supposed to be able to give you a family and we don't know if that's going to happen. I still feel so... broken."

"Baby." I breathed and pulled her closer to me. "You're not broken and you have nothing to feel ashamed about. This is just something we have to get through and we have been. Look at how much better these last few days have been."

She looked up at me with those big hazel eyes, still brimming with tears.

"But we have to get through this together, Isabella," I murmured. "I need you to let me be there for you because it's been killing me to see you like this. I just want you to be happy and at times I feel like I don't know how to make that happen anymore."

My voice cracked with emotion. It was unexpected but it was the truth. I've been trying to be a positive energy for her. I've been trying my best to be there for her lately but it wasn't always easy. I felt helpless.

"You make me so happy," she cried. "I know I've been distant lately but I'm trying."

"I know you are." I ran my fingers through her hair. "And I also know you're going to have good and bad days but you need to know that I'm here for it all. The good, the bad, the ugly. All of it. You're not alone and you never will be."

"I don't know what I would do without you."

"That's never something you have to worry about. This is forever, *mi hermosa*." I leaned down and kissed her forehead.

I kissed her forehead again. And then her cheek. And then her lips.

"I mean it, Isabella. You, me, us." I cupped her face again. "We're going to get married and it's going to be you and me till the end."

"God, I love you so much." She reached up and pulled me down to meet her lips.

She attacked me with a hungry desire that mirrored my own. With all the emotions between us, it was overwhelming and I suddenly couldn't think about anything except needing to have my way with her. I needed her. She was addictive to me and I would never get enough. I pulled her close to me, my tongue parting her lips as she gasped against me. I was always gentle with her except when it came to this. My arms came around and I lifted her, her legs instinctively wrapping around my waist. Her hands were cupping my face, then in my hair, then moving down my arms - she was trying to grasp at every part of me that she could.

I walked us over to the couch, never once breaking the kiss. I lay her down and towered over her, my hand running up her torso to reach her breast. I squeezed through the material and could already feel her nipple harden against my touch. My own arousal rushed straight to my groin and I was already aching to be inside of her. It was unlike anything I had ever felt before and I craved it. I craved her. I slipped my hand underneath her shirt, feeling her hot skin against my touch. I pushed it up till she lifted herself with enough space to toss the shirt across the room. She grabbed my shirt, tugging at it. I quickly followed her lead and removed my own shirt. Her hands found my body and she ran her fingers up and down, feeling my muscles with her nails. She dragged them across knowing exactly what that did to me. I was throbbing now against my pants but I wasn't going to give in just yet - I needed to take care of her body.

I reached for the button of her jeans and popped it open before sliding the zip down. I pulled them down her legs, her underwear following. Her breathing picked up the way it always did. Between her small breaths and the moans escaping, I was struggling to contain my own desire. I was ready to rip into her.

"You're mine, Isabella," I murmured into her ear. "You've always been mine."

She whimpered as I sucked on her skin against her neck. I slid my hand up her bare thigh, slowly running my fingers over her as I reached between her legs.

"And I'm not going anywhere. I'm yours." I reminded her as I continued to leave kisses against her collarbone, starting to move over her chest.

"Gio." She breathed.

"I'm here, baby." I felt between her legs again and she was already so ready for me. "Do you see what I can do to you?"

She tugged at her bottom lip as her gaze met mine, her eyes burning with desire. I slipped a finger inside and watched as her head fell backward, her eyes rolling in her head as she soaked in my touch. I picked up the pace against her, hitting her where she needed it. She couldn't hold back the moans on her lips.

"Right there," she moaned.

Oh, fuck I loved when she did that. I wanted to know that she was getting what she wanted. I aimed to please and when she encouraged me like that, I was just about ready to explode myself.

"There, baby?" I asked, pushing harder against her.

"Yes!"

I slipped another finger in which earned me another moan falling from those lips of hers. I crashed my lips against hers, soaking in her moans against me. I needed more of her. I needed her to surrender her body to me. I broke the kiss and pulled away, my fingers leaving her body. She jerked her head forward in surprise but I brought my fingers to my mouth, tasting her.

"Oh, Giovanni," she moaned.

"You taste fucking amazing, baby."

"When you say things like that, I-" she breathed, stopping mid-sentence as I brought my fingers back inside her.

"You what?" I probed. "You like that, don't you?"

"I fucking love it."

God, she was killing me now. I pulled away and stood up to remove my pants and underwear. They dropped to the floor, freeing myself to her. Without warning, she sat up and took me in her hand. She caught me off guard and she knew that. She had this look in her eye - intrigue? desire? Whatever it was, it was sending a rush of heat over my body.

"Isa-?" her name got lost on my lips as she brought her mouth over me.

My fuck. She slid up and down my length, pushing deeper with each movement. God, the feeling of her tongue twirling around my d-

"Fuck, Isabella," I breathed her name as she brought her mouth down, causing me to hit the back of her throat.

My hand went to her hair, gripping it as the pleasure shot through my veins. Her greedy, wet mouth working its way over me was pushing me closer and closer to my climax. She was so fucking perfect. I couldn't help but soak in the image of her right now. She glanced up at me as she continued and I couldn't help but grip at her hair, harder as I tried to soak in each moment a little longer. She wasn't going to let me though. Her hand wrapped around my base and she picked up her pace once more, this time not stopping instead, she gave me what I was craving.

I couldn't stop the moans that formed on my own lips. I closed my eyes and leaned my head back as I released myself into her mouth.

"*Joder,*" I breathed as she twirled her tongue around me one last time before removing her mouth from me.

She looked satisfied with herself. She knew she had me right where she wanted. I was bewitched by her. Whatever she wanted, I would give her. Whatever she needed of me, she would have. I was so tightly wrapped around her finger that there was no way I could ever be without her. I needed her. Every part of her.

And right now, I needed to be inside of her.

I reached for her and pulled her lips to meet mine.

"Turn around," I instructed.

"Oh yes!" Her eyes lit up.

Isabella loved to be taken from behind and right now I was eager to give her everything she wanted. She flipped her body around and got on all fours in front of me. Her body surrendered itself to me and I would never get enough of that. I positioned myself in front of her, slowly pushing through her entrance. She gasped as I filled her up. I couldn't help the small breaths of pleasure that escaped as she tightened around me. This was where I belonged. Buried deep inside of her. I grabbed on either side of her hips and started to move - pushing deeper inside of her with each thrust. She extended her hand out in front of her, gripping the couch as she moaned my name.

"Faster," she instructed. "Don't hold back."

"Never."

Faster and harder, I gave her exactly what she wanted and I was rewarded with the sounds of her moaning my name to the world.

CHAPTER 37:

Isabella

I had never given much thought to my wedding day. When I was a little girl, I didn't find myself romanticizing what a union like that meant. I had always found marriage to be something of convenience - not something that happens when you're in love.

Turns out, I was so wrong about that.

There was nothing I wanted more than to celebrate the love that Giovanni and I had for each other. It was the kind of love I never thought I would be lucky enough to experience. The kind of love that consumes you. The kind of love that you feel in every part of your mind, body, and soul. I had never cared much for believing in soulmates but when I met him, I knew that there was something about the way we connected that couldn't be explained except that our souls were meant to find each other. He accepted every part of me - the good, the bad and even the parts I wished I could have hidden from him. He made me the best version of myself.

He was my person.

So when we stood up at that altar, exchanging our vows in front of our friends and family, I couldn't hold back the tears.

"Damnit, I promise I wouldn't cry"" I said, trying to slowly wipe my tears away without smudging my makeup.

He let out a small laugh, his deep dimple showing and reminding me that it was one of the many reasons I couldn't take my eyes off him. Here he stood in a well-fitted black suit. His beard had been well-groomed to perfection and against his dark skin and deep brown eyes, I didn't know how my knees didn't give in. We stood hand in hand, looking into each other's eyes as we exchanged the promises we had for each other.

"Giovanni." I took a deep breath in. "I'm not sure about a lot in life - in fact, half of the time I feel like I'm just floating through but promising myself to you for the rest of our lives is the one thing I have never been more sure of. In you, I have found the love I never thought I deserved. You are my comfort, my friend, my love, my soulmate."

He squeezed my hand and I could have sworn he had tears building in his eyes.

"Do you, Isabella Avery, take Giovanni Velázquez to be your lawfully wedded husband?" the priest asked.

I smiled and nodded through my tears as I slid the ring along his left finger. "I do."

"Giovanni, it's your turn."

He took a deep breath in, never once breaking eye contact. "Isabella - I don't even know where to start."

A small chorus of laughter spread throughout and I couldn't help but smile.

"From the first moment I met you, I knew there was something different about you. There was something that drew me in and I couldn't shake you. I had never been one to think of marriage - I had never even been one to consider a relationship."

This time I couldn't help the small laugh that escaped my lips. He had come a long way from the man everyone warned me to stay away from. Look at how far we have come.

"But you changed it all for me, *mi hermosa*. Every day I wake up with you in my life, I fall more and more in love with you and it's not just because you're the most beautiful person in the world but rather because you make my world beautiful. There is no life without you, Isabella."

There was no way I could stop the tears from falling now.

"Life has tried to test us. We've gone through some things that we didn't need to go through but we've come out stronger - together."

He squeezed my hand. God, he was perfect.

"And no matter what life has in store for us, you and I are going to get through it because I'm never going to stop loving you. I promise to take care of you. I promise to be patient and treat you the way you deserve to be treated.

You are my world, *mi hermosa,* and I am going to spend the rest of my life making you happy - even if it means sitting through countless Twilight movie marathons."

A chorus of laughter erupted again. I couldn't hold my own laughter back and reached up to wipe away my tears again. He took the ring in his hand and slowly slid it along my left finger to join my engagement ring. "With this ring, I promise that you will never have to face this world alone."

He secured it in place before grabbing my hands in his once more.

"Today, I choose to spend the rest of my life with you and every day I will keep choosing you."

"I love you so much," I cried.

"I love you, *mi hermosa.*"

"Giovanni Velázquez, do you take Isabella Avery to be your lawfully wedded wife?"

Without hesitation, he answered, "I do."

"By the power invested in me, I am happy to pronounce you husband and wife," the priest announced. "You may now kiss your bride."

Giovanni reached for me and pulled me closer, his lips finding mine in the sweetest kiss I would ever experience. It was true euphoria. A huge chorus of celebrations surrounded us but at that moment, it was just him and I. My heart had never been happier.

He pulled away but leaned his forehead against mine. "I love you, Mrs. Velázquez."

"I love you, Mr. Velázquez."

We turned to our family and friends who were all on their feet now - shouting, clapping, and celebrating for us. Giovanni lifted our hands that were intertwined in the air as we celebrated our official union. After everything that had happened, it seemed like this day was out of reach but now here we were and we finally got what we wanted. He placed our hands back down and started to lead us back down the aisle. I used my free hand to grab the side of my dress so as to not step on it as we continued to make our way past our guests who were now throwing petals at us.

He pulled me closer and lifted my hand to his lips.

A forever with Giovanni was everything I had dreamed of and it turns out that dreams do come true sometimes.

***

Hand in hand, Giovanni led me to the dance floor. Under the beautiful chandelier that hung above us, we stopped and he pulled me closer to him. My one hand slipped into his as he pulled me up against him, my other hand resting on his shoulder. The sound of *Por Primera Vez* by Camilo and Evaluna Montaner surrounded us as I leaned my head against his chest. I had never been calmer than I was right now in his arms. We swayed from side to side, soaking in the moment.

We were married.

I couldn't believe it. This man was my husband and he would be mine for the rest of my life.

Por primera vez, yo volví a nacer contigo.

For the first time, I am born again with you.

When Giovanni first played this song to me, it made me emotional. He sat with me and took me through the translation and I didn't want another one for our first dance. The beautiful Spanish words surrounded us and I was so overwhelmed by the love I had for him. I pulled away with enough space to look up at him and he was already looking at me.

"*Mi vida es vida solo contigo,*" he murmured the words of the song to me. "My life is only a life with you, baby."

He leaned his forehead against mine. "Thank you for choosing me, Isabella."

Tears swelled in my eyes, "Giovan-"

"I'm serious, there was no life before you. You've given me everything I could have ever wanted."

"I didn't think I would ever be this happy," I admitted. "When I think back on my life before you, there's nothing - you gave me the life I've always wanted."

He cupped my face with his hands. "I love you, *mi hermosa.*"

I didn't think it was possible to feel as loved as he was making me feel right now. In his deep brown eyes, I could see that he meant every word. I would never understand how I got so lucky.

"I love you."

I leaned up towards him and his lips met mine before pulling away. "And I can't believe how beautiful you are."

A blush spread across my cheeks. "You don't look too bad yourself."

He smirked. "Turns out I clean up nicely."

I couldn't help but laugh as he leaned closer to my ear. "As much as I love that dress, I can't wait to see it on the floor."

I was happy that I finally got to wear my dress that had been hanging in the guest room all this time. It was a vintage-styled dress that clung perfectly to all the curves of my body. The lace detail on the dress trailed from the straps to the plunging, yet tasteful, neckline all the way down to the floor. It held my breasts perfectly in place and accentuated them enough for Giovanni to enjoy. A lace trail spilled over from the waist and along the floor. It was a long train but it was delicate and beautiful.

My desire kicked into first gear and I couldn't contain the excitement inside of me. I still had no idea what he had planned for our honeymoon but I was just mere hours away from finding out.

"Is it too early to leave?" I joked.

He smiled. "Patience, *mi hermosa*."

A chorus of cheers surrounded us as the song came to an end. The DJ's voice pulled us away from each other. "The dance floor is now open."

"Now's where the real party begins," Giovanni announced.

"I hope you've been practicing your dance moves."

"Oh you're not ready, baby. I might just put you to shame."

"Give me enough shots and I'll be dancing circles around you."

Giovanni threw his head back and laughed. "Then I guess we better get those going."

Reyna and Katrina made their way onto the dance floor and in true Reyna fashion, she already had a tray of shots in her hand. If you wanted a party, she would be the person to bring it.

"You're not leaving this dance floor until you've had a shot," she warned us playfully.

Giovanni and I eyed each other, smiles playing on our lips. Katrina rested her hand on her baby bump. She was starting to reach the end of her pregnancy and her bump was perfectly rounded. She still remained just as tiny as she was - it was just her stomach that grew.

"I am quite happy that I am pregnant right now 'cause she's relentless," Katrina remarked which only made Reyna roll her eyes.

"You had a great time at your wedding, Kat, and I was just as relentless."

Diego made it to the dance floor just as Reyna had started to hand out the shots. She handed one over to me as Camila and Smith popped up from behind me.

"I hope there's enough for us to join," Camila said and took a place in our circle.

It was still jarring to see my sister like this. She and Reyna were getting along better than ever and had even kept in touch since my bachelorette party. I got the feeling that Camila admired Reyna's outlook on life and she had since eased up even more than I had ever seen her before.

"You guys can grab the last two," Reyna said as she handed them the shots.

"You're going to need to order one for Sergio," Giovanni commented.

"Sergio can wait till the next round."

"Yes ma'am." Giovanni laughed.

"To Isabella and Giovanni - I can't believe this started because I dared you to have a one-night stand," Reyna laughed. "You're welcome, guys."

"We would be nowhere without you, Rey." Giovanni nudged her playfully.

"You joke but I played cupid that night and now look! But seriously, I couldn't be happier for you two." She raised her shot and we all followed her lead. "To Mr. and Mrs.Velázquez."

Mrs. Velázquez. I would never get tired of hearing that.

I brought the shot glass to my lips and tilted my head back, allowing the burning alcohol to fall down the back of my throat. I couldn't help but pull a face. I didn't recognize the taste but it was stronger than I expected it to be.

"What the hell was that?" I asked, placing my shot glass back on the tray.

"Silver tequila." Reyna said.

"That was fucking awful," Giovanni commented.

"Give it a few minutes and you'll start feeling great." Reyna grabbed his shot glass and placed it on her tray.

I could already feel it burning its way through my body, making sure to cover every part right down to my toes. I was already swaying to the music.

"Can I steal you for a dance?" I heard my father ask from behind me.

The best part of our wedding was the fact that we managed to successfully get both our families to be here - no drama included. Even Cecilio had managed to put his pride and general distaste for Marcina's new boyfriend aside for the sake of us. It was the most selfless I had seen him and even though he wouldn't admit it, I knew Giovanni appreciated it.

"Of course." I reached for my dad's hand as he pulled me closer to him. Out of the corner of my eye, I saw Giovanni offer his hand to my mother for a dance. I half-expected her to say no but she, too, had decided to put everything aside and enjoy herself.

"I am so happy for you, Bella," my dad said as we swayed from side to side. "I've never seen you this happy before."

"I've never been happier, Dad. I'm so glad that you guys are here."

"You know we'd never miss this." He smiled. "Whatever has happened with you and your mother, that's all in the past now."

"It is and you don't know how happy that makes me. She was really helpful to me during the whole -," I paused for a moment. "Miscarriage situation."

When I first found out that we had lost a baby, I went into a dark place. I didn't want to open up to anyone about how I was feeling so it surprised me when she told me what happened to her that one Sunday when they came to Barcelona. I know she was trying to help me but when I first heard the story, it just made me want to crawl into a ball and cry. Every week after that day, she would check on me and slowly but surely, it got easier to deal with. We were the closest we had ever been. In some kind of messed up way, I was thankful for what happened to me because without it, I don't think my mother and I would have become as close as we were now.

"You don't need to think about that situation now." He leaned down and kissed my forehead. "Everything is going to work out the way it's meant to."

While I didn't want to give much thought to anything beyond our wedding night, I was feeling more hopeful.

The DJ switched the music up to something more upbeat and the floor flooded with people joining in. My dad and I ended our dance just as Sergio was bringing a new tray of shots to the dance floor.

"Good luck with that," my dad commented.

I couldn't help but laugh. "Thanks. I'm going to need it."

CHAPTER 38:

Giovanni

She was on the dance floor and I couldn't take my eyes off her. I stood by the bar closest to the dance floor with Sergio, Diego, and Alvaro while Isabella stood in the crowd, waving her hands in the air from side to side. She had the biggest smile on her face and she would often throw her head back in laughter at something someone had said. She was glowing with a happiness I had never seen and it was the most beautiful sight.

I couldn't believe this woman was my wife.

I couldn't believe I was married. It was the best decision I had ever made. A part of me always knew I would marry Isabella. That was part of what was terrifying when I first met her. I had never experienced something like that before. An instant connection that couldn't be ignored. I wanted to know the woman behind those intriguing hazel eyes. She was the beautiful stranger that I just had to know more about.

Years later, I could now officially call her my wife.

"Emilio is ready to take you guys when you're ready," my father said, joining us by the bar.

"Thank you."

My father's wedding gift to us was a private jet to take us to our honeymoon destination. He had friends in many places and when I mentioned that flying on a private jet was something Isabella wanted to tick off her bucket list, he offered to organize that for us. When we first spoke about her having a bucket list, it was back when I first took her on our date by the fountain. It was before we had even officially started dating but I remembered her saying she didn't have one. I thought about how that needed to change so about a year ago while we were still planning our wedding, I bought her a small notebook I had seen in the window of some random store for just that reason.

I placed the empty notebook in front of her. She was seated at the kitchen counter and looked up from what she was working on, eyeing the notebook and then me. "And now?"

"You're going to make a bucket list."

"Am I dying anytime soon?" she joked.

"Firstly, terrible joke. Secondly, I remembered you telling me that you had never had one so we're going to change that."

She reached for the notebook and flipped through the empty pages. "Do you have one?"

"Not written down but there are definitely things I want to do before I die."

"Like?"

"Well for one, I'd like you to have a bucket list."

She rolled her eyes and smiled. "Not what I was expecting."

She reached for a pen that was on the counter and turned back to the first page of the notebook. She started to write something down. I leaned over to see what she was writing.

Get a tattoo.

"That's a great start," I commented. "I'll take you to my tattoo guy."

"I don't know what I'd get, but I know I definitely want one."

I pulled a barstool over and sat down, scooting closer to her. "What else do you have in mind?"

She thought for a moment, resting the pen between her lips like she always did when she was deep in thought.

"Skinny dipping?"

I couldn't help but laugh. "Oh hell yes. I'll do it with you."

"Have you done it before?" she asked.

I nodded which caused her to roll her eyes. "Of course you have."

"Before you get any ideas, I did it as a dare actually," I clarified.

She gaped at me, a hint of amusement in her eyes. "Who dared you?"

"Sergio, of course. We were out with a group of friends at a beach party, as drunk as ever, and he dared me to skinny dip in the ocean."

"Oh God, were there people around?"

"Tons," I chuckled. "And it didn't take security very long to chase me off the beach - butt naked might I remind you."

She burst out laughing.

"Let me just add that getting sand by your balls is definitely not recommended."

"Thankfully, I don't have those," she said in between her laughter. "I'd be happy to skinny dip with you in private."

"We can make that happen."

She continued to fill in more lines on the page. I scanned through some of them as she went along, writing whatever came to mind.

Visit Italy - specifically Florence, Rome, Cinque Terre and Positano.

"Italy, huh? That's very specific."

Her eyes lit up as she nodded. "Always wanted to go there. I've seen pictures and you know how much I love beautiful views and they seem to have a lot of those."

I made a mental note to remember to plan a trip to Italy for her. I leaned over to kiss her temple before glancing back at her list.

Try snails.

This one made me laugh. "They're actually so much better than you'd expect."

She scrunched her nose. "The thought of it is so disgusting but I'm trying to take some risks here."

"Risks would be sky-diving, baby - not eating snails."

She shook her head. "Eating snails is about as risky as I'm going to be right now. You will never find me sky-diving."

"Bungee jumping?" I suggested.

A horrified look settled over her face. "I arrived in this world on a chord, I'm not about to leave because of one."

I burst out laughing. "So, no sky-diving or bungee jumping which is what you'd usually find on people's bucket lists so what else do you have here?"

She lifted the book so only she could see the list now and peered over it. "I'll read some to you."

I waited in anticipation as she started to go through the list in front of her. "Wine tasting in France, watch the ball drop in Times Square for New Years, smoke weed in Amsterdam."

I gaped at her before I started laughing. "You smoking weed? I can't picture it."

"Hey, I'd like to try that at least once in my life, and where better to try it than Amsterdam."

"I would love to see you high."

"I'll need to add more, but I have other ones like 'fly on a private jet', 'get married', 'have babies' - you know, the usual ones."

"Soon enough you'll be able to tick off the 'get married' one," I leaned forward to kiss her as she smiled against my lips.

I was planning to tick off a lot on her bucket list with this honeymoon.

We were well approaching midnight and I was itching to take Isabella away now. We had already consumed copious amounts of alcohol and I had been sending Katrina with bottles of water for Isabella. It was our wedding night and we were not going to spend it drunk in our hotel room.

I had other plans.

"I'm going to grab Isabella. The hotel manager is doing me a favor by checking us in so late so I don't want to push my luck."

"Does she have any idea of where you're going?" Sergio asked.

"Nope. I've been really good at keeping this a secret."

My mother started to walk towards me, hand-in-hand with Sebastian which caused my father to turn and take off in the opposite direction. He had stayed true to his word when he said there would be no drama from his side. It surprised me - I didn't think he would be capable of that but I clearly underestimated him. He was surprisingly pleasant tonight.

"*Mi amor,*" my mother said and reached for me, cupping my face. "I can't believe you're married!"

I chuckled. *"Mamá,"*

She had been emotional all night but I could see how happy she was for Isabella and me.

"I'm so happy for you, *hijo."* She smiled before turning to Sebastian. "We are going to go back to our room now. My feet are so sore from dancing in these things all night." she lifted her foot to refer to high heels.

All our guests were set to stay here tonight and some had already started to make their way to their rooms. While I had considered that, I just wanted to take my wife away so we could have our own celebration. All the important parties knew that we were leaving tonight - Isabella, however, was unaware. I had been pretty good at keeping this a secret. I turned to place my empty whiskey glass on the bar counter just as Isabella snuck up behind me, wrapping her arms around my waist.

"There you are!" she exclaimed. "Come and dance with me?"

I turned around, still keeping her arms around me, and rested my thumb against her chin, tilting her face upwards so she could meet my gaze. "I was actually thinking we could get out of here."

"Oh?" She cocked an eyebrow.

I nodded. "I think it's time for you and I have to have our own fun, wouldn't you agree?"

She tugged at her bottom lip before smiling. "Hell yes."

***

We worked our way through what was left of the crowd, saying our goodbyes. Isabella was still on a level - this was evident by her adorable giggle and her arm constantly wrapped around mine. I started to lead her out of the dining hall towards the parking lot, causing her to stop. I turned back to her and she now had a look of confusion across her face.

"Our room is that way." She pointed in the opposite direction. "Why are we in the parking?"

A long black sedan pulled up in front of us. Emilio stopped the car and rolled the passenger window down. *"Buenas Noches, Señor Velázquez."*

"Buenas Noches, Emilio." I turned back to Isabella. "We're not going to our room."

"What are you talking about?"

"Everything is already sorted. Reyna made sure to give our bags to Emilio so you and I just have to worry about getting to the airport."

She gaped at me. "Where are we going?"

"Our honeymoon," I announced proudly.

She threw her arms around my neck and pulled me to meet her lips, smiling against me.

"I thought we were only leaving tomorrow," she said, breaking the kiss.

"Your husband is full of surprises, baby."

She had the biggest smile on her face as I let go of her to reach for the car door. I pulled it open and stood back, allowing her to get inside.

"I should have changed," she said.

I shook my head. "The only way that dress is coming off is when I remove it."

She cocked an eyebrow. *Oh, she liked that.* I slid onto the seat next to her, pulling the door closed behind me. I gave Emilio the go-ahead and he put foot, heading for the airport.

"I hope you're not tired," I murmured. "Because I still have a few more surprises for tonight."

"Are you kidding me? I'm way too excited to see what you have planned."

I leaned forward and kissed her temple before pulling my tie over my head. I popped open the top two buttons and leaned back against the seat, my hand resting against her dress on the inside of her thigh.

"Did you have a good time?" I asked her.

She glanced up at me, her eyes shining with happiness. "The best time. I can't believe we're married."

I chuckled. "Better believe it, *mi hermosa.*"

"Are you going to tell me where we are going yet?"

"Nope," I popped the 'p'. "You've done well up till now, I'm sure you can wait a little longer."

She sighed. "Can I guess?"

"That would ruin the fun."

"But what if I get it right?" she challenged.

"I won't tell you if it's right or wrong."

"Well that's not a fun game then." This earned me a playful eye-roll. "You're really building up my expectations here."

"Trust me, it'll be worth it." I lifted her hand to my lips.

CHAPTER 39:

Isabella

Giovanni was right.

It was so worth the wait. A couple of hours later, we had finally made it to our hotel and I was in awe. First Giovanni went and organized a private jet for us - or rather, his father did - but when we stepped onto the plane, we were treated like royalty. Royalty who ordered fast food for the trip. I often felt like Giovanni could read my mind because I needed food in my system and there I was, sitting and devouring the fries we had on the way to our honeymoon destination. There were tons of other options but fries were my go-to when I had been drinking. I could feel the alcohol leaving my system as we started to land. Still not knowing where we were going, we arrived at a private airport and there was already a car waiting for us. He really went all out with this and I couldn't believe it. I would never have expected it.

And I really never expected to be driving the streets of Florence.

"No way!" I exclaimed and turned to face him as the car came to a stop just outside the *Duomo di Firenze*. I had only ever seen this spectacular structure in pictures and now here it was right in front of me.

"I can't believe we're in Florence!" I couldn't contain my excitement which caused Giovanni to laugh as he opened the door. He came around to my side and opened it up for me. I stepped outside and couldn't keep my eyes off my surroundings. The full moon shone down on us against the clear night-time sky and there was not a person in sight. I looked around the deserted square in amazement. It truly felt as if we were the only two people in the world right now. Here we were, Giovanni still in his suit and me still in my wedding dress, standing in the middle of the empty square in Florence for crying out loud. It was like something out of a romance book. A light chill surrounded us and I took a deep breath in. I loved it. I loved the freshness of it and even though it was well approaching three in the morning, I had never been more awake.

"You ready to check-in?" Giovanni asked, forcing me to tear my eyes away from my archaic surroundings.

I nodded. "How far are we from the hotel?"

"Right here, baby." He pointed at the building directly in front of the *Duomo.*

"We're staying right here?" I gaped.

"Of course - best view in town."

He reached for my hand and started to lead me through the large, dark brown doors that were open, waiting for us. We strolled along the cobblestone path that led to the reception area.

An older gentleman peered over the counter. "Ah, *Signore Velázquez, Benvenuto!"*

"*Ciao,* Mr. Russo." He let go of my hand and walked over to greet the man. "Thank you so much for allowing us to check-in so late."

"*Certo!* We are happy to welcome you to our hotel." He glanced at me over his glasses and smiled. "Congratulations *Signora Velázquez!"*

I returned the smile. "Thank you. I'm so excited to be here."

"She had no idea," he informed the man. "It was a surprise."

"Well, I hope you'll enjoy staying here."

"We definitely will," I said.

He chatted briefly with Giovanni handing over our key and explaining a few other miscellaneous things but I couldn't contain my excitement. I was looking around, still stealing glances at the *Duomo* through the windows. We eventually had everything we needed and took the elevator up to the top floor. There was a very clear renaissance feel to the hotel from the paintings hanging on the wall to the wallpaper. While it was still a very modern hotel, it never lost its sense of culture and history. Giovanni stopped at the door at the end of the hall and unlocked it, stepping back to allow me to step inside before closing it behind us. It was a large penthouse-style room and the large windows opened directly onto a view of the higher parts of the cathedral.

There was a large bed that was raised on wooden pallets. In the opposite corner was a small living area with a couple of white, leather chairs scattered around a coffee table. I walked over to the bed, running my fingers over the soft material of the duvet. To my left was a small door that opened onto the bathroom. Walking over, I peeped into it and a large jacuzzi stood right by the windows.

"Oh my God, there's a jacuzzi in here!" I exclaimed before turning back to Giovanni. "You seriously went all out!"

He chuckled and walked over to me. "I told you that it would all be worth it."

His arms wrapped around my waist and I felt his lips against my skin as he left soft kisses against my neck. My body awoke at his touch. I could already feel the heat between us and I took a deep breath in, trying to keep my sudden arousal at bay. I would usually throw myself at him but right now, I wanted to savor each moment with him now.

I turned to face him, wrapping my arms around his neck. "I would have been happy with anything. You didn't have to do all this."

"I didn't have to but I wanted to. I want to spoil you."

My cheeks were sore from smiling. I had never been happier than I was today. Everything about our wedding was more than I could have ever wanted and I was still reeling from it.

"How did I get so lucky?" I murmured, reaching up to meet his lips.

His kiss was gentle. His hands came up to cup my cheeks as he used his tongue to part my lips. Each movement was slow and delicate. It was as if he was soaking in every moment. My breath caught in my throat as he slowly started to run his hand down my arm. He pulled away, looking down at me with a look I couldn't quite place. His eyes were burning with desire but there was also so much love. There was such an intensity to him right now that it was causing a flutter within my stomach.

"You're so beautiful," he murmured, his gaze dropping to my lips before flicking to meet my eyes again. "You're all mine."

"All yours."

His lips twitched into a smirk before he reached for me again, his hands pushing their way into my hair as his lips met mine with a new refound sense of urgency. I was so ready for him. I had been waiting all evening to be taken by my husband. He ran his hand down my arm and slipped it around my waist, pulling me closer as my tongue flicked over his. My ever-increasing arousal pulsed through my veins and my heart was pounding in my chest in anticipation. He found my zip and slowly started to pull it down, my one strap slipping down my shoulder. His lips moved from mine and started to trail along my jawline, down my neck, across my shoulder - stopping to suck against my skin as he used his other hand to slide the other strap down. The pressure between my legs was already building as I craved his touch. He started to push my dress down my body, exposing the new white lingerie set I had underneath.

"Oh, baby." His eyes dropped to my body as I stepped out of my dress.

It was my wedding night so I made sure to have something underneath my dress that he would enjoy. I had settled on an intricate lace white set that sat on my body in ways that made me feel sexy. It pushed my breasts together, accentuating them enough for Giovanni not to be able to pull his gaze away. A carnal look of pure hunger settled over his face and I wanted that. He made me feel desired and there was nothing I craved more.

"You like it?" I slowly ran my hand up the side of my leg, slipping a single finger underneath the delicate material.

"I love it," he breathed. "You're fucking breathtaking."

He didn't give me another second to say anything more before his hungry lips found mine. His strong arms came around me, forcing my legs to wrap around his waist as he pinned me up against the nearest wall. The sound of my back hitting against it caused me to gasp but it was enthralling. He was holding nothing back and I could feel him hard against me. He grabbed my hand and placed it above my head, keeping it against the wall as his lips continued to trace along every part of me it could manage. My lips, my cheeks, my jawline, my neck, my ear - he didn't leave one place untouched and I was already finding it difficult to contain the moans building on my lips. His hand tangled in my hair, causing it to fall out of its bun. It cascaded down my shoulders as I leaned my head to the side, allowing him to continue down my neck.

He nipped at my neck with his teeth causing his name to fall from my lips.

"I love hearing my name on your lips," he murmured as he gripped either side of my cheeks with one hand before crashing his lips against mine.

He didn't hold back. His voracious appetite had taken over and there was no stopping him from devouring me in any way he could. I reached for his shirt, trying to pop each button open before I eventually gave up and ripped his shirt open to expose that body of his. I ran my fingers up his torso and then across his chest. My touch burned against his skin causing my desire to pulse through me as I allowed myself to feel every part of him. I couldn't tear my eyes away from him. He was so sexy.

We stumbled towards the bed and he placed me down. I slid myself higher up, resting my head against the pillow as I watched him. He pulled his belt off and dropped it to the floor before removing his pants, his underwear following shortly after. God, he was perfect. There he stood all ready for me and I couldn't contain myself.

He climbed back onto the bed, his arms on either side of me as his lips found mine again. I couldn't hold back now. I flicked my tongue over his, nipping at his bottom lip in between. I was ready to be taken by him. My heart couldn't take the amount of love I was feeling for him. He consumed every part of me. His hand slid underneath me, reaching for my clasp. I arched my back with enough space for him to pop it open. I pulled my bra off my arms and tossed it across the room. His lips found my neck again causing my breathing to pick up the way it always did when he reached the sensitive area close to my ear. I felt his hand running down along my stomach to reach my underwear.

"Don't rip them," I warned, causing him to chuckle.

"Fine." He pulled away and started to slide them down my legs. "You can keep this one."

He ran his fingers over down my opening, parting me as he slipped one inside. I closed my eyes, already soaking in his touch. I was already ready to welcome him where he needed to be and I could feel him hard against me.

"Giovanni," I breathed his name against his skin.

"Just lie back, Isabella," he instructed. "I got you."

I rolled my eyes back in the ecstasy of his words. That was exactly what he said to me the first time he helped himself to me in a way I had never experienced before. My toes curled in anticipation. I was ready to feel his tongue against me. He moved further down and used his knees to part my legs, allowing him enough space to position himself between me. I expected to feel him against me but instead, I felt his lips against my knee. I tilted my head to watch as he moved up my leg, leaving kisses of devotion all the way until he reached between my legs. He was so close to me now, I could feel his breath against me.

"You love it when I do this to you?" He brought this tongue down against me, causing me to jerk my hips against him. "Tell me what you love."

"I love when yo-" My breath got caught in my throat as he ran his tongue up my opening. "Gio, please."

"I'm just teasing you," He murmured, his breath hot against my skin. "I know exactly what to do."

He didn't hold back before finding his rhythm against me - sucking and licking - never once stopping to give me a moment to catch my breath. I could feel my climax building. I was already aching against his touch. He slipped a finger inside to join his rhythm. The moans fell from my lips, each one getting louder and louder as he pushed me closer to the edge. I was at his complete mercy. My hand found its way into his hair, gripping it as I flicked my hips against his tongue, fighting for the release my body needed.

And he didn't stop until I found it. I threw my head back against the pillows as the delirious pleasure rolled through me, reaching every inch of my body.

Giovanni didn't give me any time before his lips found mine again.

"I need to be inside you," he breathed against my lips.

I needed him and a rush of confidence burst through me. I wanted him my way.

Without warning, I pushed my hands against his chest causing him to swap places with me. His back hit the bed as I pulled myself over him, my legs straddling either side of him. He was intrigued. I could see it in his eyes. He loved it when I took control and right now, I just wanted him. I couldn't hold back any longer. He positioned himself for me and I hovered over him. He teased my entrance at first, already causing me to tug at my bottom lip before I brought myself down on him. I couldn't hold back the small moan that already fell from my lips as he filled me up.

"Fuck yes." His eyes rolled back as he soaked in the feeling of us skin to skin.

I rested my hands against his chest as I started to flick my hips forward. As I flicked back, I lifted off of him just enough to tease him before bringing myself back down hard against him. I picked up my rhythm and I leaned my head back, reeling in the pleasure that was already building inside of me again. I didn't hold back - I was in charge now and I used this opportunity to ride my husband. His hands rested on either side of my hips as he started to push himself deeper inside of me. Small breaths fell from his lips. I loved to hear him. I loved knowing what I was doing to him.

After everything, we were officially one in more ways than one and I didn't want the moment to end. I wanted to stay like this for as long as possible. It was exhilarating. He reached around my back and tossed me around, causing my back to hit against the bed as he thrust deep inside of me.

"Yes, yes, yes," I moaned.

His arms were on either side of me, his muscles rippling with each movement. I watched as he closed his eyes, stray strands of his hair falling over his eyes and I could see him clenching his jaw as he reveled in our joint pleasure.

His eyes met mine and I had never felt more loved.

"Lift your hips, baby."

I happily obliged and hooked my leg around his waist as he reached deeper inside of me. We moved as one until we both finally found our climax. Giovanni collapsed on top of me, both of us trying to catch our breath. We just lay there. His body was still hot against mine and a new sense of calm settled over me. I felt as if I belonged. With Giovanni was where I was meant to be and I had never been more sure of anything in my life.

My eyes were closed but I felt him remove himself from me and lie down next to me. I slowly turned my head in his direction, my eyes fluttering open to meet his gaze. He was smiling over at me. A boyish grin that I couldn't help but smile back at.

"And that smile?" I teased.

He reached for me and pulled me closer to him, my head resting against his chest as my leg draped over him. "I'm just happy."

"Me too."

CHAPTER 40:

Isabella

"Can we just stay here forever?"

"You mean Italy or on this wine farm?"

"Both." I dropped my head to peek over my sunglasses at Giovanni who sat across the small glass table between us. "I don't think you'd object to living on a wine farm since that's your - second," I stopped for a moment and thought. "Or third glass of wine?"

He glanced over at me, his lips pulling up in amusement. "Is that a hint of judgment I hear in your voice, Mrs. Velázquez?"

God, I loved it when he called me that.

I chuckled. "Absolutely not considering this is my fourth."

We sat under the warm Tuscan sun that sat at its peak in the sky. The constant heat would have bothered me if it wasn't for the cool wind brushing up against my skin. It was the perfect combination. I propped my legs up onto the cobblestone wall in front of me as I overlooked the wine lands in front of me. There was nothing but the sound of indistinct chatter in the distance intertwined with a few sounds from nature - a slight buzzing in the air from whatever bugs had taken up residence as well as the slight chirping of the birds in the trees around us. There were mountains in the distance as the perfect backdrop against the blue sky. Although we were supposed to be approaching Autumn, Spring had decided to stick around on our honeymoon and I was thankful for it.

I felt like I had been living a dream. It was as if I had stepped into my favorite romance novel and I now got to call it my life. We spent the last week experiencing pure marital bliss. Giovanni took me sightseeing, allowing me to explore the beautiful archaic city of Florence and it's surrounding areas. I was in awe of its beauty and to be here with Giovanni was what made it just everything perfect. We went sightseeing, shopping, stopped by tons of restaurants to try the local cuisine, slept in late, laughed and chatted about anything that came to mind. There was never a moment where it wasn't comfortable with him. I was exactly where I was meant to be.

Oh, and we had sex.

Lots and lots of sex.

It was like being with him for the first time. I was still just as enthralled by him, if not more. We couldn't keep our hands off each other and there was no sense of slowing down anytime soon. Every chance we got, we devoured each other. It had never been more in love with him. My heart was full.

I stole a glance over at him, his side profile on full display. My breath caught in my throat. I had enough alcohol in my system to let go of my inhibitions and give in to the true desires pushing through. He was so fucking sexy.

He sat staring out in the distance with his wine glass in his hand. He wore a black well-fitted t-shirt that sat around his muscles in a subtle way. I watched as he brought the glass to his lips, his arms flexing as he went with the motion. He slowly sipped on the wine, holding the stem of the glass between his two fingers. He leaned his head back just enough to allow the liquid into his mouth and I watched as his Adam's apple moved up and down as he swallowed. His beard had grown out over the last few days and I was actually enjoying this rugged look of his. His tongue ran over his bottom lip before he turned to face me. He was wearing sunglasses but I could tell he had caught me staring at him.

I didn't care. I couldn't tear my eyes away from him.

"So, what do you say?" he started. "Should I go buy this place so we can spend our days drinking wine under the sun?"

I rolled my eyes and smiled. "Probably not the smartest thing to do. We'd never be able to get anything done."

"That's the point. We won't have to do anything."

"And how would we make money?"

He snorted. "I think we're fine, babe."

That was something that had taken me by surprise when Giovanni and I first intertwined our lives together. I had always known that he was well-off given his choice of car. The Audi R8 he used to drive was a dead giveaway when I first saw it that he lived more than comfortably. Money was never an issue for him - his businesses were successful enough and between the ongoing expansions of *Mala Mía* and the projects he was working on at *Velázquez Constructa,* he was set for life. He didn't have to work - he chose to because he enjoyed it. While it may have been appealing to get into a relationship with a man with this kind of financial security, I didn't care for his money. I was with him for him but it did make me want to bring my own contribution to our lives together. *Aroma* was a passion project but it was also my way of adding financially to our lives in some way. I didn't want to be taken care of. I wanted us to take care of each other.

My mind was already buzzing as I brought my glass back up to my lips, sipping on the sweet taste of the wine. We had tried a couple of different wines - a dry white, a very bitter - not my favorite - red wine, and finally a sweet rose. I settled on that as my drink of choice while Giovanni went for the bitter red wine. My palette was hardly as mature as his. I enjoyed the ones back home but these were not for me.

"Hypothetically, though." Giovanni pulled my attention back to him. 'Would you want to live here?"

"On the wine farm or in Italy?"

He chuckled. "Italy."

I thought for a moment. "I love it here. I love Florence but I love it as a holiday destination. I'd be far too relaxed if I lived here."

"You're probably right."

He paused for a moment as he took another sip before he turned back to me, peering over his sunglasses. "But do you still want to live in Barcelona?"

I lifted an eyebrow, confused by his question. He picked up on that and continued, "I know you love Barcelona but have you thought about a change of scenery?"

"You don't want to live in Barcelona?"

"You know I don't mind it there and obviously our businesses are there but you've enjoyed being away, haven't you? We spoke about this in Sevilla and I wanted to know where your head was at now."

I had thought about what Giovanni said that day. He would be more than happy to pack up and move anywhere I wanted. I had considered what it would be like to leave Barcelona. I loved it there. It would always have a special place in my heart but there was a part of me that wasn't opposed to the idea of experiencing what it would be like to live in another city. Besides our businesses that were set up in Barcelona, we didn't have anything tying us to one place.

"Okay, hypothetically, if we were to leave Barcelona, where would you want to go?" I asked.

"I asked you first."

I smiled and rolled my eyes. "I wouldn't mind living in Sevilla for a bit. Or even Madrid. Or what was that little place we stopped by on our way back from Sevilla?"

"Huelva?"

"Yes! I loved that place too - very small-town living."

"You'd want to settle down in a small town?"

"Settle down?" I placed my glass down on the table and shifted my chair to move under the umbrella that was hovering over us. The sun was starting to get a little too hot as the wind had started to slow down.

"Yes, where would you want to set up roots, raise a fam-"

"Giova-"

He stopped me before I could get his name out. "Just hear me out, baby."

He shifted his chair closer to me, pulling his glasses off his as he placed them down on the table along with his glass. He ran his fingers through his hair before resting his hand on the inside of my thigh. His touch burned against my skin.

"You know I love you, *mi hermosa* - more than I've ever loved anyone and I'm not trying to upset you but it is something I wanted to speak to you about." His voice was gentle and he caressed my thigh with his thumb.

I understood where he was coming from and if this conversation had come up months ago, I probably would have reacted a lot worse to it. While there would always be the constant disappointment, I had been actively trying for months to not focus on that but rather on acceptance - it wasn't easy but I was doing my best. I wanted to focus on our future together and what that would look like for us. I was also focused on the present moment. Thinking of the future was often overwhelming at times. I was thankful for the alcohol already in my system. It helped to be able to think about what he was asking me without any emotional repercussions.

A diversion, if you will.

"You know there's a strong possibility that having children isn't in the cards for us," I murmured. "You knew that before we got married."

"Of course and that doesn't change a thing," he reassured me. "But I also don't want us to give up so easily, either."

He reached for my hand in my lap and intertwined his fingers with mine. "I'm not saying we should try right now. I'm happy to have you all to myself but years down the line, when it comes to it, I think we should try whatever options are available to us. Don't you?"

Dr. Gavina had tried to take us through the various fertility procedures available. Since we weren't actively trying for children, she ended up just giving us the information for us to have a look at in our own time. I didn't have it in me to go through it at the time so I didn't know what was out there for us but I was in a more hopeful place than I was before.

"You know I'll try anything. I still want a family with you."

"You're already my family, baby, and I mean, we're definitely not going to stop trying." He smirked, revealing that dimple of his. "You know how much I enjoy that process."

I smiled. He was right. We had taken full advantage of the fact that he didn't need to wear protection. Leading up to our wedding, I had been continuing with my frequent check-ups and Dr. Gavina was happy with my progress. There were still no new issues I had to deal with so that was a step in the right direction. After what happened with Katrina being too afraid to tell me about her pregnancy, my outlook on everything in my life had shifted. I didn't want to be the one to miss out on important things because of my sadness. I actively chose to look past that.

"But that's not what I want us to focus on right now." He squeezed my hand, bringing me out of my thoughts. "I just want to know if you want to move 'cause I don't think it wouldn't be a bad thing to try another place out. Even if it's just temporary - we'd still always have the apartment in Barcelona to go back to."

"What about Valencia?" I suggested.

"Not bad. Good choice. I could see us living there."

"And you have a *Mala Mía* there so that works."

"You could easily set up an *Aroma* there too. I told you I'd buy you a building." He leaned across and nestled his head in my neck, his lips finding my neck.

I giggled. "You wouldn't."

He pulled away to face me and cocked an eyebrow. "Challenge accepted, Mrs. Velázquez."

"No, no, no! I wasn't challenging you." I shook my head, smiling. "Can we put a pin in this? I'm definitely interested in a change of scenery but we don't have to decide that today."

"Of course not. It was just something I wanted you to think about."

We sat in a comfortable silence for a few moments, soaking in our surroundings. I reached for my glass again and brought it to my lips.

"At least you can tick 'visit Florence' off your bucket list now."

"I can tick quite a few things off now thanks to you." I pointed my glass at him. "Fly on a private jet, get married."

"Not a bad start," he commented. "We've still got to do that skinny dipping thing."

"When we're done here, we can just do it in that river I saw by the entrance."

He gaped at me and I couldn't help but laugh. He was too easy to fool.

"Come on, you know I would never do that." I snorted. "I told you I want to do it in private."

"You can't say you're not into doing things in public. I know you." There was a hint of temptation in his voice that piqued my interest.

"I never said I was opposed to that," I said in a low voice.

"We can add 'hooking up in public' to your bucket list."

"Hooking up? We're married, Giovanni."

"Doesn't mean we can't hook up." He squeezed the inside of my thigh, sending a rush of electricity further up. "We can pretend we don't know each other and that we're meeting for the first time."

"And then what? Have sex with each other after just meeting?" I pretended to be shocked at that thought. "How scandalous!"

He threw his head back in laughter. "I know. I can't believe people would do such a thing."

I couldn't help but laugh. Look at where we ended up because of our attempt at a one-night stand. I did owe Reyna for her playful game. She gave me the push I needed to go after what I wanted and that night, Giovanni was just that.

"So, I say we finish up our wine here and go get something to eat. I'm sure we could find a bathroom and we can try the whole 'hooking up in public'," he murmured.

I dropped my jaw. "In a bathroom?"

"Hey, some of the bathrooms here are fancier than you give them credit for."

"Oh that makes it more romantic." I rolled my eyes.

Giovanni chuckled and squeezed my hand. "Fine - we'll stick to the bathroom in our hotel room."

"We haven't made use of that jacuzzi, yet," I mentioned, turning my head to meet his gaze.

"You're right." He slowly started to slide his hand higher up my thigh. "It would be a shame to leave that as the only place unchristened in that hotel room."

The heat spread across my cheeks at the thought of what we had done to that hotel room. We took advantage of pretty much every surface and he was right, the jacuzzi was the only place left.

"Jacuzzi sex it is then."

"Hell fucking yes."

CHAPTER 41:

Giovanni

"Welcome back!" Penelope shrieked and skipped over to Isabella, wrapping her arms around her before turning to give me a hug.

"*Hola,* Penelope."

"Marriage suits you guys," she gushed. "You're practically glowing."

"Must have been all the s-"

"Don't even finish that sentence," Penelope warned, causing me to throw my head back in laughter. "I don't need to know that, Giovanni."

A slight blush had formed across Isabella's cheeks as she chuckled. We followed Penelope out onto the patio but I stopped and reached for Isabella's hand, pulling her towards me.

"I'd much rather be back in our hotel room," I murmured into her ear, causing her lips to pull up into a mischievous grin.

"If we leave now, we can make the next flight out."

"Don't tempt me," I challenged.

I had quite enjoyed these last three weeks having Isabella all to myself. We acted like complete tourists as we explored the streets of *Florence* - stopping whenever Isabella wanted. I had gone as far as to organize a few day trips to the surrounding cities including *Pisa* where she gushed over the monument. She loved small things like that and I just wanted to make her happy. She had fallen in love with Italy so instead of sticking to our original two-week honeymoon, I decided to extend our trip by a week and decided to add *Rome* and the small towns of *Cinque Terre* to our itinerary. She was glowing as we continued our exploration of the archaic towns. Between all the typical touristy things, we devoured each other every chance we could get. I would never get enough of her. I craved her and there was something empowering about knowing she was mine in every way.

"I'm sure we could easily get another room in *Vernazza* again or even -"

"*Riomaggiore.*" She finished my thought. "That was my favorite."

"We'll just have to make this an annual thing then." I leaned down to meet her lips and she smiled against mine.

Stepping out onto the patio, Alvaro came to greet us with Mateo in his arms. He had already grown since I had last seen him. As soon as he saw me, he extended his arms to me. *"Tío!"*

"Hola, Matelio." I pulled him in for a hug before securing him against my hip. I couldn't believe he was already approaching two years old. It seemed like just yesterday I was at the hospital when he was born.

"Sometimes I wonder if my son likes you better than he likes me," Alvaro commented as he greeted us.

"Your son is smart then."

Alvaro rolled his eyes and laughed as I turned back to Mateo as he reached for my finger, wrapping his hand around it. "Did you miss your *Tío?*"

Mateo nodded excessively, his dark curly hair bobbing forward. Isabella leaned forward to kiss Mateo's cheek. *"Hola,* Mateo.*"*

"You went holiday," Mateo said, an ever so slight lisp coming through.

Mateo had become quite talkative over the last few months and although they weren't full sentences as of yet, we all understood him. While he can be considered to be quite shy and quiet, that was only around people he didn't know. With us, his personality was starting to shine.

"We did go on holiday," Isabella said, her voice becoming sweeter the way it always did when she spoke to children. "A very special one."

"Special," he repeated.

"I'm sure it was." Alvaro pipped up.

I rolled my eyes as we made our way to the table that was already filled with the setup for lunch. We had gotten back a couple of days ago but we had a lot of work-related admin to sort out since the unexpected extension of our honeymoon. Mateo sat in my lap as we continued the conversation, catching up on the past few weeks. Every now and then I would steal a glance at Isabella who was seated next to me. She was deep in conversation with

Penelope. I could stare at her all day. Her beauty never ceases to amaze me. It was effortless for her - here she sat in a simple cream-knitted jersey and her hair was tied in a low bun. A few strands of her hair fell along the side of her face and she didn't have any makeup on. Truthfully, she didn't need it. Her cheeks were a light pink and the freckles that lined her nose and cheeks had since darkened since spending time on the beach when we visited *Cinque Terre.*

"We're moving forward with the *Arenas de Barcelona* expansion," Alvaro said, handing me my glass of whiskey.

"Oh, that's great news! When are we set to get started on that?"

"A few weeks from now. We just need to run through some of the final architectural designs as well as the scheduled rollout. When are you back in the office?"

"Monday." Mateo grabbed my hand and started to twist my wedding ring around my finger. I let him do his thing as I turned back to Alvaro. "End of the month, Isabella and I have to head to Sevilla for a few days again."

"I was actually telling Penelope that I wanted to head over there soon to see the new branch."

"You really should. We might relocate there for a while."

I didn't mean to say it but it just rolled off my tongue which earned a choke back from Penelope who had just taken a sip of her wine.

"You're moving?" she gaped at us.

Isabella turned to me, clearly thrown off by my announcement. We hadn't finalized any plans but we had both agreed that relocating for a while was definitely on the cards. It was just a matter of deciding on where and for how long.

"Uh, we're still debating it." Isabella clarified, "It's just something we have been discussing."

"Nothing is set in stone ye-"

"But you're definitely thinking about moving?" Penelope asked.

I shrugged my shoulders and turned to Isabella. She was already looking at me and she nodded before responding. "We are."

"And you're looking at Sevilla?" Alvaro asked.

"It's one of our options."

"It would only be for a while." Isabella jumped in to explain. "And we'd still have the apartment here but we're looking at a change of scenery for a while."

"At least you guys will have somewhere to stay if we do decide on Sevilla." I attempted to lighten the mood. I wasn't sure what happened to the energy of the room since I mentioned our relocating plan but it definitely wasn't the excited one I was hoping for.

"It's going to be weird not having you guys in Barcelona." Penelope leaned back against her chair, clear disappointment on her face.

"I know but with everything that happened before the wedding, it just feels like it would be good for us," I explained.

I didn't feel like I had to justify our decision. As soon as I mentioned before the wedding, I knew they knew what I was referring to. They had seen how difficult it was for Isabella and I. They were nothing but supportive and we were well aware that the change would have its challenges but it seemed to be what we needed right now.

"I think that would be great for you guys," Penelope said with a sweet smile on her face.

Penelope and Isabella had grown quite close over the years and it was at least once a week that we all got together. Family was important to me - it always had been and always would be but Isabella and I needed this. Even if it was just for a while.

"Well not that my vote counts but I think *Málaga* would be a great place to live," Alvaro chimed in.

Isabella chuckled. "I've never been there before."

"You have to take her there," Alvaro said, turning to me. "I forgot to let you know that they extended our contract for the *La Sagrada Familia*."

"That's incredible news!" I exclaimed. "I'm sure *Papa* was pleased to hear about that."

The one thing our father was adamant about before handing the company over was that we needed to maintain that contract. It was the most important one to him. Alvaro continued to share more about what I had missed while I was gone but I got distracted by Isabella excusing herself as her phone rang. She stepped down the few stairs onto the grass and lifted her phone to her ear. I couldn't hear who she was speaking to but when she turned around with a surprised look on her face, I froze. It wasn't until I saw her big smile that I calmed down. Whenever she got a phone call, a part of me immediately went back to the day she found out her dad had a heart attack. The look of pure fear and devastation on her face was one I wouldn't be able to forget, no matter how hard I tried.

"We'll be there soon." She told the person on the other end, "Will call you when we arrive."

She walked up the few steps back onto the patio. "Katrina went into labour!"

"Oh my God! How exciting!" Penelope exclaimed.

"Reyna and Diego are at the hospital now. Reyna's parents have just landed from Madrid and she asked if we wouldn't mind fetching them," she said to me. "I said yes and only realized now that the car we brought only has two seats."

I chuckled. "We can stop at home and get the other one."

CHAPTER 42:

Isabella

Giovanni was turning thirty this weekend and I was finalizing the plans for his birthday party. He didn't want to call it a party and I suppose with about ten people in attendance, we couldn't really categorize it as that but it was definitely going to be a celebration. Even Katrina and Sergio had agreed to pop by for a bit. Katrina had given birth to a beautiful baby girl named Gianna and they stepped into the parent role like it was made just for them. I had somehow managed to make peace with the fact that things were just going to be a little more difficult for Giovanni and me when it came to having children. While it was still a disappointment that lingered around my heart, I didn't want to focus on the negative. In fact, I didn't want to focus on it at all and we had yet to bring that conversation up again since our honeymoon. We were on the same page though - when it came time to want to actively try, then we would explore our options but until then we just continued with life as it was.

I pulled the car into the first opening parking spot along the street outside Dr. Gavina's offices. The one thing I couldn't escape was my ongoing checkups that were scheduled every few months. Giovanni was in Valencia for the day meeting with Pedro so I was headed to this checkup alone. I didn't mind it. Giovanni had wanted to rearrange his meeting around my appointment but I assured him that I was fine to do this. I didn't feel as fragile as I once was.

I texted him to let him know I had arrived before locking the car and making my way through the entrance.

"*¡Buenos días! Señora Velázquez.*" The receptionist, Clarissa, smiled up at me as I stopped by her desk. She had been around for as long as I had been seeing Dr. Gavina so we had become acquainted over time. She was a bright, bubbly personality which always helped distract me from my nerves. We exchanged polite pleasantries before Dr. Gavina opened the door to her room.

"Isabella, you're early." She smiled at me. "I'm ready if you are."

"Let's do this."

I followed Dr. Gavina into the room before she closed the door behind us. She reached for my file from the stack that sat on her desk before sitting down across from me.

"Where's your handsome husband today?" she asked politely.

"Valencia. He had a meeting with his partner there so it's just me today."

She nodded and smiled as she opened up my file before glancing down. She was quiet for a moment before she stood up and gestured for the bed. I had been here enough times to know how this went. I placed my handbag on the chair and made my way to the bed. I lay back and positioned myself against it as I lifted my shirt up to reveal my bare stomach to her.

"How have you been feeling? Any pain or discomfort lately?" she asked as she slipped on her gloves.

I shook my head. "Nothing out of the ordinary."

"And you're still taking the pill I prescribed to you?"

"Yes."

"That's good. I don't expect to find anything new on the scan which is a good sign." She reached for the small bottle of gel. Hovering over my stomach, she slowly squeezed and it landed cold against me causing a small gasp. She picked up the probe of the ultrasound machine and brought it against my stomach. The nerves were tangled deep inside my stomach like they always were. I didn't need any further growths or complications so whenever she did the scan, I couldn't help but feel anxious at the fear of the unknown. I closed my eyes as she started to move over my stomach.

"I haven't seen you since before your honeymoon. Where did you end up going?"

"Italy. Giovanni had arranged for us to stay in Florence and then we went around visiting some other places like Pisa, Cinque Terre, Rome..." My sentence trailed off as she paused her movement against my stomach. I peeped an eye open and she was looking intently at the screen. I swallowed in an attempt to contain my nerves.

Please, don't let there be a growth.

She moved the probe against my stomach again and paused. Her facial expression gave nothing away which didn't help the anxiety building inside of me one bit.

"Well, Mrs. Velázquez, it would appear that you are pregnant," she said casually.

I froze.

"I- I'm what?" I stammered.

She turned to me, a huge smile spread across her face. "Pregnant."

I'm pregnant?

Oh. My. God.

"How?" I managed to get out, the happy tears pooling in my eyes. "I didn't even have any symptoms."

Or did I? I hardly paid attention lately but I couldn't place anything out of the ordinary. Sure, I felt nausea every now and then but that happened whenever I took too long to eat. And my period? That had always been so light and with the pill I was on, I didn't find it unusual.

"The body is a fascinating thing sometimes. Everyone is different," she explained. "Truthfully, Mrs. Velázquez, I have no idea how this happened, but I am so happy to have been wrong about this."

"I can't believe this." My hands flew to cover my mouth.

She chuckled and turned back to the screen. "You're just over eight weeks now."

I turned to face the screen. I couldn't make out anything through my tears right now. A rush of emotion came over me as the reality settled over me.

"I'm pregnant." I breathed.

"You're pregnant," Dr. Gavina repeated, smiling down at me.

She turned and placed the probe back onto the machine before turning to break off two pieces of paper towel - she used the one to wipe the gel off my stomach and the other she handed to me for my tears. She wiped the gel off and pulled my shirt to cover my stomach. I pulled myself up to sit on the bed, my legs hanging over the side.

"We're going to have to monitor your pregnancy extra carefully," she explained. "We want to avoid any complications as best as possible since we're aware of your condition."

I tugged at my bottom lip nervously. "I'm scared."

She reached for my hand and squeezed it. "Don't be. This is a beautiful thing. We just have to do what we can to ensure that you have a smooth pregnancy as best as we can."

I couldn't believe I was pregnant. We weren't even actively trying and I had pretty much accepted this wasn't meant for us. We had been having unprotected sex for months now. We didn't care to use protection since we were both well-aware of my condition. My hand went to rest against my stomach.

My miracle baby.

"I'm sure Mr. Velázquez is going to be thrilled by the news!"

I couldn't help the smile that formed on my lips. Oh my God - I couldn't wait to tell Giovanni. She handed me a small picture that was printed from the ultrasound. She pointed to the small dot against the white and black lines.

"That's your baby."

My hand covered my mouth as tears escaped my eyes.

"Congratulations!" Dr. Gavina said and pulled me in for a quick hug. "I am so happy for you two."

"Thank you. I still can't believe this."

She chuckled and walked back over to her desk. "Let's schedule an appointment for a month from now. We should have them more frequently now as a precaution to make sure everything is alright with the baby."

I nodded and slipped off the bed, walking over to grab my bag. "I'm guessing I should stop taking the pill you prescribed?"

"Yes. It seemed to have stopped the further growth of any more cysts but it definitely didn't help with the contraceptive part."

I threw my head back in laughter. "Definitely not."

We said our goodbyes and after setting up my appointment with Clarissa for next month, I made it back to my car. I pulled myself inside and locked the door. For a moment I just sat there, Dr. Gavina's words repeating in my mind as I stared down at the picture in my hand.

It would appear that you are pregnant.

"I'm pregnant," I repeated out loud, my hand immediately resting against my stomach again. I was so overcome with emotion that I couldn't hold back the tears that were now streaming down my face. I didn't know how it was possible but I was thankful. So so thankful. My heart swelled and a warm feeling spread across my chest. I glanced down at my stomach, already feeling an intense attachment to the baby growing inside of me.

The sudden ringing of my phone caused me to jump. I reached for it and Giovanni's name flashed on the screen. I was dying to tell him but I wasn't going to do it on the phone. I wanted to see his reaction in person. I took a deep breath in and brought the phone to my ear. "Hi, babe."

"*Hola, mi hermosa.*" His deep voice coming through the phone. "You done with your appointment?"

"I am. Just got back in the car."

"Anything I should be concerned about?" he asked, a flicker of concern in his voice.

I smiled to myself but gave nothing away with my response. "No. All is good. Nothing out of the ordinary."

Except for the baby I now had growing inside of me.

"Thank fuck!" He breathed a sigh of relief through the phone. "I get so nervous whenever you have an appointment."

"No need. We're all good."

"I'm so glad. That's going to make this flight home a lot less stressful."

"What time do you arrive?"

"I'll be home just after five. Should we go out for dinner?" he suggested.

"Could we order in instead?" I tugged at the inside of my cheek nervously. "Do you want anything specific?"

"Surprise me," he said.

Oh, I was planning to.

"Okay, I'll sort dinner out and see you later." I slipped the key in and turned the ignition on.

"Let me know when you're home safely, *por favor.*"

"I will. I love you."

"I love you, *mi hermosa.*"

CHAPTER 43:

Isabella

There was a quaint little family-run Italian restaurant down the road from our apartment that I decided to order from on the way home. We ended up enjoying all the different kinds of food that Italy had to offer us on our honeymoon and you'd think I'd be tired of it but no. I stopped to fetch the pasta I ordered before heading back home. Once I had made it upstairs, I leaned against the counter and took a moment to myself to process everything. Over a year ago, I was completely devastated when I was told that having children was going to be a difficult road for us. I never expected that I would be standing here now with a little one growing inside of me, especially so soon. Giovanni and I had managed to conceive and I wanted nothing more than to protect my baby. I had suffered a miscarriage before and I was terrified of that happening again. It would shatter me so I vowed to do what I could to protect this baby at all costs.

Tapping my nails against the counter nervously, I had to find a distraction until Giovanni got home. I just wanted to share the news. It took all my self-control to not pick up the phone and tell anyone. I was still in shock but I had an excitement inside of me that brought tears to my eyes just to think about. I placed the food in the oven for now - I would need to warm it up when he arrived home and instead of standing around killing time, I decided to clean up. A mini-spring clean if you would. I needed something to distract me from my excitement until my husband got home.

***

I placed the pasta in the microwave and turned it on to warm up as I heard the elevator doors open. *Perfect timing.* I reached for the whiskey and poured some into the glass I had laid out for him. I knew my husband and a glass of whiskey after a long day was exactly what he needed. He came into view and I couldn't help but smile.

"Hi, baby," he said as he placed his phone and car keys on the kitchen counter before coming around to greet me.

"Hello."

He pulled me in for a kiss and I sunk into his arms. My heart already felt like it was going to burst right out of my chest but I was trying my best to keep it together. I pulled away but he still kept his arms around me. I reached up and straightened the tie he was wearing. Giovanni wore suits so often and I loved it. The way they sat so perfectly against his body and the confident, businessman demeanor that came with it was an attractive look on him.

"You can actually take that off," he referred to his tie. "Don't think I'm going to need that for dinner."

My lips pulled up in amusement as I reached for his tie and undid it, slipping it off him and placing it on the counter.

"I ordered Italian, I hope that's okay."

"Pizza or pasta?"

"Pasta."

"Good choice."

I reached for the glass of whiskey on the counter and handed it to him. He shrugged his suit jacket off, hanging it over the nearest barstool before taking the glass from me. The microwave beeps as it finishes warming our food up. As I gathered some plates for our food, Giovanni spoke through the Valencia branch and his meeting with Pedro. I was trying my best to stay focused on the conversation at hand but I was also bubbling with excitement. I handed him his plate of food and set mine down next to him at the counter. I pulled a barstool closer to him by the corner and sat down.

"Ravioli?" his eyes lit up at the food in front of him. "Great idea, baby. I've actually been craving this since we had it in Rome."

He dug right into his meal, lifting a forkful into his mouth before turning back to me. "So everything went alright at Dr. Gavina's today?"

I nodded, poking at my food. "Nothing to be concerned about."

"Then why do I get the feeling there's something you're not telling me?"

A flicker of worry presented itself in his voice again and I lifted my gaze to meet his.

"What makes you think I'm not telling you something?"

"I know you and you're being way too quiet tonight which makes me think that there's something you want to tell me."

I sighed and couldn't help the smile that played on my lips. He knew me far too well.

"Are you smiling right now? Why are you smiling?"

I placed my fork back down and reached for his hand. "There is something I need to tell you but I don't know you're going to handle it."

Okay, I was totally teasing him right now and when his face twisted in concern, I felt kind of bad about it. He dropped his fork against his plate and shifted his body towards me.

"Whatever it is, Isabella, we can handle it, you know that right?" he squeezed my hand.

God, I love this man.

"I know that."

I slipped off the barstool and made my way over to my handbag that had the picture inside. I didn't have any special way of telling him planned. I knew the news itself was already special enough. Giovanni watched me with confusion in his eyes but he didn't say anything further. He waited patiently for me to continue.

"Dr. Gavina didn't find any new growths." I walked back over to him as he eyed what was in my hand. "But she did find this."

I turned the picture over and slid it across the counter over to him. He took the picture from me, his jaw-dropping ever so slightly before he jerked his gaze up to meet mine.

"Isabella, please tell me this is what I think it is," he breathed.

I couldn't hold back my smile and tears started to form in my eyes again. "I don't know how it happened, Giovanni, but I'm pregnant."

This time his jaw dropped further and he just gaped at me, unable to move. "You're pre-..." his voice trailed off as he looked back down at the picture before looking back at me. "Wait. Is this a joke?"

I giggled and shook my head. "No, it's not. That would be kind of cruel, don't you think?" I pointed to the small dot against the black and white lines.

"I'm about eight weeks now. That's the little one there."

He shook his head as he stared down at the picture, trying to process the information. I didn't blame him. I wasn't even sure I believed it myself right now. Glancing back at me, I could see tears forming in his eyes.

"Baby," I breathed and went around to where he sat. I reached for him, my hands cupping his cheeks. "Are you crying?"

"I can't believe this. How? I thought..." his sentence trailed off but I knew exactly what he was going to say.

"I thought so too. If it makes you feel better, Dr. Gavina has no idea how this happened."

"You're pregnant," he repeated.

"I'm pregnant."

"We're having a baby."

I chuckled. "We're having a baby."

And in one swift motion, he got up off the barstool and reached for me, his strong arms lifting me off the ground as an ecstatic laugh left his mouth. I could feel the happiness radiating off of him. He placed me back down and reached for me, cupping my face as his lips found mine. The warmth spreading across my chest was overwhelming. Any moment now, my heart would burst from happiness. I was so sure of it.

"I can't believe this - I am so happy right now."

"Me too." I nudged him playfully. "You're going to be a dad."

The reality dawned on him and his hand lifted to his mouth before resting against his jaw. There were still a few tears in his eyes and I had never seen him emotional like this before. Just when I think it's not possible to fall more in love with him, he proves me wrong.

And now we are starting a family together.

We were finally getting everything we wanted.

"She did warn that there could be complications so we really have to be extra careful," I mentioned, trying not to think too much about that.

"Of course." He placed his hand against my stomach. "Our little miracle."

Now the tears escaped my eyes as I watched him in awe. No matter what happened, this moment would be engraved in my mind for the rest of my life.

CHAPTER 44:

Isabella

"We're going to need some kind of cover story as to why I'm not drinking tonight," I pointed out as I watched Giovanni. He stood in front of the mirror, running his fingers through his hair. I leaned against the door frame of the bathroom, peering inside. He was shirtless and I watched as the muscles in his arms ripple as he lifted his hand up to apply his oil to his beard. One thing about Giovanni was that he took care of himself. As he should. I couldn't keep my eyes off his body. It was so fucking sexy that it made the pit deep in my stomach scream for a release.

"How about the fact that you don't want to?" he asked, pulling me from my salacious thoughts.

"It's a celebration. We all know I would at least have a drink."

"You can be the designated driver then," he suggested.

"That's actually a great idea. You can drink for both of us tonight."

He whipped his head around. "Do you want me to get alcohol poisoning? That best friend of yours is like a chihuahua."

I burst out laughing. He wasn't wrong. I loved Reyna with all my heart but she could be relentless at times.

"It's your birthday weekend, babe. You can let loose tonight. I promise I'll take care of you."

He turned back to the mirror but flicked his gaze to mine through it. "So you'll hold my hair back if I throw up?"

A laugh played on my lips. "Of course. Typical wifey things."

Opening the tap in the basin, he washed off his hands before reaching for the hand towel hanging on the rail next to him. He wiped the water off as he turned, his back now against the counter. He placed the towel down and gestured for me. I walked over to him and positioned myself between his legs, leaning into his chest. He lifted his hand and slowly placed a stray piece of hair behind my ear before taking my chin between his thumb and index finger.

"You sure you don't want to tell anyone yet?" he asked softly.

I shook my head. "I don't want to jump the gun."

His hands fell to wrap around my waist. I leaned into him, taking a deep breath in. He smelled of fresh body wash and his intoxicating cologne. God, that smell was enough to put me under his spell.

"We'll wait then."

He reached down, his lips finding mine. I had never been more content with life than at that very moment. I was married to the man of my dreams and we were expecting a child together. Nothing could compare to the way that bound us for eternity.

"Now I know your birthday is only tomorrow but I can't wait. Please can I give you your gift now?" I said excitedly.

He chuckled. "You really are the worst with that."

"Hey!" I slapped his arm playfully. "You'd actually be proud of me because I bought this gift a month ago and I didn't breathe a word of it to you."

"You're right, I am proud of you, baby," he teased, pulling me closer and nuzzling his face in my neck, leaving small kisses against my skin.

I pulled away but not before giving him a quick kiss against his lips. "Wait here."

I slipped outside of the bathroom and walked over to my side of the bed. Pulling the draw of my bedside table open, I pulled out the long black box I had. I smiled, proud of myself for what I decided to get him. I knew my husband and I knew he was going to enjoy it. Gift in hand, I made my way back to the bathroom. Giovanni eyed me with curiosity. I stopped in front of him and handed it over to him. A smile played on his lips as he took the box, eyeing between me and the box.

"Open it," I nudged him.

He pulled the top of the box off and I watched his jaw drop slightly before flicking his eyes back to mine.

"You didn't."

"Of course I did," I chuckled.

"You seriously got me *El Clásico* tickets?" he gaped at me.

He lifted the tickets up to inspect them. I peered over and pointed to the seats. "And not just any tickets. We're right in front. You'll practically be able to smell the sweat off the players," I announced proudly.

"This is amazing!" he exclaimed, pulling me into his arms. "You know you didn't have to do this right? I could have watched it on TV."

I shook my head. "And what fun is that? This gives us an excuse to go to Madrid for the weekend too."

He paused. "Wait? These are home tickets?" He lifted the tickets to inspect them again, clearly missing that detail before.

"Gio, do you think I don't know my husband? You would never watch Real Madrid vs. Barcelona at *Camp Nou.*"

"Your knowledge of football is seriously turning me on."

I giggled and pointed to the date. "I've sorted out the flights and accommodation. We leave next Friday."

He shook his head, that beautiful smile of his on full display. Pulling me closer to him, his lips found mine again. I wrapped my arms around his neck as I felt his body up against mine.

"Wife of the year," he said in between our kisses. "Seriously, thank you, baby. This is amazing."

"You're welcome," I smiled up at him. "But we have to finish getting ready now or you're going to be late to your own party."

I dropped my arms and turned to leave but not before Giovanni reached out and slapped my ass playfully. I jerked my head back to face him. "If you keep doing that, we're not going to make it out of here tonight."

"Cancel the party then."

"Absolutely not." I eyed him. "You'll just have to be patient."

He sighed. "Fiiiiine."

***

Okay, Giovanni was drunk.

Like drunk drunk.

And it was hilarious. Sergio had to help me get him back to the car and I had Reyna constantly apologizing for getting my husband drunk.

"Rey, please don't apologize." I reached out and squeezed her arm. "I think he had a pretty good time tonight."

"Isabella!" Giovanni shouted from inside the car. "I ne..."

The rest of his sentence became nothing more than a mumble. I turned to say goodbye to our friends before slipping into the driver's seat. Closing the door behind me, I turned to my husband who had his eyes closed as he leaned his head against the headrest.

"Gio, you alive, babe?" I rested my hand on his leg.

He turned his head, still keeping his eyes still closed. "No."

I couldn't help but laugh. I don't think I had ever seen him this drunk.

"You need to put your seatbelt on."

He didn't even flinch so instead, I leaned over and reached for the seatbelt. He felt my presence close to him and leaned forward, leaving a kiss against my neck.

"You beautiful," he mumbled.

I pulled the seatbelt across his body and clipped it in. "Thank you, my love. Now, you need to tell me if you need to throw up okay?"

He nodded, still keeping his eyes closed. "Do you think you could s-stop the world from spinning?"

"I'll try." I reached over and squeezed his leg. "We'll be home in no time."

I turned the car on, the engine roaring to life. Pulling the car out of the parking space, I took off down the road towards our apartment. It was well-approaching midnight and it was almost officially his birthday. My cell phone connected to the Bluetooth system and I flicked over to our reggaeton playlist.

"-iss a good song." Giovanni slurred. "Makes me want to party."

"We can stop at a club," I suggested playfully. "But I don't think you're going to make it there."

"Your husband is drunk."

"He is."

"-m your husband."

"You are," I chuckled.

"I love that."

"I love you."

I felt his hand on my thigh in response. I eyed him out of the corner of my eye and he was already looking at me. He may have been drunk as a skunk but he still looked just as good. His contagious smile forced my own lips to pull upwards as he watched me.

"You look good driving my car."

"Do I?"

He nodded. "You can have it,"

"You're giving me your car?" I couldn't help but laugh.

"Yup," he popped the 'p'. "I'll get another one."

I rolled my eyes and turned back to focus on the road. I had chosen a place not too far from home and I was pleased with myself for doing that. I had no doubt that at any moment, Giovanni was going to need to get rid of the alcohol in his system and I wanted him to avoid doing that in the car.

We made it back to our apartment and after I parked the car, I walked around to the passenger seat. I opened the door and leaned forward. "Gio, we're home."

He peeped an eye at me. "The world is still spinning."

"I know but we just need to get you upstairs and you'll be fine."

"Are you going to carry me?"

I shook my head and laughed. "I don't think that will go very well. I might drop you."

He reached his arms up and I slipped my hands in his, pulling him slowly out of the car. He leaned against the car and I shut his door. Securing myself underneath his arm, we walked towards the elevator doors. He was heavy against me but I had managed to get him upstairs to our couch without him falling over.

"I'm going to get you some water," I said but as I turned to leave, he grabbed my hand and pulled me closer to him. Instead of looking at me to speak, his eyes dropped to my stomach.

"There's a baby in there." He eyed me as if he was waiting for confirmation.

"There is."

"Our baby."

"Quite perceptive aren't you?" I teased.

"Do you think it can hear us?"

"I'm not even sure our baby has ears yet." I chuckled.

He pulled me down to sit next to him. I shifted to lean against the backrest, watching as he popped his elbow up, leaning his head against it. He reached out and placed his hand on my stomach. Shifting towards me, he leaned his head closer and flicked his eyes up to meet mine.

"Can I have a moment with our baby?"

A giggle formed on my lips. "And where would you like me to go while you have this conversation? We're kind of a package deal right now."

He lifted my hand and placed it on the side of my face. "You can cover your -rs,"

"My what?"

"Eaaaars," he dragged out the word playfully.

God, he was adorable.

I sighed and lifted my hands up, pretending to cover them from what he was going to say. I watched as he glanced back down to my stomach, slipping his hand underneath my shirt. I wasn't showing already but that didn't stop him from rubbing his hand gently over my stomach. His hand was cold against me but I allowed him to do his thing.

"Baby, little baby in here," he murmured close to my stomach. "Hi. It's your *papá*."

I pulled my bottom lip between my teeth to stop from allowing my laugh out.

"I don't know if you can hear me yet. Your mom says you might not even have ears yet - isn't that crazy? A baby with no ears."

He removed his hands from my stomach as he shifted so he was on his stomach, placing both elbows against the couch as he leaned his head against his hands. When you're drunk, your head feels like it weighs a ton so I knew exactly how he was feeling right now.

"I don't want your mom to hear this so I need you to keep it a secret. You can keep a secret right? Of course, you can. If you don't have ears, you certainly don't have a mouth yet."

Oh my God, he was making it so difficult to hold back my laughter right now. I inhaled, trying to keep it at bay. He was so fucking adorable. Watching him interact with my stomach was making my heart flutter in a way it had never experienced before.

"I just want you to know that I already love you so much," he whispered. "I don't even know you yet but I know that I love you. I might already love you more than your mom - don't tell her I said that."

He was so engrossed in speaking to our baby that he didn't notice as I slowly pulled my hands away from my ears.

"I hope you know I'm going to protect you and make sure you know how loved you are. You don't know this yet but you're really lucky 'cause you already have the best mother in the world."

I felt the happy tears swell in my eyes.

"Seriously, you and I are both lucky to have her."

I couldn't hold back as I reached out and ran my fingers through his hair, resting my hand against his head. He didn't seem to notice as he continued.

"She's keeping you nice and warm in there." He slipped his one hand back underneath my shirt. "Just promise that you'll stick around okay?"

A small tear escaped my eye but I allowed it to slide along my cheek. A part of me was terrified. Terrified to go down the same path but I believed it in my heart that our baby was going to be okay. I needed to believe that.

"I can't wait to meet you little one." He pushed my shirt up and leaned forward, kissing my stomach.

"Giovanni," I said through my tears.

He leaned his head against my stomach, turning his head so he could look up at me.

"All done now," he announced and closed his eyes, the same boyish grin on his face.

I slowly ran my nails through his hair, stopping to gently scratch his scalp the way he liked.

"I can sleep like this right?" his eyes flung open. "I'm not hurting our baby, am I?"

I shook my head and leaned forward, leaving a kiss against his temple. "You're all good, babe."

CHAPTER 45:

Giovanni

"Okay, I'm not going to lie, I'm starting to freak out a bit," I admitted.

Isabella turned around, her baby bump leading the way past me down the aisle as I followed closely behind her.

"Too late, *Veálzquez*." She stopped in front of a whole lot of baby bottles on display. "Now, which one do you think is the best?"

"Since I have no experience in buying baby bottles, I'm going to say I have no idea. How are we expected to know these things?"

Isabella was approaching her six-month mark and we had gone into preparation mode which only reminded me of how unprepared I felt. We were about to bring a baby into this world. A living, breathing human being.

Fuck, I was in way over my head here.

I was at least glad that Isabella was much calmer today now that we were working through the list she had stayed up writing until the early hours of the morning. If I thought normal Isabella was a nightmare with her list-making, pregnant Isabella took it to a whole new level.

She reached for a pack of bottles and dropped them into the trolley I was leaning against. She stepped closer to me and reached for my hand. "You know it's normal to feel like this right?"

"I know but seriously, Isabella, I am freaking out. We have to take care of a baby - our baby."

"I know that," she chuckled.

"How are we going to do that? I've only ever held like one baby and that was Mateo. What if I drop the baby? Oh my God - I'm going to drop the baby, aren't I?" I stood up straight as my mind was bombarded by all the fears I didn't realize had been building up in my mind.

"Giovanni," Isabella said softly and came around to stand closer to me, her one hand reaching up and cupping my cheek. "Breathe."

What a simple instruction and yet, my mind wasn't allowing me to.

"What if it shits on my hand?"

"Giovanni, did you really just call our baby an 'it'?" she gaped at me.

"Well, we don't know what it is yet so what am I supposed to call it?" I asked sheepishly.

She burst out laughing."I'm calling it 'baby V'"

"Baby V?" My eyes widened. "I love that."

A shy smile spread across her face before she reached up to cup my cheek again. "And we're still on the same page about not wanting to know until I give birth, right?"

I nodded. "As long as baby V is healthy, that's all I care about."

"You used the nickname." Her eyes lit up.

"I told you, I love it."

"We're going to be just fine." She reassured me. "Our baby is going to be fine. We have each other and we're going to learn as we go along."

"I know bu-"

She interrupted me. "No more buts and no more driving yourself crazy here. We just need to take it one thing at a time."

Her hand fell from my face and rested against her stomach. It was habit now. Watching Isabella grow our baby inside of her was the most unreal experience. I had never felt such an earth-shattering love in my life but every day I watched her, I fell more and more in love with her and our baby. She had also never looked more beautiful. No matter how much she complained about her weight gain, I didn't give a shit. She was growing a human in her body for crying out loud - she needed all the protection she could get.

"I know you're right." I sighed and rested my hand against hers on her stomach. "Should we be practicing though?"

"And how would we do that?" she cocked an eyebrow playfully.

"Rent-a-baby?"

She let out a breath of amusement. "There's no way you think that's a real thing."

"It should be. It would be really helpful to prepare." I leaned closer to Isabella's stomach. "You're already driving your daddy crazy," I murmured to our baby.

"Poor little thing hasn't even done anything yet," Isabella teased. "I'm freaking out too if it makes you feel any better."

I stood up straight but kept my hand against hers. "Two soon-to-be-parents freaking out - how is our baby going to have a chance?"

She chuckled and rolled her eyes. "Our baby is going to be perfectly fine because we're in this together."

I leaned down and left a kiss against her forehead. "I know. I'm just having a moment. I already know our baby is going to be the best baby ever born."

"You're biased."

"No way. Our genes are mixing babe - we are about to create the world's most perfect baby."

"I agree." she leaned up and her lips met mine. "Now, we've got quite a list to get through so I say we power through."

"Yes ma'am."

***

"I thought we were headed home?" she said as I took the opposite off-ramp to where she thought we were headed.

"Just have to make one more pit stop," I explained. "It's not too far and we won't be too long."

"And then can we get something to eat?"

"You craving something specific?"

"Sushi."

"You can't eat sushi, baby," I chuckled.

"I know," she groaned. "Doesn't mean I can't crave it."

I had learned a lot about pregnancy and the women's body since Isabella fell pregnant. If she was going to prepare as if she was going to be tested about this kind of stuff then I would do the same. I wanted to know everything she knew. It was my baby, too, and I was trying to calm down the freaking out part of me.

"Think of something that you're actually allowed to eat and we can get that on the way home."

She sighed and intertwined her fingers in mine as I placed my hand against her thigh. Her baby bump brushing against our hands.

"Do you feel better now that we've started to work through your list?" I asked as I indicated as we approached the traffic light.

"I do. We're probably going to have to turn the guest room into the nursery sometime soon."

"We have time for that."

While Isabella and I had discussed moving from Barcelona, when we found out she was pregnant that changed our plans. I was focused on ensuring her pregnancy was as stress-free as possible and something like moving cities wouldn't help with that. The option would still be there in the future but the more we spoke about it, the more the idea of staying in Barcelona became a welcomed one. The city had felt tainted with what she went through but now that she was carrying our baby - by some sheer miracle - things didn't feel so bad anymore.

Now I had other plans for us.

I turned up the road that headed towards the top of the hill. Isabella had closed her eyes as she leaned her head against the headrest. Her hair was loose with a few strands of hair falling in front of her face. I pulled up to the driveway and turned the car off. Her eyes fluttered open as she adjusted to our surroundings, a look of confusion presenting itself.

"Are you meeting someone here?" she asked.

"Not quite." I unclipped my seatbelt. "I want to show you something."

Her eyes lit up with curiosity as she followed my lead. She unclipped her belt and stepped outside the car. I closed my door behind me and came over to her side, slipping my hand in hers.

"What a beautiful area," she commented, glancing at the houses surrounding us.

Perched upon this hill was a string of houses that overlooked the city. We were preparing to welcome a baby into the world and I wanted to make sure we had everything in place before that. Which included moving out of our apartment. As much as I loved that place, I didn't want to raise my child in an apartment right above a club. It was convenient when I worked at the Barcelona branch full-time but between the expansions and the other projects

I was working on, I did not need to be so close anymore.

"Come on." I gestured towards the concrete pathway leading up to the front door of the house.

"Who lives here?" she asked as we reached the front door.

"Well…" I took a deep breath in. "We could."

She stopped in her tracks. "Wh-what?"

"I've been looking around at some houses for us. As much as I enjoy our apartment, I had something different in mind for when we were going to have a baby and well - surprise - look at what's happened." I rested my hand against her belly.

"You bought us a house?" she gaped at me, her jaw-dropping slightly.

"Not yet," I answered quickly. "But out of all the ones I have seen, this is the best contender but I didn't want to make any decisions without your input."

Her eyes lit up and she couldn't hide the surprise on her face. I was worried about her reaction at first but I could see there was nothing but pure excitement in her eyes. Now I just needed to see if I knew her well enough with the house I was showing her today. I wanted it to have everything she would want.

"We're buying a house?" She laughed, her hands covering her mouth.

"Yes, baby. We need a family home."

"I can't believe this!" She exclaimed, "I'm so excited."

I chuckled and grabbed the keys from my pocket, unlocking the door. I pushed it open, stepping back to allow her to enter first. She stepped inside and glanced around the entrance hall. She loved open-plan houses. That was one thing she had always mentioned to me and this one was spacious and inviting. The hallway leads us to the impressive living room as well as a separate dining room with access to the terrace and the large kitchen.

"Oh my God, Giovanni!" Isabella breathed, her hands coming up to cover her mouth. "This place is beautiful."

A large marble counter stood in the middle of the kitchen. She walked over and slowly ran her fingers over it, taking in the rest of the kitchen. There were large windows on the far wall that opened up onto the patio area. From where she stood, she could see the pool in the garden. She turned behind her to where the fridge stood. Right next to it was another counter against the wall with some other appliances - the kettle, toaster - little things like that. She had the largest smile on her face as she took in every little thing.

"Do you like it?" I asked, sheepishly as I leaned against the pillar.

"Like it?" she repeated. "I love it!"

"Oh thank goodness!" I let out a laugh and walked over to the counter where she stood. "So it has five bedrooms and six bathrooms. As you can see there's a patio and a swimming pool but I wanted to show you the best part."

I extended my hand to her and she slipped it in mine, allowing me to lead her out of the kitchen and towards the patio. We stepped onto the wooden terrace.

"This is my favorite part of this place." I led her past the swimming pool, and in the distance was the perfect view of the city and the ocean. She let go of my hand and picked up her pace before leaning against the balcony.

"This view is…" she stopped and shook her head. "Breathtaking."

"I know how much you love great views and this place had the best one so I tho-"

Before I could finish my sentence, she turned around and threw her arms around my neck. Her lips found mine and I tightened my hold around her waist, pulling her closer to me.

"I love it. I love it. I love it." She kept repeating in between our kisses and I couldn't hold back my smile.

"You haven't even seen the rest of the house," I teased.

"I don't need to. This is enough to have won me over."

She tried to lean her head against my chest but her baby bump was starting to get in the way now. She looked down at it and I started laughing.

"You're going to have to turn to the side to do that now," I teased.

She ran her hands over her bump. "Can't believe how big our baby is already."

Her eyes flicked up to mine and there was nothing but love in them. Every day I woke up, I just wanted to see that. I wanted to see her happy. Whatever she wanted, she would get. I would give her the world if she asked me.

"Can you see us raising a family here?" I asked.

"Oh yes." She smiled. "You chose a good one here."

"I just put on my 'what would Isabella want' hat and this was the place."

"You know me too well." She smiled.

For a moment we just stood there, overlooking the view. I kept my arms around her and a flicker of excitement came from within at the prospect of our future together. This was everything I could have wanted and more.

"You want to check out the rest of the house?"

"Yes please!"

CHAPTER 46:

Isabella

"Y ou can put those in the bedroom upstairs," I instructed. "First door on the left."

Alvaro and Diego nodded, boxes in hand before disappearing upstairs. It was officially moving day and we needed all the help we could get. We had been at it for hours but we were getting there. It took a few months to organize everything that was needed but we were finally moving into our family home and just in time.

Our baby was due in less than a month.

I was huge. Like I couldn't even see my feet. Baby V was not playing around with their size and it was starting to take its toll on my body. Swollen feet. Back aches. Body pains. Pregnancy was no joke but I wouldn't trade it for anything.

I rubbed my hand over my protruding belly. "I can't wait to bring you home."

As if to reply, my baby kicked inside of me and warmed my heart. Every time I felt a little movement, I couldn't help but become overwhelmed with emotion. A warm, fuzzy feeling presented itself in my chest and always caused a smile on my lips. Our baby was growing inside of me and it was the most surreal experience of my life.

"Baby V awake?" Giovanni asked as he walked through the door, a big box in his hand. He placed it down against the wall before coming over to me.

I nodded and looked up at him. "A little kicker this one"

"Probably already training to be a football player."

I chuckled. "Oh you'd love that."

"Of course I would. Our baby could grow up to be the greatest footballer of all time."

"Or our baby could not like football at all," I pointed out.

He glared at me, not amused by the possibility which only made it funnier for me to observe. "Our baby not liking football? Between me and your dad, that baby is going to be well educated when it comes to that sport."

An amused laugh escaped my lips. "You better be careful, my dad might convert our little one into a Spurs fan."

"I love your dad but respectfully, no fucking way."

This time I burst out laughing. A sudden small pain twisted inside my stomach causing my laughter to come to a grinding halt and Giovanni noticed as my hand went to my stomach where the pain was.

"And now?"

I froze for a moment and waited for the pain to pass. Thankfully, it did.

I shook my head and reached out to rest a hand on his arm. "Nothing. Just a random small little pain but it's all gone now."

The concern in his eyes did not falter. "You sure? You'd tell me, right? You can't keep that stuff to yourself."

I waited for a moment but there was nothing. The pain was fleeing and I felt perfectly normal again.

I brushed it off. "Nothing to worry about babe, all good here."

He eyed me, unconvinced with my answer but he let it slide. "Fine, but no picking up boxes. You leave that to us."

"Fine. I'll stick to unpacking."

"Maybe not even that. You should just sit down."

"Gio, I'm not going to not help. I'm fine, I promise."

"How many boxes we got left?" Diego shouted from the top of the stairs, interrupting our conversation.

"There's still a few in my car," I replied, glancing up at him.

He nodded and made his way downstairs, Alvaro following closely behind him.

"Izzy, please call Reyna and find out where she is. I'm fucking starving," Diego said as he passed me through the front door.

"I'll call her now."

Reyna had been gone for a while now so I expected her to arrive any moment now.

Giovanni leaned down and kissed my forehead before picking the box up and making his way through the lounge.

"Let me call Rey," I murmured to myself as I patted my pockets, looking for my cell phone.

"Has anyone seen my phone?" I shouted.

Alvaro walked in, a new box in his hand. "I think I saw it upstairs."

The box was marked kitchen so I asked Alvaro to leave it on the kitchen counter as I made my way up the stairs towards the first room. I had been unpacking the small things into the set of drawers we bought for the baby's nursery and found my phone on top of it. I reached for it but was halted in my tracks as another flicker of pain pierced my stomach. I waited for it to leave but it didn't and a sudden rush of dizziness rushed over me. I tried to call for Giovanni but the words couldn't reach my lips as the world started to spin. Before I knew it, I had collapsed into darkness.

***

"Isabella?" I heard his rough voice in the distance laced with a fear I had never heard before.

I couldn't make out where I was. I couldn't make out anything. There was nothing but darkness as I tried to gather my bearings. His voice disappeared, suddenly being replaced by absolutely nothing. It terrified me. I couldn't move. I couldn't do anything. I couldn't call for help.

Come on, Isabella.

I used all my strength to try and regain my consciousness. Each passing moment not being able to tell Giovanni I was here had created an increasing pressure that started to spread across my chest.

"Isabella, baby, please," his voice said, getting louder as he shouted for me.

I tried to open my mouth to call for him but instead, all that was left was the vocalization of the pain that started to pierce through my stomach again.

My eyes flung open.

"Isabella, *Jesus baby,* can you hear me?"

Tears stained my eyes as my gaze landed on the face of my worry-stricken husband. The world was still spinning but nothing was concerning me more than the constant ache in my stomach. My baby. I needed to protect my baby.

"It won't stop," I whimpered, my hand reaching to lean against my stomach. "Something's wrong."

Giovanni didn't wait a moment longer before he was slowly pulling me to my feet. Alvaro and Diego hovered around him, asking what they could do to help. He was barking orders at them as I focused on nothing but the world around me that wouldn't stop spinning. White spots blurred my vision but I didn't want to think of that. I just wanted to get to the hospital. I felt Giovanni's arm wrap around my waist as he guided my head to lean against his body. He held me up as we started to make our way out of the room and downstairs.

"We're going to go straight to the hospital now," he told me. "Everything is going to be fine."

He kept repeating that and it was reminiscent of the last time we had to rush to the hospital because of pains in my stomach. The night I lost the baby I didn't know I had and now a new kind of fear crept into my bloodstream, shooting to every part of my body. I was terrified. I was so ready to meet my baby.

Our baby.

I didn't want to think of what could happen. I couldn't allow my mind to even go there. I wouldn't be able to survive.

"Isabella, you with me, baby?"

"Yes," I managed to get out.

"Everything is going to be fine."

We reached the bottom step and before I knew it we were out the front door and Giovanni was helping me into the car.

"Reyna is going to meet at the hospital," I heard Diego say.

"Should we call Isabella's parents?" Alvaro asked.

Giovanni shut my door and their conversation became a muffled echo. Within seconds, he was in the driver's seat already pulling out of our driveway. I felt the rush of nausea come over me again causing me to close my eyes.

In and out.

"Don't close your eyes," Giovanni instructed. "Baby, I need you to stay with me, can you do that?"

I felt his hand on my thigh, squeezing to get my attention which forced my eyes to flutter open.

"I'm so scared," I whispered.

He reached for my hand this time, bringing it up to meet his lips. "You have nothing to be scared of. This is nothing, *mi hermosa.*"

The tears started to build in my eyes as the fear settled over me.

"I'm serious, Izzy. This is nothing. Probably just those Braxton Hicks contractions."

With tears pooling, I turned to face him. "How do you know about those?"

"I read those books you got."

My heart.

"You didn't."

"Of course I did. If you were going to prepare then so was I."

The tears spilled over as I clung to his hand. I was absolutely terrified right now and I knew he was doing what he could to distract me.

And I loved him even more for that.

He was always the comfort I needed. No matter what happened, with him holding my hand through it all, I felt calmer. Terrified as hell but there was a hovering calmness just waiting to settle over me if I would give it a chance.

"So, trust me when I say that you're going to be just fine. Our baby is going to be just fine. We're going to be fine."

I wanted to believe him. All the way to the hospital I desperately clung to the notion that everything would be fine. Even when I slipped from consciousness once more.

CHAPTER 47:

Giovanni

A s they wheeled Isabella through the doors, I felt completely helpless. I was instructed to wait outside as they needed to run some tests. I had never driven faster in my life and I didn't even bother parking as we arrived. I came to a grinding halt right outside the emergency room and shouted for help as I tried to get Isabella to regain consciousness. I had never been happier to see those beautiful hazel eyes flutter open but that didn't stop the fear that still lingered inside of me.

For the first time in my life, I felt truly terrified.

I didn't know what to expect and it was completely out of my control. I fucking hated it. The two pieces of my heart that made it whole had just been taken through those double doors and I had no way of knowing what was going to happen next.

"Giovanni!" Reyna's voice pulled me out of the black hole my mind had been sucked into. "Where is she?"

"They've just taken her in," I didn't recognize my own voice. "I don't kn- know what happened."

I felt her hand against my arm. "Gio, hey, everything's going to be fine. She's in good hands."

I didn't move. I stayed staring at those double doors, waiting for something. Anything. Some kind of movement or indication that she was okay.

"Why won't they let me in?" I asked, a rising frustration inside of my chest continued to spread, causing me to clench my fists. "I should be allowed. I'm her husband."

"I'm sure the doc-"

Before Reyna could finish her sentence, one of the nurses pushed through the doors. I rushed over to her.

"*Señor Velázquez*, your wife has just gone into labor."

My jaw dropped, "She what?" I shook my head. "She still has a month to go."

"I'm sorry, *señor*, there is not enough oxygen going to the baby so we need to perform an emergency C-section now. She's asking for you."

"Take me to her. *Ahora!*"

She didn't wait a moment longer before pushing through the doors as I followed closely behind her. I turned back to shout to Reyna. "Rey, please call our parents."

"On it!" she shouted back before the doors shut.

If I thought I was terrified before, nothing compared to the way it was consuming every part of me now. There was a tightness in my chest causing me to need to take deeper breaths. *In through the nose and out through the mouth.* Something so simple and yet it was proving to be a difficult task. I kept trying but it didn't work. I just needed Isabella and our baby to be fine. I didn't care what they needed to do.

"What happened?" I asked, trying to keep my voice as calm as possible.

"I'm not so sure, *señor* but we had your wife on the CTG machine and the baby's heart rate started to drop significantly. I was then instructed to come and find you."

We turned down the corridor, the blinding fluorescent lights beating down on me. I could feel my heartbeat in my ears as we approached the theatre doors. All I could think about was Isabella and how I needed her to be okay. I needed our baby to be okay.

"They've already administered her with the epidural to numb the pain," the nurse explained right before she pushed through the doors and my gaze landed on Isabella in the bed. Her fear-stricken eyes landed on me, the tears spilling over against her cheek.

"Baby," I breathed and rushed over to her side.

"Gio," she cried. "I'm so scared."

I leaned down and kissed her forehead. "No, listen to me, everything is going to be fine."

The doctor had a curtain drawn, separating us from being able to see her baby bump and what they were about to do. Isabella kept squeezing my hand and I could feel her fear radiating off her body. As terrified as I was, I couldn't allow her to know that. She needed me right now. She needed to be strong for her.

"Izzy, look at me baby," I murmured.

She glanced up at me, her eyes filled with tears that were spilling down her cheeks. I reached over and slowly wiped them away before cupping her cheek with my hand.

"Focus on me," I instructed softly. "Don't think about any of this right now. I need you to keep your eyes on me."

She nodded, her bottom lip quivering. The doctor spoke to me in Spanish and I translated for Isabella.

"They're going to start now. He says you're going to be fine - you won't feel it, only a strange sensation."

Isabella shook her head, "I can't do it."

"You don't have to do anything, you just need to focus on me." I rested my arm against the bed above her head and stroked her hair. The sweat glistened against her forehead and she already looked exhausted. The color had yet to return to her face. Fear twisted inside of me but I couldn't give into it.

"Do you know what I can't wait for?" I murmured softly to her, knowing that she needed every distraction she could get right now. "I can't wait for us to go back to Italy."

She took a deep breath in as she leaned back against the bed again, glancing up at me. She looked so drained.

"You loved Italy, didn't you?" I asked.

She nodded, tugging at her bottom lip as she tried to stop the tears from falling.

"What did you love about it?" I needed her to speak to me. She looked as if she was going to pass out at any moment now and I couldn't have that. She needed to focus on me. She needed to stay awake.

"Everything," her voice was barely a whisper. "I loved it all."

"Remember that gelato we had in Florence?"

I heard the shuffling from behind the curtain. I didn't focus on any of that. All I focused on was Isabella. I didn't pull my eyes away from her.

"Of course, I remember." A small smile presented itself on her lips. "We each had two cones."

I chuckled. "Yes we did. It was too good to have just one."

She closed her eyes as her face pulled momentarily, a physical reaction to whatever was happening behind the curtain. God, I couldn't even imagine what her body was going through right now. She looked so weak, and yet, I knew that she was the strongest person I had ever met.

"I promise that as soon as we can, we are getting on a plane and heading back just to get that ice cream," I said, leaning down to plant another kiss against her forehead. "We just have to get through this small little hurdle and everything is going to be fine. We're going to take our baby home and we are going to be fine, *mi hermosa*," I leaned my forehead against hers. She nodded, trying her hardest to keep it together.

Loving Isabella has been the most exhilarating experience of my life. I never knew what it was like to be in love like this. To have a walking piece of my heart roaming the earth was fucking terrifying. Looking at her now, at this moment, was the most vulnerable I had ever felt. I wanted nothing more than to take all her pain away.

"I love you so much," I said softly. "There are no words to describe how much I love you, Isabella."

"Giovanni," my name fell from her lips along with the tears from her eyes and before she could say anything further, we both heard it.

The sound of our baby crying.

"Oh my God!" she gasped. "Our bab- our baby is here."

Before I knew it, the nurse appeared from behind the curtain with our baby wrapped up in a blanket, the cries filling the room.

"Congratulations *señor y señora Velázquez*, you have a beautiful baby girl."

My jaw dropped at the sight of my daughter in her hands. I heard Isabella's muffled cries from beside me but I couldn't pull away from my little one. She was the most perfect little thing I had ever laid my eyes on.

The nurse handed her over to me. "Time to meet *papá*," she said.

I was careful as I slowly pulled her into my arms. I didn't even realize the tears that had started to form in my eyes but as I looked down at the baby

Isabella and I had just brought into this world, I was overwhelmed with a rush of emotions I had experienced before. I wanted to scream at the top of my lungs in happiness but also burst into tears.

"Mi niña hermosa," I gushed as I brought my hand around to slowly take her tiny fingers between mine. She was so small. So small and so perfect.

"She's here," Isabella cried. "I can't believe it."

I was so happy. The happiest I had ever been.

Until suddenly I wasn't.

As I turned to introduce her to our baby, everything changed. In the blink of an eye, the regular beeping from the machine that monitored Isabella's heart rate dropped and I watched her hand fall against the bed as she fell unconscious. I froze as the fear suffocated me, restricting my airwaves. I heard the doctors shouting all around me.

"Patient is crashing!" One of them shouted.

"Someone get me an IV now!" Another doctor ordered. "And get him out of here! *Ahora!*"

Before I knew it, my baby girl was being taken from my arms and I was being pushed outside of the theatre away from my wife.

"What the fuck is going on?" I shouted. "Someone tell me what's going on?"

But no one did, I was guided further away from the theatre towards the waiting room. '*Señor Velázquez,* we're going to need you to wait here," the nurse that guided me out the room said.

I stopped and turned to her. "No. You need to tell me what's going on! What the fuck is happening to my wife?"

"*Señor,* please. We need you to stay calm."

"Stay calm?!" my voice boomed through the corridor. "Why won't you let me see her?"

"Your wife has lost a considerable amount of blood. Her vitals have dropped and the doctors are doing everything they can to save her," she reassured me.

To save her?

No fucking way. This wasn't happening.

I swallowed, trying to stop the pain that was constricting the airwaves in my throat right now. The world started to spin around me.

"Is she going to be okay?"

Her eyes dropped. "The doctor will be out soon."

That didn't answer my question. That didn't stop the pulsing fear inside of me that continued to attach itself to every part of me. I was sick to my stomach. I didn't even notice when Alvaro had arrived at my side.

"Hermano, what happened?"

I couldn't form the words. I couldn't even move.

"Gio!" Reyna shouted, rushing over to me. "What's going on? Where are Isabella and the baby?"

"Baby's fine. Isabella's not. They're trying to save her," I managed to get out, my voice hoarse and distant.

"Save her?" Reyna exclaimed, her voice full of emotion.

I shook my head, "This can't be happening. No, no, no."

I repeated that over and over as I stumbled over to the nearest wall. I felt them rush over to me, asking me questions I couldn't answer. I slipped down the wall and onto the floor.

"I can't lose her," I choked. "This isn't happening."

The happiest moment of my life quickly turned to the worst moment and there was nothing I could do but wait until I heard the fate of whether my wife was going to live or not.

CHAPTER 48:

Giovanni

I thought I knew what pain was but it was nothing compared to the torture of knowing your wife was fighting for her life and there was absolutely nothing you could do about it.

I was losing my fucking mind.

I wanted to punch everyone. I wanted to scream and shout across the hospital until they let me in to see her. I wanted to kick the door down. I wanted to burst into tears. Every emotion I could have experienced was working its way through me and there was nothing that could stop it. Hours had passed with no word. Was it a good thing that I hadn't heard anything? Surely if something bad had happened they would have let me know right?

God, Giovanni. Don't go there.

I couldn't allow myself to think of the worst. There was absolutely no way that Isabella wasn't going to make it out of this. She had to. We had so much we still had to experience. We still had a whole life ahead of us that we had to live. This wasn't the end for her.

I refused to allow that thought to enter my mind. No fucking way.

"Hijo?" My mother's voice snapped me back to reality. I felt her resting her hand on my arm, *"Ven conmigo."*

"No, Mamá." I shook my head.

"Hijo, the nurse over there came to ask me to get you. Your baby is in the nursery."

I whipped my head to face her. "I can see her?"

My mother nodded, her eyes full of so much fear but also so much comfort. She was trying to hide her own fear over what was happening to

Isabella right now. As much as everyone tried, I couldn't be comforted.

But I needed to see my daughter.

"*Lo siento,* please take me to her," I said to my mother.

She reached for my arm and started to guide me down the corridor. I was surprised my legs had even managed to move. They felt like concrete being dragged around right now. I was using all my strength to keep it together but I was one bad news announcement from completely losing it all.

"Congratulations on your baby girl, *cariño.*" She squeezed my arm. "And Isabella is going to be just fine. You know how strong she is."

The pain in my throat tightened as I used all my strength to hold back my tears. I didn't want to cry. I needed to keep it together. I needed to believe that everything was going to be fine. That was exactly what I kept telling Isabella and yet, I knew I didn't believe it myself because I just didn't know. The world doesn't owe anyone anything and I was terrified that the most important person in my life was going to be ripped away from me. I told her on our wedding day that she was my life and I meant that. There was no living without her. She was my fucking world.

But when we turned that corner and my eyes fell on our baby girl in the nursery, I realized that my world had just split in two.

There she lay, all wrapped up in a blanket sleeping peacefully. I leaned my hand against the glass separating us and the tears came.

My mother's arms came around me as she tried to comfort me. "She's going to need you, Giovanni."

"I can't do this without Isabella," I choked on my words. "*Mamá, no puedo.*"

"*Shh cariño.*" She pulled me closer to her, her hand rubbing my back as I cried into her shoulder.

I had never cried like this before. I had also never felt the pain and fear that had currently cemented itself over my heart so this was all new to me.

"*Hijo, escúchame.*" She pulled away to cup my cheeks. "Everything is going to work out the way it's meant to. You know it will. For now, you just need to focus on that little one there."

She turned to face the glass and I followed her lead. She was right. That tiny little human in there had quickly become everything to me.

"When you have children, nothing else matters except them," my mother murmured to me as I turned towards the glass, leaning my hand against it again. "It's so so scary but oh *hijo*, it is so worth it. You and your brother are the best things to ever happen to me and I know you feel the same about that little angel in there."

I nodded. "I already love her so much - how is that possible?"

A breath of amusement left my mother's lips. "Welcome to parenthood."

For a while, we just stood there looking at her. She didn't need to do anything but I was somehow comforted by just the sight of her sleeping peacefully. She was the living, breathing embodiment of Isabella and me. I couldn't explain what that did to my heart. There were no words.

"Have you thought of names for her?" my mother asked softly.

I nodded. "We have a few options."

"She's so beautiful," she gushed.

I smiled at my baby girl. Yes, she was. Isabella had given me the best gift I could have ever asked for and I wanted nothing more than to raise this baby with her. I watched her go from girlfriend to fiancé and to wife with such ease and I was looking forward to watching her step into the role of mother. She would be a natural at it. There was nothing she couldn't do. In my eyes, she was capable of it all and I often found myself in awe of her. Truly the most beautiful soul I had ever come to know. I looked down at my left hand where my wedding ring sat. I twisted it around my finger as I allowed myself to think of her. My wife. My world. My forever love.

For hours, we stood there, watching my daughter sleep before I was finally put out of my internal misery. Suddenly there was an update on Isabella.

"Señor Velázquez?" the doctor said from behind me.

I whipped my head around. "That's me."

"I'm Dr. Molina. I was brought in to assist with your wife." He extended his hand to me and I quickly shook it. The nurse from earlier followed closely behind him before stopping in front of me.

"What happened?" I asked.

"Unfortunately, your wife suffered what is known as postpartum hemorrhaging. Multiple blood vessels tore in the uterus which caused her to suffer from excessive bleeding."

Good lord. I felt the color drain from my face as he continued.

"About five in hundred women suffer from this after birth. Thankfully, we were able to seal off the bleeding blood vessels. She's been asking for you."

"Asking for me?" I gaped at him, my heart beating erratically in my chest.

He smiled. "*Sí señor.* Your wife is okay and in recovery."

"I'll take you to see her," the nurse said.

My feet already started to move before I had been able to register everything that was said. My wife is okay. Isabella is okay.

Oh my God.

Thank you.

The tears building in my eyes were from nothing but pure relief that started to wash over me. I never wanted to feel fear like that again. I followed the nurse back up the same corridor I was chased down, somehow losing my mother along the way but I couldn't think about that. I couldn't think about anything except Isabella. I needed to see her.

She stopped outside a private ward and stepped back. "She's in there. I'll go get your little one in the meantime so she can meet *mamá.*"

"*Gracias.*" I was thankful for her kindness, I needed it right now.

I took a deep breath in and slowly pushed the door open. I stepped inside, closing it behind me before I rushed over to Isabella. She was facing the opposite side and I noticed all the machines they had her hooked up to. The constant beeping from the ECG machine was everything I wanted to hear. That meant she was alive.

I stopped by her bed and pulled the chair closer, the legs dragging against the floor unexpectedly. Her eyes fluttered open as she turned to face me.

"Giovanni?" she whispered.

"Hi, baby." The emotion got caught in my throat as I tightened my grip on her hand. "I'm so glad that you're okay."

The tears spilled from my eyes causing Isabella to slowly reach out to cup my face. I leaned into her touch, needing to soak in every moment with her. Almost losing her was the worst feeling I had ever experienced and I never wanted to feel that again.

"Our baby?" she asked.

"They're bringing her now." I kissed the back of her hand over and over again.

"Her?" Her eyes lit up. "I thought I had dreamt that."

I shook my head, a small laugh escaping my lips. "She's here, *mi hermosa*, and she is perfect."

"I was so scared for a moment," Isabella admitted. "I just remember begging the doctors to save her. They told me there was no oxygen and I was just terrified."

"Hey, you don't have to think about that now. Our baby is fine. You're fine. Everything is fine, just like I said it would be."

She ran her thumb over my cheek. "I'm so glad."

A tear escaped my eye and she noticed causing her to reach up and wipe it away. "Gio, my love, everything is okay."

"I know." I brought her hand to lean against my lips, my eyes dropping down as a few more tears escaped. "I was just so scared, Isabella. I have never felt like that before. I was terrified of losing you."

"You're not going to lose me," she murmured.

"I can't lose you. Ever. It would kill me."

"Gio, I'm right here. I'm not going anywhere."

I lifted my gaze to meet hers. "I love you so much."

"I love you."

I stood up and cupped her cheek gently, slowly leaning down to meet her lips. A sweet and gentle kiss but it was everything I needed at that moment. The door behind me creaked open causing me to turn around. The nurse waltzed in with our baby in her arms. She smiled at me before turning to Isabella. "Hi *Señora Velázquez*. Congratulations on your baby girl."

"Gracias," Isabella replied, smiling.

The nurse turned back to me and slowly passed my baby over. I slipped my hand carefully underneath her body and rested her against my chest as my other arm held her to me. Her eyes were closed as I gently rubbed my thumb over her soft cheek. They had her warmly wrapped in a blanket and a small beanie that sat over her head.

She was perfect.

The nurse dismissed herself as I turned to Isabella who was now eagerly sitting up in the bed.

"Isabella, meet our beautiful baby girl," I murmured as I leaned closer, passing our baby over to her.

Tears spilled from her eyes as soon as our daughter sat in her arms. She was looking down at her with such love and affection. Isabella brought her finger over her little hand. "Hi my baby," she said softly. "I'm so happy that you're here."

She continued to gush over our daughter and honestly, I couldn't blame her. I couldn't stop looking at her. I couldn't believe she was ours. After everything that happened in our lives, somehow we had finally gotten here. This was exactly where we were meant to be. After an attempted one-night stand, the back and forth of our relationship, the family drama, the drama with our exes, an engagement, an almost wedding, the ongoing health problems, finally getting married, finally buying a house together for our baby - we had made it. We had made it here and I didn't need more. I finally had everything I could have ever needed.

"We should probably choose a name for this little one." I leaned closer to them.

Isabella glanced up at me with a smile on her face before turning back to our baby. "I think Baby V is perfect,"

I chuckled. "I love you but that's not going to work. She's not going to stay a baby forever."

"Don't say that." She pretended to be hurt. "We just got her. I don't want to think of her growing up already."

I let out a breath of amusement. "You're right. I'm getting ahead of myself but baby V is not a suitable name but maybe Valentina is?" I suggested.

She turned back to me, her deep hazel eyes shining with a new refound excitement. "Valentina?"

"I know it wasn't on our original li-"

"It's perfect!" she turned back. "It's so nice to meet you, Valentina."

Valentina Velázquez.

Baby V.

The most perfect baby I had ever laid my eyes on and she was ours. I couldn't help but smile down at my two girls. My world. My reason for living.

"This is everything I'll never need," I murmured. "I don't need more than us, Isabella. You, me and Valentina. I'm never going to need more than this."

She smiled at me with a happiness that reached her eyes. "You don't think we're going to do this more than once?"

"You're already thinking about having more children?" I gaped at her.

She chuckled. "In the future. Some day. If the universe allows."

"Trust me, the universe is going to want more *Velázquez* babies in the world."

I leaned down and pressed my lips against her forehead. For the first time in my life, I had everything I could have ever wanted.

EPILOGUE:

5 YEARS LATER

Isabella

"Valentina? Gabriel?" I shouted, leaning against the banister of the stairs. "Are you two ready to go?"

"Coming *Mamá*!" Valentina's sweet voice shouted back.

"We don't want to be late!" I turned to make my way back to the kitchen but stopped when I saw Valentina by the railing, glancing down at me from upstairs.

"Gabriel can't find his one shoe," she said.

"Just the one shoe is missing?"

She nodded. I watched as Giovanni walked down the corridor, stopping where Valentina was to peer over at me.

"Look how beautiful you look *mi nina, hermosa,*" he gushed to Valentina as he fixed the collar of his shirt. She did a little twirl, her pink flower girl dress spinning around with her. She lifted her arms and he picked her up, pulling her into his arms. Valentina was the perfect combination of Giovanni and I. She was blessed with his darker skin tone and dark features but the big hazel eyes were all me. Our daughter was almost five years old but that didn't mean a thing when it came to being picked up by her father. She was daddy's little girl and she loved it when he carried her around.

I changed my course and instead of heading to the kitchen, I headed back up stairs to help our son find his shoe.

"What's going on?" Giovanni asked as I reached the top.

"Gabriel says he can't find his one shoe."

Giovanni followed closely behind me as I made my way down the hall to Gabriel's room. A constant banging sound caught my attention, causing me to rush over. I pushed the door open and found Gabriel kicking a soccer ball against his wall.

"Gabriel!" I exclaimed. "What do you think you're doing?"

He turned around to face me, his big brown eyes widening as he realised he got caught. He was the splitting image of Giovanni. Even down to the deep dimple he had in his left cheek. Standing in his little tuxedo and one shoe on his foot, my heart was bursting.

Gabriel came just over a year and a half after Valentina did. We had just started to feel like we were getting the hang of this parenting thing and then boom, we had to prepare for another baby. And this time my pregnancy was a lot more complicated. The morning sickness this time around was unbearable some days. As I reached my third-trimester, I was put on bed rest. My high-blood pressure and with the growing fears around my complications, Dr. Gavina refused to take chances. A few months later, after doing everything I could to ensure the rest of my pregnancy ran smoothly, I gave birth to a beautiful baby boy.

I walked over and bent down in front of him. "You know you can't wear just one shoe right? *Abuela* won't be too pleased if you hopped down the aisle."

Marcina and Sebastian were getting married, and of course, her grandchildren were going to be part of the nuptials. Valentina and Sofia, Penelope and Alvaro's little girl, were the flower girls for the ceremony while Gabriel and Mateo would be the ring-bearers. Marcina was adamant to have each of them involved and I knew it meant a lot to her. Now, I was just trying to get my children ready in time before we missed the ceremony.

"But I want to play with my ball," he complained, flinging his hands around in exasperation.

"Gabriel," Giovanni's voice was full of warning. "We can't be late to your *Abuela's* wedding. You can take your ball and you and Mateo can play after the ceremony, okay?"

His bottom lip pulled into a pout and as much as I knew I shouldn't laugh at my child, I just couldn't help it. I reached for his little hand and pulled him closer to me, wrapping my arms around him.

"*Mamá,* I want to play."

"I know you do, baby." I turned back to look at Giovanni whose lips had pulled up in amusement. "Remember what we practiced yesterday at the church?"

He nodded.

"That's all you need to do. You just have to walk with Mateo and then before you know it, you guys can go play with your ball."

"I want to play too!" Valentina said. I turned towards the two of them.

"You can both play," Giovanni assured her. "But only if you two promise to do as we practiced yesterday. Otherwise, no one gets to play. *¿Entiendes?"*

"*Sí papá."* Valentina nodded.

Turning back to face Gabriel, I squeezed his hands gently. "Do you think you could find your other shoe now?"

He sighed and let go of my hands before walking over to his bed. Lifting his pillow, he revealed the missing shoe. I tried to hold back my laughter as I watched him walk back over to me, shoe in hand, hanging his head. He really thought hiding his one shoe would stop us from going. I loved that child with all my heart.

Giovanni walked over to put Valentina down as I stood up, straightening out my dress. I had decided on a simple yet elegant black cocktail dress that hugged my curves the way I needed it to. It felt good to dress up like this again. Giovanni leaned down, one knee on the ground as he helped Gabriel put on his shoe. I couldn't help but smile as I watched something as mundane as that. I would never get tired of watching Giovanni in the role of father. He stood up and instructed our children to gather what they needed because we needed to get going. I started to make my way out of the room, Giovanni following closely behind me. He stopped me at the top of the stairs, his arms wrapping around my waist as he pulled me to his body.

"I don't think I've told you yet how beautiful you look and that's a damn shame." He nuzzled his head in my neck, causing a rush of goosebumps over my body.

"You don't look too bad yourself," I teased as I reached for his tie, straightening it.

I felt his hand slide further down my back to rest over my ass. "I might need to steal you during the party later so we can have our own fun."

I leaned closer to him, feeling him come alive against me. My own desire was creeping up on me as I flicked my gaze to meet his.

"What is it with us and having sex at our people's weddings?" I said playfully.

"That's just our thing, baby." His breath brushed against my skin. "And honestly, with that dress on, I don't think I'm going to last very long without having my way with you."

He leaned down and his lips found mine. He used his tongue to part my lips before nipping at my bottom lip, causing a light moan to escape.

"If you carry on like that then we're really going to be late for the wedding," I said between our kisses.

"*Papá!*" Valentina shouted, breaking us out of our trance.

"That's just one of the many reasons why we wouldn't be able to do exactly what you're thinking right now," I teased as I leaned into his erection.

Giovanni sighed. "I love them to death but that really killed the mood."

I chuckled. "That's what happens when you have children, babe."

"Trust me, I know." He leaned down and rested his lips against my forehead. "But I wouldn't trade this for anything in the world."

THE END

A NOTE FROM THE AUTHOR:

When I started writing "More Than Once" over three years ago, I never thought it would amount to anything. I certainly never thought that I would be here, finishing the third and final book of Isabella and Giovanni's love story. They have lived in my mind and in my heart for the longest time and I am so happy that I have been able to share this with you. I just want to thank each and everyone of you for your support of me and this series. I know I am a writer but I don't have the words to describe to you what your support means to me. I could never have done this without you. You have changed my life.

To Traci and Delaney - thank you for coming into my life. It's thanks to you that I have been able to achieve this and I cannot express to you how thankful I am for both of you. You have helped me make my dreams come true and for that, I will be eternally grateful.

Thank you to Bob and Cassie for their work on this series. Couldn't have done this without your contributions.

To my parents. Michelle and Andrew - thank you for allowing me to be me. My whole life you have allowed me to chase my dreams, even if at times they may have seemed unrealistic. You have always allowed me to explore my creativity and supported me with unconditional belief. I am the person I am today because of you two and I couldn't be more thankful to have you as my parents. I would be nothing without you.

To my friends and family - you know how important you are to me. Your support means everything. Having you cheering me on as I tried to make my dreams come true has truly meant the world to me. It's always easier when you know you have people in your corner.

To my soulmate, Miguel - you are everything to me. I would always read these books of these epic love stories and deep down I longed for that. I never believed it would be possible to find that kind of love but then I met you and you changed it all for me. You make me feel like I am living a real life romance story. You love me more than I deserve sometimes. You are patient with me and I couldn't have done this without your support. You are my biggest hype man and I don't know what I did to deserve you. I love you more than you will ever know.

And a final thank you to the readers - my life will never be the same because of you and I couldn't be more thankful. I have so many more stories to share with you and I hope that you'll stick around for the ride. A word of advice - don't settle for anything less than the love that you deserve.

With all my love,
Dominique Wolf.

Manufactured by Amazon.ca
Bolton, ON

24191392R00159